LOVE AND COUNTRY

ALSO BY CHRISTINA ADAM

Any Small Thing Can Save You

LOVE AND COUNTRY

Christina Adam

LITTLE, BROWN AND COMPANY
Boston • *New York* • *London*

First Edition

The characters and events in this book are fictitious. Any similarity to real persons, living or dead, is coincidental and not intended by the author.

Library of Congress Cataloging-in-Publication Data

Adam, Christina.
    Love and country / Christina Adam. — 1st ed.
      p. cm.
    ISBN 0-316-73500-0
     1. Teenage boys — Fiction. 2. Mothers and sons — Fiction.
   3. Single mothers — Fiction. 4. Ranch life — Fiction. 5. Idaho —
   Fiction. I. Title.

    PS3601.D36L68 2003
    813'.54 — dc21   2003040148

10 9 8 7 6 5 4 3 2 1

Q-FF

Printed in the United States of America

for
Don Watson
and
Dianne Benedict

He must go unprotected that he may be constantly changed.

— *Gerald Heard*

Innocence and violence are terrible things.

— *Louise Bogan*

PART I

Autumn

1

At the edge of town, a yellow school bus swung north and picked up speed. On each side of the highway, sage flats sloped away to mountains, and under the twisted sagebrush shreds of early snow lay scattered like rained-on tissues. Kenny Swanson shoved across the hard vinyl bus seat, a muscle working just above the angle of his jaw. He slid the dirty window open a few inches, and a cold stream of October air stung his eyes. When he blinked, a curve of eyelash rested on his cheek.

Kenny had never ridden this bus before, but he knew it stopped high in the valley near the old rodeo grounds where, even with the arena trampled into craters of frozen mud, it might be his last chance to see Roddy Moyers practice. In the winter Moyers followed the rodeo circuit south. The county was building a new arena and grandstands, but they wouldn't be finished for some time.

The bus jolted over a stretch of pavement buckled by frost, the windows chattering so loud Kenny thought they might shimmy out. Other kids packed the seats three deep, but Kenny didn't know their names. The space next to him was vacant. Even so, he worried that somebody could still sit there and ask where he was going. But he was used to being new. Before his dad left, they'd been transferred with the air force four times in eight years, the last time to Mountain Home, on the other side of Idaho.

Whenever a house or ranch gate came in sight, the driver double-clutched, jammed in the gearshift with a ripping metal sound, and let the bus wheeze to a stop. The air inside heated up and thickened with the smell of stale dust and cracked seat covers. It soured with the smell of leftover lunches, white bread and banana peels closed up in paper bags.

He stared out the window. In the distance, he thought he saw a coyote, a gray outline against the sage. He paid closer attention, searching for the buff light color of an antelope. The bus swayed onto a gravel road, crossed the river, and angled north again.

Ahead, a heavy, blunt-nosed dog raced down a dirt lane, running low. When it reached the road, it flattened to the ground, its eyes on the bus, set to dart out snarling at the tires, but the bus slowed down and stopped.

The dog leapt up wagging his tail, and Kenny noticed that he was an old dog, grizzled gray around the mouth. A tall, blond girl, her hair nearly white, crossed in front of the bus and shifted her books under one arm. She started up the lane toward a low brick ranch house at the mouth of the canyon. She trailed a hand to pet the dog but went on walking. The dog leapt ahead, turning to bark over his shoulder. It made him seem as if he were running backward and forward at the same time.

Kenny knew that girl, Cynthia Dustin. He had watched her from a distance leaning against the senior lockers and laughing with one of the teachers. Being new in a place gave him a kind of extra vision. He always understood from the first few days who belonged and who did not. Seniors like this girl seemed as foreign as adults to him. As he watched her walk up the hill, he thought the old dog must have raced down to meet her ever since he was a woolly pup. It struck him as sad, but he was too excited to feel sad.

When the school bus finally stopped and turned around, Kenny climbed off and walked along the narrow highway. Dry weeds had broken through the crumbling asphalt, and the mountains looked smaller and far away. A cold wind pushed at his back, rattling in the weeds, and it seemed to take no time at all to walk to the gates of the old rodeo grounds.

Long abandoned in the center of a hay field, the arena and bleachers looked like a shipwreck of rotten poles and silver boards. Over the chutes, the announcer's stand listed at an angle, the roof torn off by wind. Still, the chute gates were decorated with five-point wooden stars, the paint flaked and faded pink and pale blue.

He walked partway across the stiff hay stubble and wedged his schoolbooks under the ticket booth. On the far side of the arena, a man was fighting a yellow hammer-headed horse down the ramp of a stock truck. Behind the big truck, a pickup and horse trailer had pulled in, and Kenny watched a fat man tie a saddle horse to the back and leave it. The horse lowered his head and cocked one hind leg, the hoof tipped into the mud, as if he planned to wait there a long time.

When he was close enough to see the faces of the men, Kenny stopped, his stomach uneasy with excitement. He knew both men by sight and reputation. The man with the dirty yellow horse was Billy Wiley. When Kenny and his mother had first moved to town, Billy went on trial at the courthouse for helping poach a moose. He had short, bowed legs and a vague, lost expression. His dark eyes and little mouth looked like *o*'s on a cartoon face.

The other man, Al Horton, ran a dairy. He was unshaven, with a tidemark of tobacco juice dried under his lip. His belly was so big and hard that his jacket never buttoned all the way. When Kenny first saw him ride, he thought Al Horton was too fat to stick. But he'd seen him ride a wild colt to a stop.

Al and Billy weren't what made him nervous. If they were here, Roddy Moyers would be with them. Just under thirty, Moyers was pretty well known, not only in town, where people said they'd have big crowds again for football games if Moyers was still playing, but also outside the state. Moyers rode roughstock, saddle broncs and bareback, and nearly always finished in the money.

Their landlord had laughed and shaken his head. "The whole damned town turned up to watch him play," he told them, "and he wasn't even that good a ball player." Kenny had heard about him long before they moved into the valley, and since then, he watched for Moyers's dirty white sports car in town, even though it shook him up to see it.

His mother teased him, saying Kenny had a crush on Roddy Moyers. But she didn't understand. He tried to explain about the way Roddy Moyers rode. How it was like fishing. Two years ago when he was twelve, his dad had taken him to Montana to teach him how to fly-fish, but Kenny couldn't learn. All morning he kept snagging his dad's flies in the weeds and willows.

But late in the day, they had walked to a wider place in the river, and he learned in only a few minutes — from watching his dad cast. He remembered the sheet metal glare off the water, his dad's old bamboo rod gleaming, pheasant colored, in the light. It was the shape and the rhythm, even the sound of it, that taught him. How the line sailed out in a long *S* curve and the fly touched, weightless, on the water.

He didn't think his mother ever understood what it was with Roddy Moyers. But any time he tried to tell her something and she got confused, she'd make fun of him, saying, "I know, I know — it's *just like* fishing," and Kenny would have to look away to keep from laughing.

Kenny found a place behind a post on the near side of the

arena where the men wouldn't notice. Moyers was there, but Kenny never looked right at him. He watched Al and Billy work the horse into the chute.

Moyers leaned on the rail, a beer can dangling between his thumb and first finger. He was not as tall as he'd first seemed to Kenny, and he wore his hair thick to the collar. His hair was true black, dull black like dog fur. Kenny had thought only Indians had hair that color — black hair was really dark brown when you saw it in the light. At school they said Moyers wore his hair so long to cover a scar. He'd cut school to ride in California, and when he reappeared, he had a square white bandage where his ear had been torn off and sewn back on.

Kenny believed the story. Everybody who rode roughstock had accidents. His mother wouldn't let him ride because of accidents. Early in the summer, just after they moved, she sat him down in the kitchen. They had painted the table in the morning, and the top still showed the wrinkle of a thumbprint where he'd touched it accidentally. His mother hardly ever wore old clothes, but she was wearing a faded blue shirt with drops of white paint spattered down the front, her hair pinned up and loose strands curling down her neck.

"We won't have insurance," she said, "until I've had this job six months."

"So?"

"So, could you wait? Not go out for rodeo this year?"

"Okay."

"It's not forever, just until we get a little bit more settled."

He could hear the worry in her voice. She didn't care for rodeo, not the way his father did, but she wasn't saying he could never ride. They were too far away from a base to use an air force hospital. She didn't have the money to pay if he took a bad fall.

Kenny had just turned fourteen. He could have found a way to ride and his mother would never know, but he didn't. Partly it never occurred to him to go against his mother. And partly he was worried, too. What would happen to them if he did get hurt?

He watched Al untie his horse from the trailer and lead him into the arena. When he stepped into the stirrup, the saddle creaked over sideways and threatened to slide off. At the same time, Moyers straddled the chute and set his rigging. The little man, Billy, stood ready to swing the gate. Moyers eased down on the back of the horse. A hoof struck hard and splintered wood — Billy scrambled back. Roddy tugged his hat down low, and Billy looked up, waiting for his nod. At the barest signal from Moyers, he hauled on the rope and the gate swung wide. But nothing happened. Moyers tried to spur the bronc out, but the dark yellow horse locked his knees and stood stiff. He rolled his eyes and tipped his ears, one forward, one back. Kenny pressed into the rail, to see better, to be closer. Then Billy slapped the buckskin-yellow rump with a rubber boot. "Get! You son of a bitch!"

Moyers's spurs raked forward and the bronc crow-hopped into the arena. The horse ducked his head, twisted in midair, and kicked out both hind legs. He reared and came down hard on both front hooves, then set off bucking in the frozen mud. The men yelled and Kenny saw the big horse slip and lunge on the ice. He ached to be where Moyers was.

All Kenny's muscles tensed against a fall. He tried to loosen up, to get in time with the ride. But in seconds Al crowded the pickup horse in close, and Moyers dove off. He swung over the rump of Al's horse and landed on his feet. Al chased the bronc, leaned down from the saddle to slip the bucking strap, and trotted his own horse back to the chute. Roddy was at the rail, calling for another beer.

The bronc circled the arena, bucking harder than he had with

Moyers. When he stopped, the skin on his neck quivered. He put his nose to the mud and shook, starting with his big square head and ending with his tail, like a wet dog. The men laughed, and Moyers noticed Kenny.

"Hey, kid," he called, his voice so sudden and loud that Kenny jumped. Moyers nodded at the horse. "He's ready to go again. You want a round on Mustard here?"

"No," Kenny said, but Moyers couldn't hear him. "No, thanks," he said, louder.

Moyers waved him over, beckoning with the whole length of his arm. Kenny felt stranded. All three men were watching. He began the slow circle around the arena. It seemed to take so long. He could hardly take the last steps, as if some kind of charge, like a magnetic field, kept pushing him away. But Moyers only held out a beer. Kenny shook his head.

"No, thanks," he mumbled. But Moyers didn't take the beer away.

"Go ahead," he urged. "Hell. I won't tell on us if you don't." He thrust the beer closer. Kenny reached out and wrapped his fingers around the icy can.

Moyers saluted with his beer and took a swallow. "You've been out here before," he said. It might have been a question or an accusation. Kenny wasn't sure. Seeing Moyers up close confused him, made him afraid to look around. He nodded.

"You ride roughstock?"

Kenny hesitated. "No," he said.

"You don't sound convinced — what is it, yes or no?"

"Yes," Kenny said.

Moyers let out a laugh, and Kenny laughed, too, from relief. But Moyers was looking down at him, at his school clothes and worn, gray gym shoes.

"I used to," he said, but Moyers wasn't listening. He'd turned to watch Al and Billy muscle a raw-boned sorrel horse out of the stock truck. The horse threw his head, jerking Billy Wiley off his feet, and Moyers moved to help.

Kenny stepped back, hoping Moyers would forget about him. He set the beer can on the ground.

"Who's up next?" Moyers asked.

"Ain't me," Al grumbled. "Can't sit down from last time. Put the kid on."

Billy Wiley looked over with his vague expression. "Put the kid on," he repeated.

Moyers spoke over his shoulder, not turning around to look at Kenny. "Sure you don't want a try?" he said.

"No." Kenny said it clearly, but he could hear his voice rise with the start of panic. "I can't."

"Sure you can." The men all spoke at once.

Kenny backed up. He shook his head no. "I can't," he said, and Moyers turned to look at him. Kenny couldn't meet his eye. Billy gave a slow nod.

"Go ahead, boy," he said. "I'll go out and pick up all the rocks. Won't hurt so bad when you come off."

The men laughed at the old joke, and Kenny heard Al Horton suck in juice and spit. They all stared at him and waited.

Kenny grinned, his eyes on the ground. A dark circle, like he got from staring at a lightbulb, was closing in around him.

"I can't," he said. He looked at the raw-boned horse, and from the horse to the men. "I promised my mom."

Before the words were out, he knew he'd said the wrong thing. He wanted to stop and explain, but before he could, the men looked from one to the other and bent over laughing.

"I promised *my* mom," Billy said, "but she ain't here right now."

Kenny grinned harder, as if it could make him invisible.

"You see this boy's mother here?" Al Horton said. He pretended to look around for her, then he caught Billy's eye and winked. "Ain't his mother that new one at the courthouse? The blondie?" He was short of breath from laughing. "Hell," he said, "if my mother looked like that, I'd ask her permission to *spit*!"

Kenny felt the blood rise in his face, prickle the skin at his hairline. He was trembling. The men went on joking, but he couldn't hear. He wanted to stop them, say something to turn the joke around, but he was afraid if he tried to talk he might start to cry.

"How 'bout a date with your mother? Think you could fix that up?" Al leered at him, his teeth brown with tobacco juice.

Kenny tried to speak, but the words caught in the back of his throat. Al leaned closer. "What? What'd you say?"

Kenny couldn't think. The men were yelling at him. Blood pumped in his ears.

"I guess," he said.

"You guess?" Al Horton repeated. He whooped, and Billy bent over double, helpless, as if he could picture fat, greasy Al with Kenny's mother. Kenny's face burned with a sting like hot ant bites. When Moyers cut in, his voice was so low Kenny wasn't sure he heard him right.

"It's getting dark. Let's get to work here or go on home."

He tossed his empty beer can at the bottom of a fence post and started toward the chute.

When Kenny finally looked up, it seemed as if he'd stepped out of the movies in the daytime, surprised to see the light. But the sun had fallen below the peaks in the west. He was standing in blue shadows, tinted pink. Al and Billy turned back to the sorrel horse, laughing to themselves.

Kenny wanted to disappear. But he stood where he was, waiting for the rushing in his ears to stop. Several minutes passed before he felt safe enough to move away.

He retrieved his schoolbooks and walked out to the blacktop, to the place where his mother had promised to pick him up after work, and looked down the empty road toward town. His mother was late. He wished she'd never made them move here. She was only a secretary. She could have been a secretary in Mountain Home. Where was she? He couldn't remember his mother ever being late.

He wished he'd ridden the damn bronc, just to show her. He swore to himself that he would never promise her anything again. He cursed through his teeth and threw his books down on the road. He drew back his foot and kicked one of the thick, gray-covered books so hard it cracked in the spine and scraped, the pages fluttering and flapping white, across the asphalt.

His anger fell away, like the sudden dropping of a trapdoor in his guts. The men had tricked him, and he had hurt his mother. The way the men had talked about her felt to him dark and dirty. For the first time in his life, he saw his mother as someone, like him, who could be hurt or scared. He felt cold, and a dark space seemed to loom just outside his field of vision.

Pages from the broken book had scattered up and down the road, white and luminescent in the dusk. He went after them, scraping his knuckles on the asphalt, and tried to fit them back together, but the covers wouldn't close. The book seemed swollen with too many pages. He clamped it under his arm with the rest of his books and started walking down the road toward town.

Bands of smoky clouds pushed over the peaks in the west, and a glow from behind the mountains, from beyond the round curve of the earth, washed the valley blue. The air itself was blue, the color of a shadow in a snowdrift, and it smelled like ice and wood smoke.

When a loud heckling call, like the barking of small dogs, broke out somewhere above him, Kenny stopped and looked up. At first he saw nothing. Then, low over the river, he saw a ragged line of Canada geese, their long necks stretched out toward the south, their set-back wings pushing them through the air. In the near darkness, Kenny shivered. He wondered where the geese went at night. He was suddenly afraid of the geese, not that he might be *like* them, but that he might *be* them. That his skin was not strong enough to keep him separate.

He shook the feeling off and began to walk again, searching in the distance for the headlights of his mother's car.

2

The county courthouse stood on Main Street behind a lawn burned dry by drought and frost. Two spindly, ancient spruce trees flanked the door, mineral blue against the faded brick. Inside, heavy woodwork had darkened with age, and by late morning the rooms filled with a high golden light and the pinching smell of varnish heating in the sun.

In the recorder's office, Lenna Swanson bowed her head over a battered desk, inking numbers into a ledger bound in rusty-red cloth. She glanced up and saw a man blocking the dusty tunnel of sunlight in the doorway. He appeared to be near seventy, but he could have been much younger. He wore a fleece-lined denim jacket and work jeans buffed across the knees with powdered clay. As he crossed to the counter he lifted off a stiff, straw hat.

Lenna scraped her chair back, rose, and approached the counter. "Can I help you?"

"You can't," he said, "you better hunt for different work."

His eyes flashed blue, and Lenna stepped back. She suspected he was teasing, but she wasn't sure. Bareheaded, he looked ashen and unfinished. His forehead was divided by a straight hat line, white above and red below, but his cheeks had faded to the gray that comes from age and too much sun. He stood at the counter curling the brim of the hat in both hands. The hat was sweat-stained around the band, the color of blackened, moldy hay, and when he set it on the counter, Lenna heard it rock, like a penny spinning to a stop. Beside the hat he placed a small, square leather wallet.

"How are you this morning?" she said.

"Oh, I get around. I take nourishment if I can find it." He leveled his eyes at her, and she noticed the blue had faded milky at the edges. She raised an eyebrow, ready to take more teasing. But the skin around his eyes wrinkled, and he gave her a grin so unexpected that she felt herself smile back and nearly laugh, as if the room had filled with lighter air.

"Came here to pay my taxes," he said.

"You have your notice?"

"Wish I didn't," he said. He thumbed through the folded papers in his wallet, as if they were greasy-soft, familiar playing cards.

Lenna took the notice from his hand, straightened the folds, and read his name. "Mr. Dustin?"

"That's *one* of the things they call me," he said.

Lenna smiled and asked him to wait just a minute. She carried the notice back through the long, high-ceilinged office, where two older women worked in a maze of metal filing cabinets. Below the tall windows and darkening honey-colored woodwork, six worn velvet ledgers were ranged along a shelf, collecting dust. She lifted the first one open and found his name, smoothing the printed notice flat on the page to check it against handwritten figures. She was tempted to read down the columns below his name, Earl Dustin. To see how many years he had been paying taxes, how large a place he ranched. But out of some kind of shyness, she didn't allow herself to look.

In a town so small, she'd thought she would know nearly everyone by now, but she didn't. People in this high valley joked with her and seemed easy, but there was a point of demarcation, a place where each one turned back to his own. Though she knew they kept it secret, maybe even from themselves, the other two women resented an outsider taking the courthouse job. They wouldn't hinder her, but they hoped that by some chance or accident she wouldn't make it through her trial months. They had been murmuring all morning about a funeral, a service for a toddler. Lenna knew the woman whose baby had been run over, knew her by sight. But she hadn't been expected to go.

She walked back to the counter, laid the notice flat, and slid it across to Mr. Dustin. He lifted the paper to the light, reading slowly, as if he'd never seen the document before. His broad fingernails were opaque and yellowing, like chicken fat. Lenna wanted to say something to him, to engage him in some easy conversation. But nothing came to her, and he was silent, concentrating on his business.

He slipped the notice in his wallet, licked his thumb, and drew out brand-new hundred-dollar bills. He creased them into a boat with two fingers and set them on the counter.

He unnerved her, studying her hands as she made change from the cash box, but he took no notice while she counted his change back into his palm. He folded the bills and tucked them under the flap of his shirt pocket. Finally he lifted his hat with a palm curved over the crown, nodded at her, and turned to go. Lenna watched him walk away, his back rigid and slightly bent. Like so many ranchers, he walked as if his bones had ached for so long he never thought to mention it.

At her desk, she fanned a thick stack of receipts and let it drop with a galloping sound on her desk before she tapped the edges flush against her palm. She had to sort the month's receipts, but she went on thinking about the rancher. In spite of his age, something about him drew her. The fleece inside his jacket was worn flat, like a drab, overwashed stuffed animal. But someone had laundered his shirt and pressed it with an iron so hot the fabric shone like roofing tin. Lenna thought of his narrow build, how his shirt tucked straight into his belt. An engraved brass oval lay flush with his jeans. She felt a longing, a desire in the body she hadn't felt since her divorce. She blushed, a tingling heat traveling up the back of her neck, resting at her throat. She looked up sharply, as if someone might have seen her. But the room was still. She forced her thoughts back to the papers on her desk.

The women in the office talked in low voices about the funeral they had gone to earlier in the day. The burial of a toddler. Rich Lattimore had run over his own baby. He'd left the house to make a quick trip to the store, thinking the kids were inside with his wife. But the toddler had followed him out, and over the long bed of his truck he couldn't see the little girl.

When the sheriff had first announced the news, Lenna found herself crying. The tragedy hurt her, like a deep bruise to the bone. She thought of Kenny as a toddler. A serious boy, he had stopped and stared in wonder at ordinary things, a pencil sharpener, a baby in a carriage on the street. "Mom," he'd say, pronouncing each word distinctly, "the *baby's* sleeping." As if he weren't still a baby himself.

But the next day, her sense of the tragedy dulled. She was ashamed of the numbness she felt, and more ashamed of the anger that replaced it. She had been raised by her grandparents in a small farming town, and like her neighbors there, these people had too many accidents. They were always being crushed by tractors or turning over pickups on the highway. She wasn't being fair, she knew, but now it made her sick to think about the Lattimore baby. She shut out the talk in the office to concentrate on sorting receipts. After a time, she lost herself in the quiet and the rhythm of the work. She was proud to have her job.

When she raised her head again, another man stood in the doorway. A dark, unshaven man with glossy hair slicked back in short, wet quills. He wore an orange hunting vest, heavy with ammunition. He cleared his throat, and the other two women looked up from their desks.

"Lenora?" he said, his voice echoing in the room.

Lenna pushed back her chair, the sound scraping loud across the wooden floor, and the other women turned to stare. She could feel hot color rising again along her throat and flushing her cheek.

She was so ashamed that she lifted her purse from the floor and stood with no explanation. Hardly breathing, she walked to the coatrack and tugged a navy wool coat from its hanger. The empty metal hangers clattered and rang. She took the time to slide her coat on before she walked past her ex-husband out the door.

She walked quickly down the hall, past the long glass case of pioneer relics she looked at every day — cracked plates with dark blue Chinese trees and bridges bleeding into white porcelain; ornate, dusty flowers woven out of human hair — through the door, and down the short, wide set of steps.

When she reached the curb, she stopped. A sharp wind funneled between the storefronts on Main Street, and the skin on the back of her arms pulled taut and crept with gooseflesh, as if she hadn't worn a coat at all. She turned her back to the wind, to the courthouse, and waited. She heard the sound of Kenneth Swanson's heavy boots behind her.

"Hold on," he said.

Lenna pressed her lips together, her whole body going rigid.

"Came to take Kenny hunting." Ken's voice was deep and casual.

"No," she said and turned around to face him. He blinked in

surprise. Then his face closed against her. His eyes went hard, the eyelids wide and unmoving. A knot pumped in the muscle below his cheekbone.

"Why not?"

"Because . . ." she started to say, but at that moment, the sheriff and deputy jogged down the steps of the courthouse. They stared at Lenna, then suspiciously at Ken, but they went on across the street.

"However you got here," she said, "turn around and go back."

"I have a right to see Kenny," he said.

"Every two years?" The words burst out, and her eyes felt warm with tears.

Ken spread his feet on the sidewalk, centered his weight, and gave her a look she hated. He looked at her the way he would at someone he suspected had had too much to drink.

"Quit that," she said. She shook her head to clear it. But she didn't know what to do next. She glanced at the buildings up and down the street. She saw the squat fire station, the brick insurance office. On both sides of the street, muddy cars angled into the curb.

"Come on," Ken said. "I have a ride." He walked down the line of cars to a rusted-out green pickup. The passenger door had been patched with smooth gray putty and pink primer. He stepped on the running board, stretched both arms over the roof of the cab, and waited. In the back of the truck, two mud-encrusted brown horses hunched under heavy saddles. They hung their heads over the bars of a peeling red metal stock rack, their eyes squeezed shut. Under their noses, Ken slapped his palm down on the roof of the truck. He began to drum out a flat, hollow rhythm, as if he were bored. At the first slap, the horses jerked back, but they lowered their heavy heads again.

Lenna looked once more up the street before she approached the truck. When she pressed her thumb into the stiff chrome door latch, Ken lowered himself behind the wheel. She climbed onto the seat, the hem of her coat snagging on the muddy edge of the door. She jerked it loose and sat staring straight ahead, where the wipers had smeared a milky fan of mud and yellow bugs across the windshield. Ken Swanson started the engine and backed the truck in one swift motion. Gasoline sloshed in both tanks, and the horses lurched and shifted, rocking the whole truck from side to side like a half-swamped fishing boat. Lenna braced her hand against the dash.

Ken straightened the wheel, and the truck lumbered forward. The dusty saddle blankets on the seats smelled of hay chaff and horses. In an instant, they brought back to Lenna the smell of a room shared with a man. Not the sharp smell of sweat, but a more private one. The smell of skin that rose from his shirt collars before she dropped them in the wash.

"Where to?" Ken said.

3

On the same day, Cynthia Dustin cinched her bathrobe tight and sat down, the plastic cover on the kitchen chair crinkling underneath her. Across the room, her mother was wrapping a baked chicken to drop off at the Lattimores before the funeral, and the smell of roasted fat in the air made it seem like Sunday afternoon. Her mother swept a long sheet of foil from the roll, sheared it off, and crimped it over the pan. Under her apron, she wore a nubby dark blue dress, the limp hem riding higher in the back than the front. Rust-dark stockings squeezed the plumpness behind her knees.

Cynthia felt restless, as if she were coming down with something. In the dry fall air, her skin had pulled tight and her eyes seemed to ache behind the sockets. "I'm not going," she said.

Her mother turned, wiping her hands on a towel. Her hair, swept up and lacquered, gleamed with a dull film, like tarnished silver, but her face was round and smooth. "Let's not have any words," she said. "Go on upstairs and get dressed. Earl will be in pretty quick now."

As if Cynthia had called him up, they heard his footsteps in the mud room. In a minute he'd have his boots and coveralls off. The muscles in her neck tightened.

"Cynthia," her mother said, "don't torment your father. Go on upstairs." She glanced at the door.

"I don't feel good," Cynthia said, just as her father appeared, slamming the hollow door shut. He tested the knob and slammed it again before he turned to Cynthia.

"You don't feel good," he said. He wasn't asking, only repeating what he'd overheard.

"No."

The air seemed to thin in the room, but Cynthia met her father's look. His wavy hair, flattened by years of wearing hats, had gone completely gray, and he looked tired.

"Go on and dress," he said. "It's not a party. You're not supposed to feel good."

He moved off toward the stairs, shuffling a little in his thick socks. She waited until she heard him in the bathroom before she climbed the stairs.

After they delivered the foil-wrapped chicken, they joined the crowd at the cemetery, Cynthia standing halfway back, between her parents. The sunlight hurt her eyes. She let them rest, unfocused, on the dark shoulders of the suits in front of her. The suits were dull and chalky, as if dust and dandruff had recently been brushed away. She glanced around. Most of the men had raw new haircuts showing crescents of pink skin above their ears. The women wore winter coats, their hair protected by thin scarves.

The families had walked up the hill between the polished gravestones and, as if they were in church, left an aisle down to the parking lot. They stood without speaking, facing the new grave and the arc of white folding chairs set up behind it.

Across the aisle, Cynthia saw her science teacher and remembered a dance that night. She'd promised to bring music. Mr. Everts turned as if he'd felt her looking at him, and mouthed a "don't forget" at her. She nodded and he turned away.

She looked at the flagpole at the crest of the hill. There was no flag, but the ropes and hardware chinked from time to time against the metal pole. Beyond, the mountains spread sideways in overlapping curves, dark with swaths of dull black evergreens. The growth of trees had the shaggy moth-eaten look of the hides of buffalo. But the clefts in the canyons overflowed with luminous gold and yellow aspen trees.

All together the crowd turned sideways, as if they'd heard a swell of music and hoped to catch sight of the bride. In the parking lot below, two deacons opened the rear door of the hearse and lifted out a folded chrome table, springing it upright with the metallic slide and click of raising up an ironing board. They placed the small white coffin in the center and wheeled it to the curb.

On the grass, Rich Lattimore and his brother grasped the handles on each side of the coffin and started up the hill. Rich looked straight ahead, his chest caved in as if he might cry, the skin around his mouth pulled tight. As they walked past her, their heads bowed low and their fingers blanching white around the knuckles, Cynthia looked down at their shoes disappearing in the short green grass. The shoes were blunt and black and very shiny.

Her own shoes were black. Black pumps she never wore except to church. The sharp heels kept punching into the grass and tilting her off balance. She looked up again toward the flagpole.

In the fall she liked to glance up at the cemetery when she drove past, a green patch against the fields of barley stubble. After hunting season, elk sometimes drifted down from the mountains to paw through the snow to the clipped grass. She'd seen them in the early winter standing among the headstones, as still and dignified as lawn ornaments.

When the minister began to speak, she bowed her head, but she didn't close her eyes. Her father gave her a grim "That's what I'd expect" look. If he had his eyes closed, she thought, he wouldn't have noticed me. When she closed her eyes, she felt surrounded by his aftershave, the packed-away smell of his suit.

She tried to listen to the minister, but she could barely hear him, his high voice drifting away. "Suffer the little children to come unto me." Cynthia couldn't believe him. She played the piano in church and sang in the choir and knew what he was really like. When she talked to him, his gaze kept shifting away, over her shoulder, as if someone more important might appear.

Her eyes would not stay closed. She looked again at the people around her. Harold Cray stood nearby, which had to be a mistake. For no apparent reason, her dad had always held a dislike for Harold, though she sometimes sang with him in choir. He looked strange, maybe retarded, and showed up at rehearsals in his motorcycle leathers. But his voice was beautiful, clear and steady, as if he might have trained for years.

It was 1984, but nearly all the girls her age wore turquoise eye shadow and white-pink lipstick that had been out of style for years. Their hair was swept back in wings, spun large, and sprayed stiff with hair spray. The faces she could see looked solemn, close to tears. She never wore makeup, and she cut her own hair in a short, angular style, one side longer than the other. Dressing for the funeral, she'd tried to brush it smooth, make it hang straight in a wedge across her cheek, but the air was so dry it lifted single hairs and floated them around her face like dandelion fluff. Her mother complained the haircut made her look unfeminine, but her father never said a word about it.

The minister talked on, his maroon robe hanging straight down, the long satin lapels gleaming, as if they were damp, in the sun. Raised up on a blanket of artificial grass, the tiny coffin looked like a cake on a trolley.

She remembered a picture from Bible school. A picture of

Jesus with long red hair and blue robes, squatting on a stool while fat little children gathered at his feet. His toes were long and squared off at the ends, his big feet crossed with leather sandals. It made her think about Curly Lattimore, the little girl in the coffin. She pictured her walking up to Jesus — and Jesus reaching out his hand. Her throat tightened. Before, she hadn't even thought about Curly or the Lattimores.

The Lattimores sat in folding chairs behind the grave. Carol shushed an infant in her lap. Rich looked angry, his forehead bunched as if he were fighting not to lose control in front of all these people.

The minister raised his hand to give the benediction. Cynthia muttered under her breath, "In the name of the Father, and of the Son, and of the Holy Ghost, Amen," and that was the end. Nobody walked up with flowers, and the coffin wasn't lowered into the grave. The Lattimores rose from their chairs and filed down the hill. In the parking lot they climbed into a big copper-colored car. Then everyone else began to shuffle down. Somehow Cynthia and her parents were stuck in the back of the crowd, and she had to take small steps to keep from bumping into the woman in front of her. Off to the side, she saw two girls from school, their arms around each other, weeping. They were enjoying any excuse to cry. It made her want to laugh.

She climbed in the backseat of the car behind her father, his hat blocking her view. She tried again to smooth down her hair. The skin around her eyes felt even tighter and more pinched, and her lips were chapped. Her mother wondered out loud if they should go down to the hotel for dinner. "That's where everyone will be," she said.

Cynthia pictured the café, the ranchers and their wives all arriving as they normally would after church. They'd leave their

own tables and stand around in their church clothes talking —
about the same things they talked about when there wasn't a
funeral.

"Don't think I'd better," her father said. "I've got a steer needs
doctored."

"Maybe we should just stop by?" her mother said.

"I'd better not," her dad said. "But you two go ahead if you
want. You can drop me off at the place."

"No," her mother said, "let's all go home."

They drove into the ranch yard, and she and her mother climbed
out to let her father put the car away. Inside, her mother hung up
her coat and slipped her apron on. Cynthia kicked her shoes off
and carried them up the stairs in one hand. The shoes smelled of
new leather and the inside of a department store. She dropped
them in the bottom of her closet.

She jerked her dress off over her head, the material alive with
snapping sparks, and her slip and stockings clung to her fingertips when she tried to fold them in the drawer. She took off her
bra and pulled on a flannel shirt, worn thin across the shoulder
blades, and jeans. The shirt was soft and cool on her back and on
her chest. She sat down on the edge of the bed and scuffed her
bare feet on the stiff nap of the carpet.

It felt strange to be home on a school day. She didn't know
what to do with herself. She wanted to go practice, but she waited
until she heard her father change his clothes and go outside.

She pulled a sweater over her shirt, so her mother wouldn't
notice she'd taken off her bra, and went downstairs. Her mother
was sliding a black-speckled roasting pan into the oven. Cynthia
walked through the kitchen into the front room.

Cynthia hated everything about the new house, except the
view. The house had been built over a raised basement on the

ridge of the canyon, only a few miles south of the cemetery. Out the plate glass window of the front room, Cynthia gazed across the valley to the river and the mountains beyond. She walked over to the piano, a small upright the ash-blond color of church furniture.

She slid the bench out and sat down, lifting back the hinged cover and spreading her fingers over the keyboard. Lightly, she let her hands hover, barely touching the keys. Without making sounds, she moved from chord to chord, up one octave and back down, feeling the memory in her fingers flex. Finally, she pressed her fingertips cleanly down, one chord. It rumbled through the house, resonating in her spine. She stepped heavy on the pedal, to make the strings vibrate like an organ, and started into a hymn. She stayed in the lower registers and made the bass notes roll and thunder. Abruptly she stopped. Her mother was standing in the doorway.

"Play something more appropriate," she said.

Cynthia began to play an old English carol, a piece composed of single notes and a repeating chorus. It was very simple, and she played it once through at the right tempo. Then she began to vary the timing, to stretch out the rests until it seemed like a new and modern piece of music. When she looked again, her mother had an unhappy, disapproving look on her face. Her nose seemed swollen and red, as if she'd been crying. As if she knew how easy it was for Cynthia to make people sad, and she was disappointed by it. She turned back to the kitchen.

Cynthia stood and almost closed the piano. Instead she rifled in the piano bench for the music she was practicing, set the pages on the piano, and began to play. She played best in the early morning, just after her father went out to do chores. Her head seemed clearer in the cold, thin light.

When she was small, there had been a place far down in the fields, off their land, where willows had grown up to hide a spring. She called it a spring, but it was only a seep, a low, muddy place where someone had built a chicken house with a small fenced yard. She'd gone back to find it once, but the coop was gone. Under a mat of long, flattened grass, she'd found pieces of dark orange wood that turned to powder in her hand. She was amazed at how small the yard must have been, how she could have spent so many hours there. Often, as she started playing, she went back to that place, the way it had been.

She worked on the piece in parts. Then she played it straight through, to hear it as it might sound in concert, as if someone else were playing. When she heard her father's voice in the kitchen, her fingers stiffened and lost their confidence. She tried to go on, but he called her from the kitchen.

She put her music away, closed the piano, and went to see what he wanted. He was bent over on the bench in the mud room, one leg across his knee, tugging off a black rubber irrigation boot.

"You didn't feed your animal," her father said.

"I'll go right now," she said.

"Already turned her out," he said.

Cynthia felt numb. The old horse was full of tricks. It would take an hour to catch her in the morning.

4

Lenna directed Kenneth down a side street, a wide street paved with a thin layer of light-colored concrete. Hers was an old neighborhood of small frame houses set far apart, without foundations or porches or shrubs. Only a few spent lilacs stood in the yards, their blossoms dried and shriveled into curly knots. The whole neighborhood looked temporary, as if the houses could be pushed from one yard to another. For the first time, Lenna felt ashamed of where they lived. She tried to take comfort in the massive cottonwoods rising over the roofs of the houses, shimmering with heart-shaped yellow leaves.

The house she'd rented stood alone on the far edge of town with only pastures and low barns beyond it. The small gray house, just one floor and an attic, had been newly painted. But rain had weathered the front door in black streaks, and one of its small windowpanes had been replaced with a blind square of plywood. She never noticed these things; her habit was to drive in back and park beside the caved-in chicken coop. But Ken parked the truck in front, and she had to let him follow her across the dull, spongy grass and through the front door. It wasn't locked.

Their footsteps echoed across the linoleum in the front room. Except for a black wood-burning stove, the room was empty. For lack of funds to ship it, she'd left behind what little furniture they'd had. He followed her into the kitchen.

The kitchen was painted pale yellow all around the bottom,

but above the wainscotting, a different pattern of wallpaper survived on three of the four walls. With age, the roses and plaids and forget-me-nots had faded and blended. The kitchen seemed to gather in around a wooden table she and Kenny had painted white. Two chairs were pulled up to the table: her small spindle chair with its steeple back, and the wide-armed rocker where Kenny sat to write out his homework. Kenny had draped a chocolate-gray cotton blanket, a boy's Indian blanket printed with lightning and arrows, over the back.

Automatically Lenna began to pick up the breakfast dishes she and Kenny had left out that morning when both of them had overslept. Even the milk carton had been left standing out, and a sweet, souring smell clung in the air. When the table was clean, she pulled her coat around her, crossed her arms, and looked at Kenneth Swanson where he stood on the other side of the table.

Ken didn't speak. He lifted one boot up on the seat of the spindle chair, crossed his wrists on his knee, and regarded her. His dark, muddy boot made her chair look undersize, a chair built for a child, and his hunting vest cast watery orange reflections on the walls. She and Kenny spent all their time in this room, and it never struck her as too small. But with Kenneth Swanson in it, the kitchen felt cramped and shabby. She stared back at him. At his square, unshaven jaw, where beard stubble glistened through dirt and sunburn. His hair was reddish-brown, but slicked flat, wet and shining, it seemed black. Against the darkness of his face, his eyes seemed lighted from within, like winter sunlight passing through a pale blue bottle.

"Why not?" he said, as if he'd just told her he was taking Kenny hunting.

"How did you get here?" she demanded.

"Where's Kenny?"

"I don't know." She looked around the room, as if the furniture might tell her. "What time is it?"

He lifted his shirt cuff with two fingers and glanced down at a heavy silver watch. "Five o'clock."

"He'll be home soon."

"You don't know where he is," he said flatly.

"How was he supposed to know you were coming?" She hated the whiny sound of anger rising in her voice. She took a breath and tried to speak slowly. "He's just late from school. He's playing basketball or something."

"It's not basketball season."

"How did you get here?"

"I got leave," he said. "Hitched a ride on a transport plane. Borrowed the truck and horses from a master sergeant in Farson. Picked up a map."

Lenna had forgotten the lazy southern drawl that came into his voice after he joined the air force — the same southern accent most pilots use when they radio the tower. His family was from Nebraska, the same as hers was. He grinned, proud of himself and trying to look innocent, even boyish. It almost worked on her — she felt her throat catch. He looked so much like Kenny. But the accent grated on her, scraped against old angers.

"Beer?" he asked her. But his look said he knew her so well he didn't even have to ask. She shook her head, and he stood abruptly and walked out of the room. She heard the front door slam.

As soon as he was gone, she saw the window glass had turned to cobalt blue, and she was standing in the dark. She switched on the light and the room jumped back, large and familiar but cold. She hadn't stopped to light a fire. She hurried into the bathroom and looked at herself in the mirror. She ran a brush through her hair, where the wind had tangled it around her face and dulled it to a dry wheat color, and looked into her own deep-set blue eyes. Her eyes were not transparent like Ken Swanson's, but the flat, dusky blue of a feather from a bluebird. She pinched her cheeks to bring some color and thought of putting on lipstick. But Ken would notice lipstick.

She was ashamed of herself, of her furtive trip to the bathroom, but she couldn't help it. Exactly why she wanted to look prettier she didn't know. She leaned down to hide the hairbrush out of sight in the cupboard. When she stood, she saw the note taped to the mirror frame. It had been there since that morning. It said "rodeo grounds." She had promised to go after Kenny.

She nearly ran back into the kitchen, but once there she couldn't find her purse. She looked on Kenny's rocker and under the table. Finally, she saw the handles of the purse standing up behind the folded laundry on the dryer. She grabbed it and started out, rummaging for car keys, but at the door she stopped. Her fingers couldn't find the shape and weight of keys. She turned back, pried open the mouth of the purse, and dumped its contents on the kitchen table, pennies rolling off onto the floor. Her car keys weren't there. The keys were in the car. And the car was parked where she'd left it, across from the courthouse.

She stood for a moment feeling panic rise in her, like soda shaken in a bottle. She would walk back to the courthouse. It wasn't that far. Or she could force herself to wait there for Ken. She grasped the back of Kenny's chair and rocked it back and forth.

The front door slammed, and Ken returned, cradling a six-pack under his arm and using both hands to open a beer can.

"How long will you be gone," she asked, "if you take Kenny with you?" She tried to stop them, but as she spoke, tears caught in her throat.

"Oh, hell . . . forget it. Don't cry." Ken swung around the table and enclosed her in his arms. She stiffened, but he held her so tightly she could feel the shotgun shells in the compartments of his vest. They made sharp knobs that cut right through her coat.

"That's not why I came," he said. "I won't take him. Don't cry."

"Why?" she said. "Why did you come?"

"To tell Kenny I'm getting married."

"What?" she said, and heard the back door slam behind her. She shoved Ken hard, twisting out of his grip, and faced the door.

Kenny stood in the doorway, his eyebrows drawn together in a moment of confusion. He didn't look at Lenna. His eyes were fixed on the man beside her. As she watched, he pressed his lips together and his mouth began to tremble and pull sideways. She thought he might break into a grin — or cry. But she was wrong.

He did something she'd never seen him do before, even as a baby. He threw himself at his father. Ran at him like a small boy. And his father lifted him right off the ground.

5

Cynthia wanted to argue with her father, but she knew there wasn't any use. And Goldie was already turned out in the pasture. She watched Earl work off his coveralls, gray railroad coveralls with a herringbone stripe in the weave. Even after chores, he had the neat scrubbed look he'd had at the funeral. His cheeks were closely shaved, and she could still smell the too-sweet tang of his aftershave. At that moment, his eyes seemed to match the blue-gray of his coveralls. He looked as if he'd soaked out all the color in his face when he washed up for the funeral.

"Go set the table," he said.

Cynthia almost reached for the Sunday china before she remembered it was Friday and brought out everyday plastic plates instead. She thought about Goldie, her old horse. Dill gave her Goldie after his accident, when she was hardly big enough to ride. Her dad talked against it, told Dill the horse was worth real money, but he and Dill Nethercott didn't fight. They'd been best friends all their lives.

She never forgot to feed and water Goldie, but somehow the change of routine, coming home early and going to a funeral, had thrown her off.

She set three places at the table, her mother and father at each end, and sat down. Her father sliced into his baked potato and wedged in a square of margarine, but it didn't melt. He cupped the potato in his hand, holding it up to demonstrate that it was cold. Then he set it back on his plate and held the plate high.

"Mother," he said, "go heat this up."

"How is yours?" Her mother turned to her. "Cold?" Cynthia fingered her potato and nodded.

"I've got some others in the oven," her mother said. She gathered the plates. In a few minutes, she was back distributing hot potatoes. Her father doctored his again and started lifting forkfuls to his mouth.

Cynthia studied her mother's calm face. Her parents weren't going to let her go to the dance. Not when they'd been to a funeral. "I'm supposed to go to school tonight," she said. "There's a dance. They asked me to bring some tapes."

"I wonder . . . ," her mother said. "What do you think, Earl?"

"Who's taking you?" Her father talked through a mouthful of beef.

"Nobody. I was just going."

Her father finished chewing his meat before he spoke. "Might as well go," he said.

"People will talk," her mother said.

"What people?" her father said. "How would a person know Cynthia went to the funeral this morning — unless they went there too?"

Her mother gave a slow nod of agreement.

"You go on ahead." Her father dismissed the subject. Cynthia listened to them talk about the Lattimores for a while before she asked to be excused. She cleared the table and washed the dishes. When she finished, she carried the scraps outside.

She found the old dog curled in a nest against the house, twitching in her sleep. "Hey, girl," she said. "Supper's here." It took a long time for the dog to straighten up and find her bowl. Must be the cold, Cynthia thought. She should have stayed, given the dog a pat, but she went back inside.

In her room she pulled on new jeans and a clean black sweater. She dampened her hair and brushed it until it hung shiny and thick in a slant across her cheek. She didn't usually go to school dances, but she'd promised the tapes, and tonight she wanted to get out of the house. She'd felt better after practicing, but the sense she'd had after the funeral, an unreal restlessness, had come back. She could always leave the dance and walk uptown. Or she might drive around.

She parked her dad's car in the wide gravel lot behind the high school and walked between the rows of pickup trucks and cars toward the gym. The sky was black, and it seemed colder than it would be later, in the winter.

Inside, the gym was brightly lit, as if a basketball game instead of a dance were going on, and the overheated air was yeasty with the smell of sweat and stale gym clothes. On one side, the bleachers had been left standing, but they'd been folded away on the other to make room for the sound system and refreshments.

Cynthia hung her jacket on the rack by the door, circled around the dancers in the middle of the court, and dropped off the tapes. She found a spot where she could lean her shoulder blades against the wall. She crossed her feet at the ankles and shoved her hands down in the pockets of her jeans.

It gave her a pleasant feeling to be there with the lights gleaming in long streaks off the high varnish on the floor, something familiar going on all around her. The music thumped through the floor and buzzed in her bones where she leaned against the wall.

She saw Mr. Everts moving through the dancers. He was a dark, heavy man who, even at eight in the morning, had a blue-black shadow of beard, like iron filings. He wore shoes with thick pink rubber soles that made him seem to stick a little as he crossed the gym floor.

It made her nervous, watching him turn and come her way. He'd made her his lab assistant, but she never knew what to say when he tried to make conversation. Though she got good grades, he was the first teacher who'd ever seemed to like her. He approached and turned his back, leaning against the wall a foot or two away.

"Good crowd," he said.

Cynthia looked down at her shoes and let her hair fall. "Looks like it," she said.

"I wish you kids wouldn't play the music quite so loud," he said. But he said it as if he was sticking up for the adults out of habit. As if he didn't really care.

Cynthia tilted her chin up and let her hair fall back. "We only do it," she said, "to drive you nuts."

"That's what I thought," he said, laughing and pushing himself upright. "Back to work," he said, and nodded before he resumed his slow vigil around the gym.

Cynthia folded her arms across her chest and watched the dancers. The sense of comfort she'd had when she arrived was gone. Her sweater itched where it pulled tight at her neck and wrists. There wasn't a single person in the gym who she didn't see every day. She looked for a shirt or a dress or a pair of shoes she hadn't seen before. The girls were flirting now. Her father was right, half the kids on the dance floor had been at the funeral. Cynthia couldn't find a trace of tears. She started for the door, stopping a few times to nod hello to kids she knew, retrieved her jacket, and walked out.

The night air hit her chest like a wall of ice water. She struggled to zip her jacket before the sweat on her back could freeze, shoved her hands deep in its pockets, and started walking toward town. When she exhaled, her breath steamed warm and white.

The lights at the hotel and farther up the street shone a liquid orange, like fires in the night, but otherwise Main Street was deserted. For a second, she had the sensation of walking alone in a big city — as if huge buildings and empty streets loomed just beyond the dark. The icy wind burned her ears. They ached down close to the eardrums.

Near the hotel, she could hear voices. Dark figures leaned on the hoods of the cars parked at the curb. A shard of laughter broke out above the talking. In the light of the pink neon sign for the café she could make out who was there.

She didn't speak, but heads looked up. She recognized two girls from her class and Roddy Moyers. He leaned against the hood of his car with an arm draped around the neck of a girl she didn't recognize, a girl with long dark hair and glasses. She was wrapped in a white shaggy coat, like a sheepskin rug.

"Aren't you guys cold?" Cynthia said, and one of the young men held out a paper bag crimped around the neck of a bottle.

"Not yet," he said.

But Roddy Moyers disengaged himself from the girl and stood up straight.

"I am," he said. "You going in?" He looked directly at Cynthia in a way that made her want to look to see if somebody had walked up behind her. He hadn't said a word to her in years, since she was a little child.

"For a while," she said.

"Hold on," he said. "I'll come with you."

Cynthia glanced at the girl in the shaggy coat. Behind her glasses she had big dark eyes and cheekbones like a model. But she didn't pay any attention when Moyers walked away and Cynthia turned to follow him. He wore a white long-sleeved shirt but no jacket, and the threadbare hems of his jeans hung over the heels of his boots. He pushed through the glass door and reached back to brace it open, just long enough for her to get a hold on it herself. Then he went on up the narrow hall and disappeared through the door to the right — into the bar. The café door was on the left. That was the door she'd expected him to take. She wasn't old enough for the bar.

She stood still, stunned, as if he'd slapped her, heat pumping into her cheeks. She'd made a mistake. When he said "going in," she thought he meant in off the street. She didn't know what to do, standing in the hall where anyone could see her, her weight shifting awkwardly over her shoes. She had to get out. She spun around and nearly ran.

She pushed open the door and, without glancing at the people leaning on the cars, turned sharply and started down the street. She took long strides and felt the muscles in her calves burn. She covered one block, then crossed to the other side of the street. Even when she was a safe distance from the hotel, her heart pounded.

She was nearly back at school, almost at the parking lot, when Roddy Moyers pulled up at the curb just ahead of her. Despite the cold, he had the top down on the car, a small white car with deep seats, like a powerboat. He cut the engine and tilted his head to look over at her.

"What happened to you?"

The truth jumped up at her. He thought she'd just disappeared for no reason. He didn't know she was underage. She'd made a big deal out of nothing, and Roddy Moyers knew it.

She searched for something to say, some lie to explain. But he was watching her intently, and she saw the truth slowly come to him.

"Jesus," he said, looking down at the gearshift. He looked at her again. "Jesus," he said, "I'm sorry." He reached over and shoved the car door open. "Come on," he said. "I'll give you a ride."

She looked down at the open door hanging over the curb. "No, thanks," she said. "I can walk."

"Come on," he said. "We'll go for a ride. It's early."

Cynthia grasped the frame of the open door and pushed it closed. It slammed with a heavy, muffled sound. "No, thanks," she said, a tight sarcasm coming into her voice. "Past my bedtime."

Moyers frowned. "Some other time," he said, not asking but telling her, before he twisted the key in the ignition.

"Fine," Cynthia said, but he gunned the motor so loud she didn't think he heard. He pulled away from the curb, circled in a wide U-turn, and drove back toward the hotel. The engine in the car growled with a tinny rattle, and a backfire echoed off the storefronts.

She walked back to her father's big Chevrolet, wanting to run, and drove it slowly out of the lot. The power steering was so loose she always felt as if she were driving a wide float in a parade. She liked the big, lumbering slowness of the car, the way it glided along the highway with no sound, but tonight she slowly pressed down on the gas until the car was speeding through the dark.

She drove across the valley and turned north on the oil road toward the ranch, but she went on past the gate and turned up the track to the graveyard. The tires crunched across the gravel parking lot. She found the service road in the headlights, an over-grown dry track winding to the top of the hill above the graves. Tall weeds slid and broke under the frame of the car, scraping along the doors. Where the road ended, she backed the car around and got out. Just below her the tall flagpole was anchored in a concrete platform. She walked across the spongy grass and sat down on its edge. Behind her, she could sense the mountains, a massive weight of darkness rising up behind her.

The damp feel of the concrete turned her hip bones into hard knobs, and her arms and legs seemed to disappear in the cold. She heard a scrape, the step of something wild behind her. She flinched before she realized it was the rustle of her own jacket. She wrapped her arms around herself. The moon came up, round and white over the mountains in the east. It outlined the peaks and dropped a gauzy mist into the canyons.

She thought about how you freeze to death, how you just lie down in the snow. She felt so dark, so black inside. She never did the right thing. The heat of being left out in the hall, of Roddy disappearing, came back, shame rising inside her like seepage. A basement of black water. But running away was worse. Roddy knew. He knew there was something the matter with her.

If she'd only stayed there and waited, he would have come out to find her. Why didn't she just go in the bar and get him? Tell him she was underage?

She thought about Goldie, going hungry all through the funeral, and her mother's look when she was playing the piano. There was something wrong with her. Her parents had wanted a boy, and she wasn't a boy. She had believed that story for so long and, at the same time, known it wasn't true. It didn't explain anything. It didn't tell her what was wrong. No one trusted her. Most of her aunts and uncles and the teachers at school and at church had always been suspicious.

She thought about Curly Lattimore, the white coffin like a cake, and her father carrying it up the hill himself. The whole town coming to her funeral. She couldn't imagine anybody, ever, loving her that way. Somehow, if she died, they'd say it was her fault.

The moon hung, smaller now, suspended over the mountains and threw the shadow of the flagpole long across the hill. Below her she could see the raw new grave, a mound of pale earth against the grass. Beside it they had left a tractor, the raised elbow of a backhoe still attached. It loomed up in the moonlight like a praying mantis.

6

At first, the window was a square of blue slate. Kenny pulled the worn, cool quilt up around his face and watched the dawn sky over the mountains slowly turn the color of a healing bruise. He floated in the hollow of the mattress, half awake, as if he were resting at the bottom of a pool, breathing underwater. Across the room, the pattern on the wallpaper stood out in glimmers of white against the shadows. The pattern repeated round, white movie reels, unwinding like springs in a clock. And he could make out sets of vacation postcards hanging down in accordion folds. In the dim light, Kenny couldn't see the figures on the cards, but he knew them by heart: a man on horseback; a sportsman fishing from a rock; a woman in a bathing suit, diving like a jackknife. The pictures made him think of the damp, pitchy cold in the shade of pine trees. And of the other boy, the boy who had the room when the wallpaper was new. Kenny thought he must be grown by now. On the ceiling, leaks had left receding waves the color of tobacco juice, and the roof sloped just above his head. He sat up carefully, swung his feet over the edge of the mattress, and stepped on something hard and alive. It rolled underfoot like a marble, or a snake. He jerked his feet back. Then he remembered. His father had come upstairs late the night before; the gray cocoon of his sleeping bag took up all the empty floor space in the room. Kenny heard his father groan, struggling in his sleep. His shoulders and elbows jabbed bulges in the canvas bag. Rising from the floor, the sour smell of last night's beer on his father's breath seemed to use up all the air. Kenny opened his mouth to breathe and stepped, teetering off balance, over the sleeping bag. He lifted up on the doorknob to keep the hinges from creaking and edged out onto the upstairs landing. His father sleeping in his room made him feel shy and formal, as if a total stranger had come to spend the night.

He crept down to the kitchen, his feet turned nearly sideways on the narrow steps, and started the coffee heating in the kitchen before he built a fire in the stove. Thin sheets of ice covered the insides of the windows. The empty living room felt cavernous, but Kenny liked the ice. It made him feel as if they had moved far-ther north, to a cabin in the mountains or a ranch in Canada. He was tempted to shave it off, to carve his initials on the glass, but he couldn't bring himself to leave the stove. He'd come down-stairs in the bottoms of his long johns, and his feet were bare. He stood in front of the black cast-iron stove, his neck and chest muscles clenched against the cold — hoping his mother would wake up before his dad.

He waited until the coffee started to bubble and perk and the smell of roasting coffee seemed warmer than the heat from the stove before he made a dash for the kitchen and pulled clean clothes from his stack on top of the dryer. He worked his legs into a pair of stiff new jeans and put on a frayed woolen shirt. When he finished dressing, his socks hung limp at the ankles, but he tugged them up and went to fill a cracked blue mixing bowl with cereal. He carried the bowl back to the front room and ate standing up, his back to the fire. The milk had begun to turn sweet and cheesy, but he finished the cereal and tipped the bowl to drink off the rest of it. As the frost began to melt, scallops of lacy crystals formed on the windows. When the windows began to glisten with sunlight, like a coating of blue sugar, he poured a mug of coffee and carried it back to his mother's room. He knocked softly on the doorframe, but he didn't hear an answer.

"Mom?" he said.

When she still didn't answer, he turned the doorknob. The door was locked. Kenny felt the resistance on the knob like a fist punched, not hard but unexpected, high up in his stomach. His mother never locked her door. He didn't know what he should do.

He stood in the hall, feeling the cold from the linoleum chill the bottoms of his socks and spread up into his feet. He tried to listen through the door, but all he could hear was the rush of his own breathing and the small bones at the base of his skull creaking, settling like odd noises in the quiet house. He wandered back into the kitchen and poured his mother's coffee back into the pot. He sat down on the rocker to pull on his boots. Then he bundled up in his old ski jacket and gloves and went outside.

His boots made dark, wet footprints in the frost, and he could smell the wood smoke from the chimney. The air seemed to crackle with cold. Except for a wisp of dark, trailing cloud over the mountains, the sky was blue now, and the air so clear that objects in the distance looked close up. Kenny saw a road he'd never seen before running straight up through the foothills like a piece of frozen twine. He began to feel excited, like being the first one up on Christmas morning. If his father woke up in time, they were going hunting.

He walked back to the sagging sheep-wire corral, where his father had left the horses for the night. They stood dozing on their feet, their soft, triangular eyelids wrinkled shut. Except for the scooped-out marks where their saddles had been, they were coated with damp, gray road dust. Kenny went to the truck to hunt for a brush. He searched behind the seat, rummaging through the empty beer cans and wadded-up paper bags, but he couldn't even find a rag to wipe the horses down with. He gave up, gathered an armful of hay, and opened the gate to drop it in a pile before each horse. They opened their liquid, melancholy eyes, and began to lip at the alfalfa. The grinding of their teeth, high up in their jaws, made a sound like footsteps marching down a gravel road. He leaned into the tall shoulder of one of the horses and breathed in the smell of dried sweat. Then he tugged off a glove and ran his bare palm along the horse's neck. Under the coarse weight of its mane, his hand grew warm with steam.

Kenny heard the screen door slam and turned around to see his dad stamping his boots on the concrete step. He already wore his orange hunting vest. "Let's go, let's go," he said. He clapped his hands together. "We're losin' daylight." He acted as if Kenny had been outside goofing off, holding them up.

Kenny blinked, confused by his father's sudden hurry. But he shrugged, relieved that somebody was finally awake. He gave the horse a pat and followed his father back inside the house.

His dad stood at the sink and finished the last drops of his coffee. His shaving kit was balanced on top of his sleeping bag, where he'd piled his things beside the door.

"I guess Mom's sleeping in," Kenny said, apologizing. He crossed the kitchen, clicked open the door of the refrigerator and looked inside. "I think we've got some eggs. I could cook you some breakfast."

"She needs her sleep," his father said. "We were up late." He glanced at Kenny.

Kenny stood at the refrigerator, holding the door wide open.

"Don't worry," his dad said. "I'm the one in the doghouse, not you."

"Why are you in the doghouse?"

His dad clinked his coffee cup as he set it in the sink and suddenly looked tired. He shrugged his shoulders and laughed. The laugh was dry and almost silent. Kenny let the refrigerator door swing closed.

"Let's get on the road. We can stop someplace to eat," his dad said. "I'll go out and load the horses, get the truck warmed up. You round up your gear."

Kenny waited while his dad hoisted his sleeping bag and elbowed his way out the door. Then he ran up the stairs two at a time. Halfway up, he stopped, worried the thumping of his feet might wake his mother. He dug through his bottom drawer and found two extra pairs of socks, rolled them in his sleeping bag, and carried the bedroll downstairs. Out the kitchen window, he watched his father coaxing the second horse into the truck. The horse balked and shied away, but his dad kept a grip on the halter, turning the horse in a tight circle before he sent him scrambling up the ramp. He lowered the stock rack gate and latched it. Kenny wanted to go one more time to his mother's door, to see if she was awake. But he didn't have time. All he could do was scribble "Be back late tomorrow" on an envelope and leave it propped up on the sugar bowl. He grabbed his sleeping bag and ran out to the truck. He was barely six feet from the door when it slammed so hard he heard the glass panels rattle in their frames.

His father drove north out of town, one hand gripping the wheel and the elbow of his left arm leaning out the open window. Main Street was wide and empty. The only other cars they saw were parked in front of the hotel coffee shop, where the plate glass window, silvered with steam, looked like a pocked antique mirror. His dad let the truck creep along until they passed the courthouse before he started to speed up. On the open highway, wind rushed through the cab and slapped

Kenny's hair around his face. He brushed it back with his hand, but a strand cut across one eye, as sharp as a blade of swamp grass. Kenny blinked back tears, but he didn't roll his window up. He was relieved the wind and the rattle of the truck made so much noise he didn't have to worry about making conversation.

After a few miles, his father cleared his throat and raised his voice.

"So tell me how you're getting along."

"Okay, I guess."

"No, tell me. How's the new school?"

"It's all right."

His father rolled his window up, and Kenny felt he had to roll his up as well.

"What's your favorite subject?"

"Lunch."

It was an old joke, but his father gave him a quick smile anyway.

"Give me some facts," he said. "Is it a good school?"

"Not very," Kenny said and immediately wished he hadn't. His dad would blame the school on his mother. The school was worn down and dirty; all the books were old and out-of-date. "It's okay," he said. "Just different from the last one."

"How so?"

"It's small."

"Well, that's good," his father said. "Any girls in it?"

"No." Kenny lied deadpan, and his father laughed out loud.

"No girls?"

"Haven't seen any."

"I bet you haven't," his father said, then added, "but you will."

Kenny grinned and looked out the window at the pale blur of sagebrush going by. Thousands of tiny purple asters, the last wildflowers, had shriveled in the short, dry grass beside the road.

"Well," his father said, "don't worry about it. Pretty soon, the girls are going to see you. But that doesn't answer my question. How are you and your mother doing? Tell me the truth."

Kenny glanced over at his father. White squint lines radiated from the outside corners of his eyes. His face was so burned by the sun and wind that it looked smudged and dirty. Kenny remembered that his father had been traveling and hunting by himself for a week now. It made Kenny feel left out. He wondered why his dad hadn't come to get him sooner.

Kenny shrugged. "We're fine," he said. He stared through the murky windshield, wishing he'd thought to hose it off while he was waiting for his dad to get up. He knew his dad was frowning — he felt it without having to look over at him. "Tell me about the time you took Mom up in the trainer plane."

"You're changing the subject."

"We're fine," Kenny said.

For a minute, Kenny thought he'd made his father mad. But his father laughed, low in his throat, as if he were laughing by himself, and started to tell the story about the two-seater. Kenny had heard it so many times he knew it almost word for word. But he wanted to hear it again. If he could get his father telling airplane stories, he wouldn't have to answer questions.

Kenny twisted around on the seat so he could watch his father's face and listened to the story. His dad had endless stories about landing airplanes in Nebraska — on dirt roads, and fields, and frozen ponds — when he was young. Three times he had walked away from planes that crashed. He had two scars Kenny knew about. In the winter when his face was clean and shaved, a thin white scar pulled at the corner of his mouth and zigzagged over the edge of his chin, like a crack in an eggshell. If you glimpsed it quickly from the side, you got the impression his dad was drooling, and when he was mad, the scar made him look a little sad, and not so frightening. It was ugly, the way the scar pulled down on the edge of his lip, but it only made Kenny want to stare at his face, as if he could never see it for long enough. The other scar made a raised, thick rope from his hip to his knee where he used to have a steel rod implanted. He walked with a limp when he was tired, but he wouldn't admit it. Kenny's mother said he'd lied about his leg for so long to pass his air force physicals that he'd convinced himself there was nothing wrong with him.

"You were just a baby," his dad was saying. "I was still stationed in Nevada, way out in the boondocks. And I talked your mother into going up with me. The first, and the last, time. I don't remember where you were. We must have left you with a sitter."

His parents had taken off over the desert in an old trainer, his dad in the front and his mother in the seat behind, and circled around the airport, chatting back and forth to each other by radio. So when his dad came in for the landing, everything was fine, except he forgot to switch off the radio, and the tower could hear what they said. As the wheels touched down, his mother shouted, "Oh! That was a good one, Daddy!" For months after that, every time his dad made a landing, the tower would come in saying, "That was a good one, Daddy!"

His dad finished the story, laughing. Kenny started to ask him about another time, when his squadron stole a jeep and hid it in the bomb bay. But by then, the road had started a steep climb, and his dad pulled off at the Food Ranch. They filled both gas tanks and went inside for groceries. Kenny wandered around the store while his father waited to pay. There wasn't much to look at on the dusty shelves. He walked over to the gun counter to look at fishing lures and flies. The lures hung on a rack, wrapped in plastic envelopes so dim and grimy he could hardly tell what kind they were. He looked in the flat case of flies on the counter, but the separate squares were nearly empty. In one he saw a real fly, a housefly, dead and curled up on its back. He almost went to get his dad to ask him, "How much you think they want for that one?" He would have done it if his mom had been along, but his dad was different. Instead, he looked at the rifles in the locked gun case. He didn't know much about guns. His father had never taken him hunting for big game before. They'd gone fishing, and one fall he went along with his dad and some men from his squadron to shoot ducks. His father was stationed in Florida now. He said he'd gone out deep-sea fishing on a charter boat.

When they were back in the truck, his father rolled his window down again, and Kenny put his hand up to keep his hair out of his eyes.

"Too much wind?" his father asked, and rolled his window halfway up. Then he pulled an orange hunting cap from the grocery sack and presented it to him. "Here," he said, "put that on. But if you're ever hunting where it's crowded, leave it home. It'll only make you a better target."

"It won't be crowded where we're going?"

"Not a chance."

"Where is it, again?"

"The Big Hole, in Montana."

"Why are we going so far?"

Kenny pushed his hair back and fitted the hat down snug over his forehead, tugging on the bill. He didn't honestly care how far they went. He was fascinated by the names "The Big Hole" and "Montana." He pictured a narrow valley with high white mountains all around. For some reason, it made him see tall, wavy grass, toasted gold and brown like shredded wheat. But his father had an answer.

"A major in my squadron has a brother-in-law owns a hunting camp up there. Must have been three years ago we got invited. I didn't get a thing," he said, "unless you count a hangover and a rotten disposition."

The truck began to climb up the pass, where snow had pooled and frozen under the trees. Tall spruce trees appeared beside the road, black against the snow, and the air smelled different. Kenny rolled his window down and stuck his head out. He could feel the cool air seep out from under the trees. It felt like standing in front of the open refrigerator in the summer, looking at what there was to eat. Kenny ducked his head back in the cab, and the truck ground into second gear, then finally into first, and crawled up the winding road, the engine scrambling like a rusty, mechanical crab. They passed a sign that said "Continental Divide," and then they were sailing down the other side of the pass, on a two-lane road cutting straight across a wide expanse of shale and sagebrush. Kenny turned and saw his father holding back a grin, as if he was keeping back a secret.

"You want to drive?" he said.

"Sure," Kenny said, but his father gave him a look and he changed it to "Yes, sir."

They pulled over, got out, and walked around the truck to switch sides. The high, arid plains seemed suddenly flat and very quiet. He took hold of the wheel to swing himself up on the truck seat and stretched his foot down toward the pedals. But he couldn't reach. Both of them had to throw all their weight to get the rusty seat to slide a little forward. Kenny grasped the gearshift and tried three times before he finally jammed it into first. Then he eased up slowly on the clutch. But the truck lurched off the shoulder, spraying sand and gravel off into the sagebrush.

Kenny glanced sideways, but all his father said was "Take it easy with the livestock." Kenny slid the gearshift into second, and finally into third.

"One of these days, if I'm brave enough, I'll teach you how to fly."

His dad and uncle Jack had grown up flying airplanes. Their father had owned a garage and John Deere dealership, and the two of them covered the entire county delivering parts and repairing tractors right out in the field. Later on, they flew to different rodeos. Kenny had his uncle Jack's old bareback rigging.

His uncle Jack was dead. He'd died a long time ago, before Kenny was born. But his dad still bragged about how they both had their pilot's licenses before they got their licenses to drive. Kenny liked to hear the story, but he didn't even have a driver's license. And his dad had been promising for years to teach him how to fly.

"Now, take it easy," his dad said. He flicked on the radio, leaned back on the dusty seat cover, and snapped open a beer can. "Just keep going straight," he said, laughing, because there wasn't any other way to go. After a while, Kenny looked over and saw he was asleep.

Kenny drove and listened to the radio. A wind came up. It buffeted the truck and threatened to jerk the wheel out of his hands. The volcanic plain stretched as far as he could see, a flat, dull-colored strip of land under a pale blue sky. Misty clouds stretched along the horizon, and dust devils twisted far off in the distance, like smoke from cooking fires. A tumbleweed skittered in front of the truck, bounced as high as a basketball, and caught in the barbed-wire fence along the road. He gripped the wheel hard to keep the truck from swerving. When the radio announcer spoke, Kenny was amazed to hear the broadcast came all the way from Calgary, in Canada. The station was playing corny old cowboy songs. He listened to "Timber Trail" and "Empty Saddles." He laughed and tried to whistle a high harmony along with the yodeling in the song that came on next. But he couldn't whistle very well. His mother could, but she wouldn't teach him how. He started to think about Roddy Moyers, and he found himself clamping his fingers too tight on the steering wheel.

His pulse raced, and he thought about straddling the chute, waiting for a signal. How the fear coiled in his stomach and he fought to keep from squeezing his eyes shut. Somehow, the tense pull — half terror and half excitement — was mixed up now with Roddy Moyers. He had to find a way to get back to it. A new fear, like the fear of forgetting a test at school, crept up the back of his neck. Something might happen, and he would never ride again. He lifted his fingers off the wheel and fanned them out, hanging on with his thumbs. He slumped down, to get more comfortable in the seat, and tried to relax with the music. But after a few miles, his hands were tight on the wheel again and he was sitting up with air between his backbone and the truck seat. He had to relax all over again.

It was after dark before he found the road up to the hunting camp, and his dad had to drive the last few uphill miles on a logging road so rutted and washed out the truck jolted over boulders as if the wheels were square instead of round. Finally his dad squeezed the brake and they unloaded the horses. Kenny took hold of a halter with each hand and led them up on foot, following the rocking, red embers of the taillights.

He was disappointed to reach The Big Hole after dark. He lay in his sleeping bag surrounded by a blackness so thick his eyes felt closed, though they were open. Overhead, dense white stars shivered in a solid mass and made the night seem blacker. They had built a fire, but it cast no light.

"Dad?" he said into the darkness. "You awake?"

A grunt came back from across the campfire.

"What's it look like in the daytime?"

"What?"

"The Big Hole."

"Huge black hole in the ground. As far across as Boise."

"Be serious."

"Indians dug it."

Kenny shook his head, smiling.

"Blackfeet." His dad let out a laugh.

"Come on." Kenny shook his head again, but the picture in his mind of Indians with dirty feet sneaking up to dig a hole made him laugh, too. "What's it really look like?"

"Another bunch of mountains," his dad said. "We're not right in the hole."

"Where's the hole?"

"West of here."

"What's in it?"

"Big ranches . . . and mosquitoes. Worst mosquitoes you ever saw. Pack a man right off his tractor. Then go back for the tractor."

Kenny laughed until his ribs hurt. It wasn't the joke, it was his father telling it.

"Dad?"

"What?"

Kenny took a breath, not sure he could trust his voice. "You ever getting stationed back up here?"

His father didn't answer. The mountain was very still, and the stars seemed to quiver and plunge down closer to his face.

"Shouldn't count on it," his dad said.

For no reason Kenny felt dragged down by sorrow. He swallowed hard. "Why not?" he said. For a minute he had the feeling nobody was out there in the dark. That he was alone on the mountain. Finally his father answered.

"I don't have that much to say about it. I just go where Uncle Sam tells me."

"But couldn't you ask to come back?"

His father cleared his throat. "If you ever need anything. Anything at all. You call me. You know where I am."

"Go to hell," Kenny said, low under his breath. He rolled over on his stomach.

His father gave the "if you ever need anything" speech every time he saw him. At first Kenny thought it meant he should call if he needed something, like new gym shoes. But when he got older he understood it meant good-bye. It was like saying "See you" or "Be sure to write."

"Kenny?" There was a hardness in his father's voice, as if he was starting in on a lecture.

"Yeah?"

"Can you hear me?"

"Uh-huh." He squeezed his eyes shut.

"You awake?"

Kenny didn't answer. He heard his father scuffle out of his bag and get up to toss a branch on the fire. He could hear it crackle and burn.

He tried to concentrate on the steep climbing they would do the next day. His dad had ended up with only one permit — to shoot a mountain goat — but goats were the hardest game to locate in high country.

When his father called his name again, he pretended he was sleeping.

7

Roddy Moyers sat up as if he were raising one sore rib at a time, opened his eyes, and squinted against the glare of white light in the cell. He held his hand up as a shade, surprised to see it wrapped in thick gauze and adhesive tape, the edges of the bandage rusty with dried blood. He flexed his fingers and winced. The jail cell was familiar — small, rectangular, the concrete walls glazed with so many layers of paint they glistened like yellowing cream. He swung his feet to the floor and stood. When his head cleared, he stepped over to the tin mirror screwed into the wall above the sink. A long scratch, beaded with crystalline blood, ran down his forehead and across one cheek. He reached up and touched a small flap of skin hanging loose near his chin. Down the hallway, he could hear the squawk and crackle of a two-way radio. He turned around slowly, opened the cell door, and walked out.

Following the sound of the radio, he passed two other cells, the windows barred with woven strips of steel. In each one, a sleeping body was rolled up in a blanket on the cot. He turned into the sheriff's office, a cubicle of gray metal furniture, the air parched with the smell of dust and old paper. The deputy sat at the radio, his khaki uniform creased sharp along the sleeves and a heavy black holster shifted around to fit under the arm of his chair.

Roddy lifted the hinged section of the counter and let himself in. The deputy glanced up, jerked his head in the direction of the coffee pot, and went on talking into the microphone. Roddy filled a brown-stained mug and carried it back down the hall to his cell.

He lowered himself onto the cot, holding the mug, feeling the heat of it seep into the bandage, and tried to recall the night before. His memory kept approaching a sense of blackness, then backing off. All he remembered was heading out to the county line, to the Midway Bar and Grill, and a redhead leaning on the polished bar. He didn't know how he'd come to be in jail. He set the coffee down and patted his back pocket. His wallet and keys were gone, and without these familiar things, he was overtaken by a vague feeling, a sense of not knowing who he was or where he belonged. He'd learned to know this feeling from riding in strange towns and waking up in unfamiliar hospitals. This time, at least, he didn't have to trust some stranger to tell him what bones were broken, or how he'd have to quit the circuit if he wanted to grow old. He picked up the warm coffee mug and took a sip. The deputy leaned in at the door.

"Mornin'," he said.

"Drunk and disorderly?" Roddy asked him.

"Worse."

"Let's have the good news."

"Better ask your friends."

"Who else have you got?"

"Al Wilson. One of the Jimpson brothers."

"What day is it — Sunday?"

"All day."

The deputy moved off down the hall, clanging the cell doors open hard enough to wake the dead. Roddy finished his coffee, stretched out on the cot, and crooked an elbow over his eyes.

The night crept back. He remembered being too drunk to drive, catching a ride with Al and Jimpson. They were all laughing, crowding into the truck cab. He had a brief recollection of a long curve of highway, his head swinging heavy against the sway of the truck. The dullness of waiting, half asleep, to get dropped off, and wondering how he was going to make it to the bunkhouse.

That's when he saw the deer, a dark shape looming up beside the road, weaving and running. It careened in from the berm, out of the blackness, and collided with the truck. The dull thud swung the truck sideways across the road, its headlights beaming off into the sage, shining on the red glow of eyes — large animals frozen by the light.

"I got a tag! I got a license. I'm legal!" He remembered Al hollering, and then the confusion in the truck, arms and legs scrambling, Al reaching for the gun rack. The first shot exploded close enough to slam his eardrums.

He stumbled down the roadside ditch behind Al, blinded by his own shadow in the headlights, and hit the barbed-wire hard, the rusted barbs burning where they tore his skin. Drunk as he was, he knew to lie still, not to struggle. Overhead, the stars spun slowly clockwise, and then he heard the thud of hooves on frozen ground, the sound of running horses. They were close, but he couldn't tell in what direction they were running. He shoved his face in the dirt, fighting the wire to get an arm over his head.

Behind him, he heard the squeal of locked brakes and the sudden crash of the collision, ripping metal and exploding glass. He must have passed out. He woke up at the sound of sirens and saw the sheriff's outfit and a fire truck. No ambulance.

There hadn't been an ambulance. He opened his eyes. His mood lifted almost perceptibly.

The deputy knocked on the open door and tossed him a white paper bag folded over at the top. "Get cleaned up," he said. "Café's sending over breakfast."

The thought of food made him queasy. He emptied the bag on

the cot — a razor, shaving cream, a toothbrush and paste, a plastic comb. He went to the sink and bent to lower his head under the faucet. He closed his eyes and let the icy water run.

After he shaved, he sat back down on the cot and leaned against the wall. The concrete was so cold it sweated dampness through the paint. He heard the deputy's stiff leather shoes coming down the corridor, and an unfamiliar voice.

"Doesn't matter," the deputy said. "They all get the same."

He appeared in the doorway carrying a heavy cardboard box in both arms, and he had a woman with him, a pretty blond woman in a powdery blue sweater. She lifted out a plate with a cracked plastic cover and waited until he levered himself up and walked over to take it from her. While he set the warm plate on the cot, she reached back in the box and held out a paper cup of coffee. The woman smelled like soap, a smell so unexpected in the stale air of the jail that he could hardly look at her.

"Thanks," he said, but she only glanced at his bandaged hand and followed the deputy to the next cell down the hall. The eggs on the plate had congealed and the toast was cold. He had a hard, empty pain at the bottom of his stomach from the first cup of coffee, but he ate everything on the plate. There was no telling when they'd get out.

Later, the deputy went from cell to cell repeating the news that the judge wouldn't be in town until Monday to set bail. They might as well relax. He stopped again at Roddy's cell and filled in the details of the night before. They hadn't hit a deer. They'd hit a horse. The animal had to be put down, but Al hadn't shot anything.

The worst of it was that an old couple had plowed a camper truck into Al's. Both outfits were a total loss, but nobody hurt. Al would get hit with drunken driving, destruction of property,

everything in the book. Roddy still didn't know why he was in
jail — he hadn't been driving. But the deputy was saving that for
last. They'd all been in a stolen vehicle.

Later, he called the ranch from the pay phone and let the foreman know where he was. His parents kept two other houses, one
in Arizona and one in L.A., because his father played golf. At the
moment, he didn't actually know where they were, but at least
they weren't around close.

Before lunch, the deputy passed out mops and buckets. "Might
as well work while you're killing time," he said.

Roddy filled the galvanized pail with steaming, soapy water
and wheeled it down the hall to the front door of the courthouse. It hurt to bend over, and it hurt to mop with one hand, but
he'd taken too many hard falls to pay much attention. The sore-
ness would last a day or two; the best thing was to ignore it. He
swept the heavy mop in wide circles, spreading a thin chocolate
film on the tiles. He rang the mop out and started over. He had all
day. The courthouse was dead quiet, the halls filling with the sick
smell of disinfectant rising from the bucket at his feet.

Out of the corner of his eye, he had the quick, eerie sense of
movement where it shouldn't be. There was nobody around. He
lifted the mop and glanced in at the recorder's office. At the
counter, the woman who'd brought breakfast was shuffling
through a stack of papers. He wondered what she was doing in
the courthouse on Sunday.

He stood just out of sight, not meaning to spy, but watching
her. She glanced up at the clock and seemed to lose her place.
She stared at the papers on the counter, but she didn't seem to
see them.

8

Early in the morning, Kenny explored around the hunting camp, a hard-packed clearing in the trees surrounded by squares of flattened grass where canvas tents had stood. He found a narrow, rocky creek to the south, and near the creek, poles lashed high between the trees for hanging deer and elk.

Right after breakfast — hard, sticky donuts they ate right from the box — they saddled the horses and rode out of camp. Since they only had a permit for a mountain goat, they left the shotgun locked inside the truck. His dad carried lunch and rope and his buck knives. Kenny rode with his dad's new Winchester in the scabbard on his saddle.

The plan was to get up high, above the game, and they rode up the steep side of a mountain, through a field of dead wildflowers, long-leafed mules-ears blown flat in one direction. Kenny stretched his legs down in the stirrups and began to feel awake. The view angled down through an open meadow and across a wide valley to another set of hazy mountains, so far away they looked like dirty clouds on the horizon.

He'd stayed awake in the night, after his father fell asleep, thinking of his mother. Ashamed for wanting to be back home. His mother never locked her door. It made her seem like somebody he didn't know, and the dark feeling loomed again. He wished he'd had a chance to say good-bye.

He followed Kenneth's horse into a stand of quaking aspens as the sun broke out from behind the peaks. Wind gusted in the

tallest yellow tree, and the leaves caught the sunlight. It poured
through each round leaf until the whole tree shimmered like a
treasure of gold coins against the high blue sky. As if by signal,
both Kenny and his dad reined in their horses and let them stand.
The wind hissed and whistled, churning and tossing in one tree,
then another, like something alive. Then they were riding up the
mountain again. The trees turned to lodgepole pines, growing
close together and thick with fallen timber.

Kenny watched his dad's wide shoulders bend forward as the
haunches of his horse gathered to jump a fallen log. Kenny followed after, his horse in perfect rhythm with his dad's. He
couldn't figure out how they could find a mountain goat in all
this country, but he didn't really care. If all they did was ride all
day, he wouldn't be unhappy. But he wished they had a permit to
shoot elk. The veiny yellow leaves underfoot were dotted everywhere with nests of dark clay beads.

At the tree line they unsaddled the horses and hobbled their
front legs. Kenny lay down on the thin mountain grass. His dad
sat leaning up against a tree, his bad leg stretched in front of him.
He'd broken most of his bones flying or riding rodeo, but only the
one leg bothered him, and only when he was tired.

His dad handed him a thick piece of salami and a cracker, and
Kenny washed it down with warm, metallic soda. The sun was so
hot he could smell it baking the nylon on his jacket sleeves. It
smelled like a short in the toaster cord. The warmth made his
eyelids itch with heaviness. He could have gone to sleep, but his
dad stood up stiffly, ready to go. They left the horses hobbled
under the trees and started up the mountain on foot.

Kenny climbed after his father, the rifle bumping on its strap
behind his shoulder, the air so thin it was hard to breathe and
keep up. He was glad when his father's boots slid and a small

avalanche of rock and shale came rolling down. He stopped and stood aside.

"Hey," his dad said, "you didn't say anything about riding this year. Don't they rodeo at school?"

"Yeah."

The climb grew steeper. His dad stopped talking and used his bare hands to haul himself up through the rocks. When he found a place to rest, he stood, one khaki leg out straight, the other bent and braced against a rock.

"You won't ever be any good unless you keep at it," his dad said. "When I was your age, we rode every day."

"You lived on a farm."

"A ranch," his dad corrected. He stopped talking and his eyes narrowed. "What happened?" he said. "You didn't make the team?"

Kenny took his hat off and wiped hot sweat out of his eyes. "No," he said, "that's not it. My mom wants me to wait until we get a little bit ahead. In case I have a wreck." He settled the hat back on and looked up.

His father was staring down at him, one eyebrow raised. A dark look passed over his face and was gone like the shadow of a trout deep in the water. Kenny saw his mistake in a second, calling his mother "my mom," as if he didn't have a dad. But his father only turned and clambered faster through the rocks. Kenny had to scramble to keep up. Sweat stung his eyes, and the rifle strap seemed to cut right through his jacket.

They climbed onto a flat table of rock where they could stand up straight. A cone-shaped gravel peak rose behind them, but over the cliff edge of the rock the solid ground dropped straight into a deep canyon ridged with rocky ledges. He stood at the rim and tried to catch his breath, but a wind swept up from the canyon and grabbed the air from his lungs. He thought the wind might lift him like a paper kite and push him off the rock. He stepped back from the edge and felt his father's hand clamp down on his shoulder.

"Kenny," his father said, having to shout into the wind. "You have a wreck. I'll pay for it. What's your mother up to?"

Kenny faced his father, the wind rushing in his ears.

"Never mind," his dad shouted, shaking his head. "I'll talk to her."

"Don't —" Kenny started, but his father hissed for quiet and jerked his chin toward the canyon.

Far down on the opposite wall, Kenny saw a tiny white dot, a piece of glistening quartz. He slipped the rifle strap off, and his dad took the gun, using the scope to sight with.

"Can't get there from here," he said, and handed the rifle back. Kenny shouldered the gun, and his dad placed his hands over his and moved them to the right positions. He adjusted the scope.

Kenny found the white dot, but it was so distorted by distance it shimmered in an oily rainbow. Even through the scope the mountain goat was only a tiny white carving you could hold between your thumb and fingertip.

The pinch of his father's hand on his shoulder came again, harder. He lowered the rifle. His father's eyes were open wide and the muscles in his face were set so hard he looked unfamiliar — a man with darker eyes and eyebrows. Kenny followed his gaze down into the canyon.

Two mountain goats, a big one and a smaller one, had appeared on a rocky ledge no more than a hundred yards below them. The big one raised his bony face and gazed into the distance, his angle of beard trailing in the wind. Then he lowered his head and began to nibble at a tuft of grass. Kenny froze. His heart pounded so hard he thought it might jolt him off the rock. He'd never seen a mountain goat this close before. He was stunned by how perfectly white and clean they were.

His father motioned for the rifle, raised it to his shoulder and readjusted the scope. His movements seemed so slow to Kenny. He thought his dad must be thinking of the wind, of where to place his shot, and of how the goat would fall. But all he could think was *hurry, hurry, hurry.* The goats might vanish into air.

The rifle went off loud in Kenny's ear and reported back from high up on the mountain. The small goat leapt and disappeared among the rocks, but the big goat stood square, as if he hadn't even heard the shot. Then his knees buckled. He crashed forward on his chin, like a running calf jerked backward off his feet. The wind died, and Kenny could hear the echo of the other goat's descent, the trickling fall of loosened rock, long after it was gone.

Then his dad was yelling and slapping him on the back, as if Kenny had shot the goat.

"I can't believe you got one!" Kenny yelled.

"One in a million chance," his dad said. "One in a million."

They were so excited they hardly noticed how long it took to work their way down to where the goat had fallen. All the time, Kenny worried how they were going to climb back out of the canyon, but he could hardly wait to get there.

When they finally found the goat, his dad grasped the front legs in both hands and flipped the carcass over, to gauge the weight and size, to see if the fleece was good enough to keep. It was a big, male goat with black spike horns — nearly two hundred pounds, his dad thought — but Kenny was surprised how small it looked up close. He watched his dad slide his knife out of the scabbard.

His father kneeled down and started cutting back close to the chest to sever the head. The hide was so thick he had to stab to make the first cut. Then he plunged the knife in so deep he had to work his watch strap over his bloody hand and hold it out to Kenny. Kenny slipped the heavy watch over his own wrist and pushed it up on his arm, but he never took his eyes off the goat. He could hardly believe they had it. It seemed still alive, its black and gold eye shiny and wet. When he knelt to touch it, the fleece was still warm, and it glowed from within, yellow close to the skin and pure snowy white at the edges.

When the head was free, his father drew out a smaller, sharper knife and began to cut the fleece from the muscle. When he finished, Kenny helped him fold the hide into a square envelope and secure it with rope. With a second length of rope, they tied the head and fixed a sling so his dad could carry it.

Kenny realized his dad meant to leave the carcass on the ledge. "Can't we eat it?" he asked.

"Some people do," his dad said. "It's pretty strong."

"I'll eat it."

"You want to carry it?" His dad looked at Kenny and down at the goat. The skinned carcass had a pearly blue cast and bits of grass and rock were sticking to it.

"I guess not," Kenny said.

They worked their way down a narrow ravine where deep snow and ice had collected in the shadows. Kenny carried the hide slung up high on his shoulders like a rucksack. He thought he could feel sticky blood trickling down his neck, but it might have been his own sweat. His dad labored behind him, carrying the head.

Kenny wasn't sure his dad knew where they were going. For a long time they struggled down through rocks, following a dried-up creek bed, but finally they struck a ridge of dark timber. They hiked the crest of the ridge and emerged on a narrow game trail.

The sun sank below the trees and lit up the mountain behind them. It radiated, warm and pink, as if the whole sheer slope were made of salmon-colored seashells, but shadows fell across the meadow and Kenny was cold. His neck felt sticky, and icy trickles of sweat rolled down his ribs.

"Listen," his dad whispered and stopped still. Kenny pulled up and heard the loud snap of branches. Something big was pushing through the trees. He glanced at his dad. His dad's mouth was pulled taut in a strange half-smile.

Fallen branches cracked and snapped. Then the elk began to bugle. At first Kenny couldn't imagine what could make a sound like that. It didn't seem to come from anything alive. He heard the elk again, squealing into the darkness in a drawn-out wail. It sounded like a heavy door creaking open — at the bottom of a boiler. He shivered, but his dad stood motionless. Kenny started to speak, but his dad held up his hand, and after a long silence, an answering call echoed out of the trees.

"Come on," his dad said. He hitched his makeshift pack up higher on his shoulder blades and moved toward the sound. They jumped a creek where the water ran clear over a bed of smooth amber stones and struggled up an embankment. Below, the grass had been chewed down in a natural, round clearing surrounded by young pines. At the edge of the trees, Kenny saw the elk.

They were two buff-colored shapes, just lighter than the dry grass and the tree trunks, until one of the elk stepped into the clearing. The young bull raised his long, curved neck toward the sky. He lowered his head to feed, the white of his rump turned toward the trees.

His dad signaled for quiet, and the second elk, a lighter-colored animal with a rack of massive horns, moved into the clearing. He angled around to face the young bull. Slowly he lowered his head, and the two bulls crashed together. Three separate times they lowered their racks and — moving like women with huge, heavy baskets balanced on their heads — swung up until one rack of antlers struck a hollow glancing blow against the other. Then they stopped. The young elk drifted a few steps away. The older one went back to feeding.

Kenny waited in the silence, watching. Slowly the elk approached again. The huge racks cracked together. Then, again, they stopped. Kenny was surprised, and disappointed, by the elk. They didn't seem to care if they finished the fight or not.

Something else kept his eyes on the clearing. Not the fighting, but the sound. Each time the massive horns collided, the hollow, rackety blow echoed off the mountain — like a battle fought with bamboo poles. There were no other sounds — no birds and no wind. The sound of the cracking antlers was so pure and ringing it seemed to suck up all the air, like lightning.

All the way back to the horses they could hear the fighting. The sound seemed to grow louder as the mountains darkened; like a radio signal, it had more power in the night. It made Kenny feel clear-eyed and alert. As if his blood had been replaced with icy water.

By the time they found the horses and rode back to camp, it was pitch dark. His dad took care of the horses, and Kenny searched the ground for wood, following the sound of the creek. He dragged two long, dry branches back to camp and built a fire. When it was hot, he opened two cans of chili and set them in the flames. His dad wrapped the goat's head and the hide in pieces of canvas, and went to lock them in the truck. When he came back he was limping like a man with one leg shorter than the other.

He sat down hard on the ground, and Kenny used a pair of pliers to lift a can of chili from the fire and pass it over to him. When he ate his own chili, it was bubbling at the edges and congealed in the center. He thought it tasted better than anything he'd ever eaten.

His dad picked up the empty cans and the rest of their food and locked it all in the truck cab. He said he hadn't seen any sign of bears, but there was no sense taking chances. As soon as he came back, they unlaced their boots and crawled inside their sleeping bags beside the fire.

Kenny ached in every muscle, and his legs twitched with sudden itches, as if his sleeping bag was full of sand. The wind had burned the skin on his face and pulled it tight across his cheekbones. If he held his palm above his eyes, he thought he might feel heat waves radiating off his forehead.

He was exhausted, but he wasn't sleepy. He was worried about his mother. She didn't know where he was. The note said they'd be back tonight. It was Sunday, and he had school in the morning. He'd thought they would at least drive down the mountain to a place where he could call.

He lay very still, listening to the creek talking, murmuring and rushing over rocks, sometimes loud and sometimes softer. He imagined he heard actual words. Then a twig snapped somewhere in the underbrush, and his heart collided with itself. He tried to stay calm, but he was wide awake.

"Kenny?" He heard his dad call, and thought it must have been the noise that woke him up. But his dad didn't mention the noise.

"There's something I need to ask you about," he said.

"Yeah."

"I wanted to talk last night, but you fell asleep."

"What is it?"

"How would you feel . . ." His dad's voice disappeared in a cough. He cleared his throat and started again. "How would you feel if I got married again?"

"To who?"

"It doesn't matter who. I just want to know how you feel about it. In general."

"But who?" Kenny said. "You never told me. You never said anything."

"A lady. A lady I met in Florida."

"What's her name?"

"Louise."

"How old is she?"

"Never asked her."

"About how old?"

"She has a kid. A little girl." His dad was quiet for a long time. Finally he said, "Corey. Her daughter's name is Corey."

"When are you getting married?"

"I don't know. Soon."

"Okay with me."

"You can come to the wedding. I'll send you a ticket."

"Okay."

"You sure?"

"Sure."

Kenny closed his eyes and listened to the creek. It made him think of the day his dad showed up, his parents in the kitchen talking. Their voices rose and fell in the night, and upstairs in his bed he'd tried to make out the words. His parents' arguing had made him feel afraid. He knew there was something going on. He'd been waiting for two days to find out what.

"Dad?"

"Yes."

"Is she divorced, Louise?"

"No. She was married to a pilot."

His dad didn't say her husband was dead, but Kenny knew that was what he meant. Of all the things he'd said, this one thing made Kenny want to cry. Louise wasn't divorced like his mother. But he didn't cry. For the first time, his dad was speaking to him like an equal, as if Kenny might be more than ten years old.

"Does this mean," he asked, "you won't be *my* dad?"

"No," his dad said, suddenly angry. "I never want to hear you say a thing like that again. I'll always be your dad. You hear me?"

"Yes, sir," Kenny said.

He thought about what his dad had said, up on the mountain, about paying if Kenny had a wreck. His mother tried to keep it secret, but Kenny knew his dad didn't always send the checks he was supposed to. Besides, his mom would never take what wasn't due her. It made him sad all of a sudden that his father didn't understand. He felt sad and hopeless. His parents were never getting back together. He hadn't even realized, until this moment, that he thought they would. After a while, he heard his father snoring. But the sky was a soft, muffled gray above the trees before he fell asleep.

On the drive back his dad said only a few words. They were both tired and sunburned. His father didn't ask if he wanted to drive, and Kenny didn't bring it up until he saw his dad brace a hand on his hip to rest his leg. They traded places, and Kenny drove for an hour, but his father wouldn't let him drive over the pass.

So his dad was driving when they pulled in behind the house in the late afternoon. His mother appeared at the back door and was at the window of the truck before Kenny could climb out.

Her hair was twisted up in some new way, and she wore a full pink dress he'd never seen before. She looked pretty, he thought, but different. A strand of hair had come loose from the pins, and Kenny knew she must have stayed home all day worrying.

He was so tired and dirty he hated the feeling of his body moving in his clothes, but he told his mother how they shot the mountain goat, talking fast, as if his excitement could wash right over her concern. She stood in the yard and listened, but her hand kept moving to her face to push the strand of hair behind her ear. She kept looking down, and he could never catch her eye.

"Dad gets the head," he told her, "for a trophy. But he's going to get a rug made from the hide. For me."

His dad stood at the truck working the knots that tied the goat's head, still wrapped in gray canvas, to the bars of the stock rack. Kenny could feel excitement coming back. His legs felt longer and seemed to want to move all on their own. He could hardly stand still while his father laid the heavy package on the grass and jerked the ropes away. Kenny brought his mother over and knelt to lift off the stiff wrapping. As he picked up the last flap, he could hear the sizzle of flies trapped underneath, and when he flipped it back, a swarm of green-black flies shot out, blind, into his face. He threw his hand up and his mother backed away.

The goat's head lay on the canvas, the fleece gone tallowy yellow and the face mashed cold and flat along one side. The black, shining eye had caved in, dull and pitted with specks of grit, like a lump of dirty asphalt. It stared away at nothing, with no more feeling than a fish eye. Kenny looked up for his dad.

His father wasn't there. He'd started for the truck to unload the horses. His mom came up and slipped an arm around his waist. He caught a quick smell of shampoo.

"Don't," he said, twisting away. "I'm dirty."

She dropped her arm and stood beside him. He could hear her breath go in and out. They watched his dad limp around the truck.

"You better go," his mother said. "Go help your dad."

She walked back to the house, and the kitchen light came on, casting a square of yellow on the grass. The sun was almost down, watery and round behind gray clouds. He looked at the goat, its whiteness glowing in the sudden dark. His nose was running and his long fingers were cold. They ached inside, along the narrow bones.

9

Though she couldn't see them, Cynthia Dustin could feel the high windows in the back of the prep room darkening. She squeezed between the wooden shelves, gluing new labels on specimen jars, curled and floating fetal pigs, nearly colorless, suspended in murky formaldehyde. Rusty lids sealed the old jars tight, but she still smelled formaldehyde, almost felt how it stung her nostrils and puckered the skin of her fingers. The white fluorescent lights in Mr. Everts's office cast dark shadows behind the shelves. She could sense the building emptying around her. If Mr. Everts didn't come back soon, she'd miss her bus.

His gray desk filled most of the office part of the room, its surface so vast and flat she thought of aircraft carriers. She sat down in his chair and studied the yellowing periodic table on the wall behind it.

At first, she had hated working in the science lab at lunch and on free periods while other seniors drove home or walked downtown. But last year she'd dished up food behind the line in the cafeteria, a net over her hair. No matter how many times she ran them through the wash, her jeans and sweaters never lost the sticking smell of rancid grease.

It was a thing her dad insisted on. If she wanted piano lessons, she had to pay for them. He acted as if she played the piano to get out of chores, as if she were shirking.

She shoved at the floor with her shoe and spun the chair in a circle, raising a breeze that lifted her hair. When she heard the door, she braked to a stop and watched Mr. Everts come in. He could hardly see over a stack of notebooks in his arms. He dumped the folders in a carton on the floor and brushed his hands together.

"Cynthia," he said, announcing her name as if he'd forgotten he'd asked her to wait for him.

She moved to give him his chair, but he waved her to stay and slid open the top drawer of a filing cabinet. Black stubble shadowed his jaw, and his shirttail had bunched up and come loose from behind.

"Where are you going to school?" He spoke with his back to her.

"What do you call this?"

"Penance," he said.

He turned and hitched himself up on the corner of the desk, a fat manila folder in both hands.

"This comes up every year," he said and handed her a pink printed page. "I've got a brochure someplace." He held the file high on his chest and riffled through the papers.

"You interested?" he said.

"Don't know." Cynthia tried to read the pink paper, but she couldn't quite figure it out. "I'm going to be late," she said. "What is it?"

"You have plans for college?"

Looming above her, he suddenly seemed too close. His smell of dust and chemicals and sweat was too strong. She shifted back in her chair, but she was afraid to move away, afraid she might embarrass him.

"I'll miss my bus," she said.

"Go ahead, then." He located a black-and-white brochure and handed it to her. "Read through this material. Let me know."

She gave him a smile and gathered up her coat and books. "See you tomorrow," she said and pushed out the door using her shoulder.

Outside, the sun was down behind the mountains, and the yellow curb where the buses should have been was vacant. She tried to open the door and go back in, but the steel doors had locked from inside. She'd have to walk to town and call her mother. A tingling sensation crept up her neck — Mr. Everts might be watching. Feeling truant — guilty but free — she hurried across the parking lot, laughing to herself, as if the quick turning of her back rendered her invisible and he wouldn't notice she'd missed the last bus.

At the hotel, she took a booth at the back of the café. While she waited for the waitress, she watched two dairymen come in. Their down vests and plaid shirts were smeared with grease, and their boot soles encased in dried mud and manure. They sat down on stools and hunched over the counter.

When the waitress approached her, Cynthia ordered coffee, and the plump, tired-looking woman gave her a look. As if she were too young to order coffee.

"Black," she said.

She flattened the pink sheet on the Formica table. Across the top, it said "Scholarship" in capital letters, and it went on in official-sounding words. The language scared her. The paragraphs looked more like a test, a punishment, than an award. She couldn't see what it had to do with her. She'd never fit all the rules and regulations.

The school counselor had made college appointments for her, but she hadn't gone. Her mother assumed she would go to music school, somewhere in the East. But no one at home had brought it up, said where the money would come from, or how she'd get to an audition.

When the waitress returned with a cup and a stainless steel pot of coffee, Cynthia hid the sheet in her notebook.

"Thanks," she said.

She reached in her pocket and placed all her change on the table. Three quarters and a dime. She needed to phone her mother. But she might get her dad. He wouldn't even ask her why. He'd say something to her mother like, "Girl's managed to miss her bus."

Her coffee was too hot to sip. If she left it and started walking now, she wouldn't be that late getting home. Out the plate glass window in front of the café, a streetlight flickered. A car passed with its headlights on, and all the parking spots had emptied. What if she never went home? What would they think then? When she thought of doing her homework, waiting in her room for dinner, her head felt too heavy for her neck.

She watched each car that passed, hoping someone she knew would stop and come in. She wished Roddy Moyers would walk in now. She'd take that ride. His voice came back to her exactly. "Some other time," he'd said.

Even from the back of the café, she heard the low throb of a motorcycle echo in the street. The bike coasted to a stop, and Harold Cray climbed off. He glanced at her as he came in the door but didn't wave. He took a seat in the front, slid back in the corner of the booth, and unfolded a newspaper. She watched him tip his head at a slight angle.

Harold Cray ran the tack and saddle shop, in an old stone building with cowboy-pajama paper left over from the forties on the walls. He lived in a shack outside of town, not far from her place. Harold could give her a ride, but she wasn't sure she could ask him.

Harold seldom spoke to anyone. He'd come back from Vietnam

with one eye injured, but from what she'd heard, he hadn't been much different before he went away. She knew him from church. Officially, he was a baritone, but his range was so wide and his voice so steady and clear that it always shocked her when he started a song. Other members of the choir, especially the old women, had voices so reedy and uncertain they made her tense; she never knew if they would hit the notes or not. People thought Harold was dumb, maybe even retarded, but in music he was always there ahead of her.

Even so, she'd never said more than hello to him. He looked strange, his head shaved and one eye always looking slightly the wrong way. The waitress served him a Coke in a bottle, but he didn't look up from his paper.

She worked up her nerve, left her coffee and books, and walked down to stand at the end of his table. When he noticed her, she wasn't sure which eye to focus on.

"Harold?"

"Hello."

Her eyes wanted to shift, to slide away from his face, but she forced herself to look at him with no expression. She started to explain how she'd missed the bus.

"I'm sorry," she said, and she was sorry. She wanted to retreat back to her table.

Harold cleared his throat. "What do you want?" His voice was so flat and forthright, almost angry, she knew she had to ask straight out.

"I need a ride home."

"Why should I?"

"Why not?"

"Eating," he said.

"I'll wait."

Harold looked back at his newspaper. He lifted a hand and motioned for her to sit down. She went back for her books and coffee cup and slid in the booth across from him. The waitress brought a heavy plate of meatloaf and potatoes, and Harold washed the meal down with Coke. She kept thinking maybe she should open her notebook and start working math problems, but that seemed rude. It was getting late. She'd have to explain at home where she'd been all this time.

Harold cleaned his plate with a piece of bread, folded his newspaper, and went to pay the check. He left a dollar on the table and nodded for her to follow.

Standing beside the bike, he shifted out of his leather jacket and handed it to her. It was large enough to slide on over her own coat. He climbed on and kick-started the bike, knocked out the stand, and balanced on his thick legs. She got on behind and found two footrests.

The sound of the bike and the wind in her face were so loud that she couldn't have heard if he spoke. At the first sweeping turn, she cringed. Her footrest scraped the ground. She ducked her head behind his back to block the wind and thought, He must be freezing. But on the old swamp road, he dropped his speed, and she let her hair fly flat back from her face. She closed her eyes to feel the coolness.

She leaned in close to his ear and yelled.

"Let me off. Stop here."

They had just passed the dump, and it occurred to her like a grand reprieve — she could go to Dill's. She could call from there, say she'd been visiting with him since school let out.

Harold dropped her off where Dill kept a chain stretched across the track to the dump when he wasn't open for business, which lately had been more and more of the time. When she tried to thank him, he did something strange. He shoved his gloved hand into hers and shook, clasping hard as if she were some kind of comrade. He nodded and drove on. She walked down the dirt track to where Dill kept his trailer. Dill and her dad had grown up together on adjoining sections, but Dill had sold his family place years ago and taken over maintenance of the dump. He'd had an accident; a colt that he was breaking for her dad had reared and fallen backward, the saddle horn striking and bruising his heart. But Dill found he liked the new job. "Lonesome up there on the hill," he told Earl. "Get a better class of visitor down here."

Dill's tiny trailer was thick with his smell, a smell like fresh pencil shavings but stronger, and crowded with stacks of faded magazines and newspapers, blank paperbacks with the covers torn off. Only the cot where Dill slept was free of his accumulation. Cynthia sat there while Dill poured her a cup of coffee and seated himself on a stack of papers. He scratched at his yellowing white beard and blinked at her. She wanted to come right out and tell him why she was there. He was more a dad to her than her own was. But if she told him now it would offend his sense of the proper visiting time, make him think she wanted his help more than his company.

Not fooled, he asked her, "What's the trouble, sweetheart?"

10

In the next weeks, snow fell, sifting onto the shoulders of the canyons like powdered sugar and collecting in north shadows in the valley. Kenny waited for a letter from his father, or a call. He made a point of stopping at the post office most days, but there was seldom a letter in their box.

In the mornings, he walked to school along a tire track behind the houses and the stores on Main Street. Frozen snow flattened the weeds beside the track, and fields of barley stubble moldered damp and gray in the west. His boots shattered star bursts in the ice underfoot.

The high school was a dingy yellow-brick building, with blue and orange plastic panels decorating the front. Behind the windows, heavy beige drapes had been yanked in some places from their hangers. A long crack in a window had been mended with a dogleg of silver duct tape. Kenny shoved open the front door and walked down the hall. The linoleum seemed to give under his feet and muffle the sound of his shoes.

He leaned against the wall outside his homeroom, tipping back on his heels, until he heard the tardy bell. It buzzed twice as long as normal, like a fire alarm. At the end of the bell, he slipped through the door and into his chair in the back. His homeroom teacher droned through the attendance, and then the day's announcements came over the speaker, but he barely listened. After the cold walk to school, the warmth in the room made him feel heavy with sleep. The bell rang. Chairs scraped and fell over. Everyone was rushing and talking, but Kenny didn't move.

The last announcement on the loudspeaker had taken him by surprise. The rodeo team was meeting out front after school. Some kind of field trip. He thought they'd have broken up with winter coming on. Every morning, all through the fall, he'd listened to the announcements, the times and places for 4-H, football practice, and drill team meetings, without paying much attention. But the notices for rodeo made his heartbeat skip.

Since the hunting trip, he'd had strange dreams where he'd joined up with the team but never knew what they were doing. He'd wake up, shamed that he'd ridden against his mother's wishes. But his father would be riding, too, and neither one could walk away from that high, racing fear and elation. That's why, he thought, the rodeo announcements shocked him, as if his name might be called any second.

He crossed the hall to the science lab, opened the door, and went in. The room was deadly quiet, the tables and stools all occupied and everybody watching him. Mr. Everts smiled from behind the zinc-topped table at the front and waved at him to hurry up. Kenny blinked and hesitated. The whole class burst out laughing.

"Good morning, Ken." Mr. Everts laughed himself, but kindly.

"Sorry," Kenny mumbled.

"Take a seat," Mr. Everts said. He marked something in his roll book.

Kenny climbed up on the stool beside his lab partner and opened his notebook.

Without speaking, Mr. Everts turned and disappeared through the frosted glass door into his office and prep room. The class stared at the open door in silence. They knew better than to talk.

When Mr. Everts returned, he was holding upright a green canvas cot. He unfolded the two halves, pried out the legs, and stood the cot on end like a begging dog. It seemed to have no weight at all when he set it down on the linoleum and shoved it aside with his foot. He addressed the class.

"First aid," he said, "can make the difference between life and death." He paused and looked round the room. "What," he went on, "is the most important word in first aid?"

"First," the class murmured.

Mr. Everts nodded, turned his back, and began to write on the blackboard with a stubby piece of chalk. He wrote fast in a thick white scrawl, the marks all up and down like letters in a foreign code. The class waited for him to turn around and translate what he had written.

"Take out your notebooks," he said and waited while a *whoosh* of fluttering pages swept through the room. A pen dropped and rolled along the floor. Kenny tried to write and keep up with Mr. Everts's voice. He scribbled, "Mouth-to-mouth resuscitation. Head back. Airway clear. Nose pinched. Vomit." Then the point of his pencil broke off clean, just below the sharpened wood. He picked up the tiny point of lead and wrote with that until it was too small to grip. He glanced over at his lab partner. The boy was scribbling fast, and before Kenny could borrow another pencil, Mr. Everts stopped.

"All right." Mr. Everts came around and leaned back on the table. "Here's the situation. You're swimming in the quarry. Your friend dives in. He doesn't come up. What do you do?" He paused before he answered his own question. "One," he said, "you send for help. Two, you dive until you find him. Three . . ." Mr. Everts stopped and looked out into the class, waiting for someone to answer the question. Kenny lowered his eyes and stared at his notebook.

Finally a hand went up and one of the girls repeated what Mr. Everts had said. Kenny relaxed and stopped listening. He pictured the rodeo team meeting after school. He knew from his last school that nothing much went on. Guys stood around and practiced roping wooden steer heads, or a burro. Or they talked about rides they'd made or seen. He wondered what a field trip meant.

When he looked up again, something had changed in the room. Mr. Everts had set up a second cot. The two cots stood, centered in the open space in front of his lab table, like a scene on a stage before the play begins.

Mr. Everts called back into the prep room and started to talk again. He didn't pause or look over when the two seniors came through the door. One was the class president, a tall basketball player with short, dark hair. The other one was Cynthia Dustin.

Kenny stared at her. A white lab coat hung down to her knees, blue jeans showing underneath. She stood beside the lab table, with no expression on her face. Mr. Everts turned finally and nodded. The two seniors walked to the cots. Cynthia sat down carefully on the edge, testing her weight before she swung her legs around and lay down.

The class was silent. Kenny felt his heart knock in his chest like blocks of wood clapped together. Mr. Everts knelt behind Cynthia's cot and slid a hand under her neck. He lifted, tilting her head until her shoulders arched and her chin pointed at the ceiling. She looked broken, like the breech of a rifle. Her hair fell back on the cot in a pale, silky wedge. With two fingers, Mr. Everts pressed her nostrils together, and with his other hand, pulled down on her chin. He mimed the motion of putting a finger in her mouth. Slowly, he began to lower his dark face toward hers. Kenny stopped breathing. Just before his lips touched Cynthia's, Mr. Everts stopped. He breathed out loudly then tilted his head sideways like a swimmer. He gasped a lungful of air, dropped his face back over Cynthia's, and breathed out again. Kenny was almost limp with relief. Mr. Everts was only imitating the movements.

He grasped the edge of the lab table and pulled himself up, resting for a minute before he gazed out over the class, his eyes moving from face to face.

"Volunteers?" he said.

The class sat rigid and silent. Kenny could feel the tension travel from the front of the room to the back. He stared down at his notebook, as if he could will Mr. Everts not to call on him.

"Relax," Mr. Everts said. "Everybody, I mean everybody, is coming up here. It's not if — it's when. We have all week." He stared around the lab again. "Sorry, Cynthia," he said. "They're going to let you drown."

The class laughed, and Kenny watched the shoulders of the kid in front of him relax. He forced his own shoulders down. A girl in the front row raised her hand. The class watched Mr. Everts guide her through the procedure. Cynthia never moved. Kenny looked up at the black-and-white clock in the front of the room. In ten minutes, the class would be over. Kenny prayed for someone else to volunteer, for the bell to ring.

Another girl volunteered to practice on Cynthia, and Mr. Everts pointed at a boy. The boy stepped up and knelt beside the other cot, like a football player crouching down to pray before a game, and looked up at Mr. Everts.

"Neck," the teacher prompted.

But Kenny watched Cynthia. The volunteer slid her hand under Cynthia's neck, but she couldn't seem to fit it under her hair.

"Ouch," Cynthia said, and the whole class gave a tiny jump. Then everybody laughed. It was like a scene in a movie where the body in the coffin sneezes. The boy cocked his elbows up toward the ceiling and breathed loudly into the face on the cot.

"Shit," Kenny's lab partner whispered across the table. "Hope he hadn't got bad breath." Kenny had to strain to hear the whisper. When he did, he smiled, his lips pressed in a straight, embarrassed line. He didn't hear Mr. Everts call his name.

His lab partner was nodding and bobbing at him. "You," he said. "He's calling you." He tried to stifle a giggle.

Kenny climbed off his stool and moved slowly toward the front of the room. Where the lab tables gave way to an open space of alternating liver-colored and dirty white squares of linoleum, he glanced at the door. For a second he almost turned toward it. He actually felt himself swing out into the hallway. But Mr. Everts was waiting.

Kenny took a step toward the class president, but the other boy was still practicing. Mr. Everts pointed at Cynthia.

Kenny heard his knees make cracking sounds when he knelt by the cot. The face below was perfectly still. Cynthia's eyes were closed. Kenny thought she might be sleeping. He wished he could see the clock behind him. It had to be time for the bell.

"Let's go." Mr. Everts nodded, impatient.

Kenny breathed in and slid a palm under Cynthia's hair. It parted, the way falling water parts when you slide your hand in. It lay on his skin, strangely cool and weighted, but the nape of her neck was warm. He lifted, watching the smooth hair swing back, holding her head in his hand, and reached around to press two fingers against her nose.

"No, not like that." Mr. Everts placed his own large hands on either side of Cynthia's face, tilted her head, and let it rest on the cot. "There," he said. "Now both hands are free."

Kenny had pulled his hand from under Cynthia's hair. But he

couldn't bring himself to touch her face. His hands were doughy and chilled.

"Let's go." Mr. Everts's voice was low and even, as if he might stand there forever.

Kenny leaned down toward the pale face on the cot and raised both his arms. His elbows stuck out like wings, as if he could touch her without touching her. As fast as he could, he pulled down on her chin with two fingers and pressed closed her nose. He breathed down, then up, like he was swimming the last lap of a race.

"Again," Mr. Everts said.

Kenny tilted his face again toward the face on the cot. He exhaled loudly, and felt the buzzing of the bell ring through the room. Cynthia's eyes opened, her face only inches from his. He was staring into blue eyes the color of a gas flame turned down low. He jumped back, as if a dead animal he'd been poking with a stick had jerked to life.

He straightened to his feet. The girl on the cot smiled slowly, as if she didn't see him. She reached for Mr. Everts's extended hand, and swiveled around to sit up.

"Quiz on this tomorrow," Mr. Everts shouted at the class.

"But I never went up," somebody whined. The class was shuffling books together, scraping stools along the floor, everyone moving at once toward the hall.

"Have a nice nap?" Mr. Everts was talking to the two seniors. The boy shook his head in an "I don't believe we're doing this" gesture. Kenny glanced at Cynthia. She was smiling in a way that seemed to Kenny very private and unconcerned.

Kenny walked back to his lab table and picked up his notebook. If he held out his hand, he knew it would tremble. When he tried to pick up his pencil, it rolled off the table and hit the floor with a loud, hollow sound. He left it there and followed the rest of the class out the door.

It wasn't until late afternoon, in his last class, that he had time to look in his notebook. The words he'd written in science took up less than half a page. He would flunk the quiz. All afternoon he'd been waiting for the blood to stop rushing in his ears and his head to clear. He couldn't recall the order of the procedure, what he should do first, but he felt he could run all the way home without stopping. He didn't care if he passed the test or not.

After his last class, he wandered to his locker. For days he'd been expecting something, not a letter from his dad, but something. All the rush of his blood seemed to drop away. He wanted to see Cynthia. To touch her. Nothing, he knew, would ever feel that way again.

He stood at his locker a long time, trying to think what books he needed to take home. He couldn't remember his assignments. Finally, he let the locker door clang shut, all his books inside. When he looked around, the hall was empty. At the far end, by the gym doors, the janitor was pushing a wide broom. Kenny turned in the other direction, shoved open the heavy door, and stood on the stairs leading down to the parking lot.

A cold wind blew across the valley, white clouds moving fast overhead. The foothills were in shadow, but a beam of white light struck the clouds. In the parking lot, ovals of snow glistened against the wet asphalt. A few kids stood by their cars, the motors warming up and sending clouds of steam into the air. A bright pool of light swept over the parking lot and shifted back to shadow, as if a window curtain had billowed open and closed. The sunlight seemed mechanically connected to the wind.

He took the stairs two at a time and turned in the direction of town. At the edge of the parking lot, a short yellow bus had pulled to the curb. As Kenny came near, he recognized a boy in a shiny red jacket embroidered with a bucking horse. Without thinking, Kenny followed him up the metal stairs of the bus. Everyone looked up, curious. Mr. Gallagher, the advisor, shifted around in the driver's seat and frowned.

"Could I just come along and watch?" Kenny asked him.

Mr. Gallagher hesitated and looked down at a clipboard on his knees.

"Yeah," he said. "But only watch. I got no permission slip on you."

Kenny took a seat in the last row of the bus and shifted over to the window. For the first time that day, the muscles in his neck and arms seemed to warm up and relax. He had no idea where the bus was going.

11

The next cow — not much bigger than a heifer — balked in the chute and refused to stretch her neck out through the head catcher.

"Get to goin'," Earl yelled. *"Get!"* The vet twisted her tail up and shoved. Dill beat on her hip with a short, flat board. The cow ignored them all. Then, as if listening to some inner voice, she stepped up to the trap. Roddy stood back and looked up at the low, darkening sky. It began to snow again.

"Here we go," Dill said. He stood at Roddy's shoulder. "Now we're gonna get some weather. Let's get a move on." He jerked his chin at Roddy and stepped up to the chute. "Give me a hand here."

Roddy moved in close, where Earl had the cow held fast by a nose ring. The chrome horseshoe-shaped clamp stretched her nostrils sideways and looked like it might slip loose, but Earl had the rope snubbed down taut around the corner of the chute. The young cow had two thick, misshapen horns turned in and growing toward her skull. Moving fast, Dill unwrapped his dehorning saw from a length of rust-stained toweling.

He laid the short saw flat against the cow's skull, and with a few short strokes, cut the horn away. He worked so fast Roddy could smell the burning hair and horn. The cow bellowed and tried to jerk free. Then blood began to spurt from severed veins near the hide. Three tiny red fountains arced into the air, spattering the ground, Roddy's boots, Dill's green rubber chaps. Roddy tugged his glove off with his teeth, stepped in close, and pressed a finger against one of the bleeders, just above the cut. He held it there until the pressure of his finger stopped the bleeding. He touched a second vein, and then a third. The warmth of the blood under his fingertip surprised him. It pumped against his skin and felt like his own pulse. Some ranchers pulled out the severed veins with tweezers. But Roddy had always preferred to do it this way. In all the nasty business of working cattle, this one thing made him feel good. He knew the cow didn't appreciate his efforts. But it always struck him as a tender thing to do.

Earl sprayed the wound with antiseptic, pressed a cotton ball over it, and jerked the cow's head around so Dill could reach the other horn. Roddy looked away while Dill sawed, but the sound of it, the saw working its way through hide and bone, was worse than the sight. This time, Dill, who rarely made a mistake, cut too deep.

"Shit," he said. "We got a bleeder. Get the iron."

Roddy swung around the chute, hauled a branding iron out of the propane flame, and carried it back to Dill. Dill grasped the long, rusty handle and touched a hot corner of the iron to one bleeder, then another, until he thought he had them all cauterized. The cow dropped her jaw and bellowed. White lather foamed from her pink mouth. One small vein began to bleed again, spurting red.

"You want a hotter iron?" Roddy asked.

"No," Dill said. "Let 'er go, Earl." He took a step back. "The best thing now is just to let her settle down. That last one should stop on its own."

Earl slacked up on the nose ring and let it fall to the ground. The cow whipped her head from side to side, flinging blood and stringy white saliva. Roddy and Dill jumped back out of the way. Earl released the cow and hazed her out the gate.

"What you want to do here," Dill said, "is molest 'em as little as possible. That's the kindest thing. Just get 'em in and out as fast as you can."

The manure at their feet was powdered white with snow, and the snow was spattered red with blood. Roddy looked down at his boots, where the blood had dried in perfect dark coins on the lighter brown leather. He looked up as the next cow hit the head catcher and Earl slammed it shut with a clang.

They worked cows all morning, and by lunchtime, the mountains had disappeared under a low ceiling of gray. Snow covered the fields all around them, with gold straw stubble and wild oats spiking through. Roddy heard the weaned calves bawling for their mothers. The falling snow muffled sound, and the calves seemed far away. The path to the barn had been churned into clinging mud and manure. It struck Roddy that every other thing he saw, every roof, every truck, every blade of grass, had, in just so few moments, turned white.

Inside the barn, he removed his hat, slapping it on his pants to knock the snow off. Lunch was spread out on a sawhorse table, and two or three wives were dealing out plates of dessert and pouring paper cups of coffee.

"Hey, look who's here," Dolly McReynolds, a pretty woman with tight-curled silver hair, called out when she saw him. "I'd better run on up to the house and build some more sandwiches. This won't be nearly enough!" She handed Roddy a paper plate crowded with two thick sandwiches. "You think that'll get you started?"

"Ought to," he said. "I'll let you know."

"You do that," she said. "Henry," she said to the next man, "how the hell *are* you?"

Roddy managed to balance his teetering plate and carry it to a half circle of straw bales set up around a smoking kerosene heater. All the ranchers traded help, but it always amazed him that they helped McReynolds wean and cull his cattle for sale in the fall. It always took a full, long day, sometimes more, to get all the cows tested, inoculated, doctored, or dehorned. Everybody liked to say McReynolds knew about as much about cows as a goose knows about Jesus — and still, his cattle weighed out better than any in the valley. Roddy had ridden his horse over because McReynolds and his dad were friends, but he suspected all the others came for Dolly.

One by one, the other men filled their plates and joined him. Dill sat down with a groan and spat tobacco juice at the stove. He'd taken off his hat, and his yellowing white hair and beard made him look like an old terrier. He pulled a wrinkled blue handkerchief from his back pocket and wiped the snow and ice from his face.

"Hell of a deal," he said. He leaned back behind the straw bale and spit out the rest of his chew. "In the old days," he said, "we used to graze all the cattle right out on the sage flats. Then, when it came time to work cows, we just drove 'em into town. Worked 'em right there in the stockyards, and when the train came, we just bought 'em a ticket. Remember that, Earl?"

Earl nodded. Roddy thought the two men must be roughly the same age. Earl moved like a younger man, but people treated him with the kind of respect they'd give if he were the oldest. He stood taller than Dill, but he sat bent over with his shoulders pinched in around his chest. Dill took a bite of his sandwich and went on talking.

"Remember the suppers?" he said. "I remember Dolly used to drive out and serve a spread from the back of her station wagon. She put out a hell of a meal."

"Ribs," Earl said.

"Hell, yes," Dill said. "We had ribs the size of my hand." He held up his hand to demonstrate.

"Bet they had more meat on 'em," one of the other men said.

"And less dirt," Earl said. Roddy saw him grin for the first time all day.

"That's true," Dill agreed. He laughed along with the other men.

Sitting close to the heater, Roddy began to warm up in the dark, drafty barn. The greasy smell of kerosene rode over the barn smells, and the light was dim, hazy with dust and hay chaff. Outside, driving snow slanted sideways in a luminous white curtain. He was staring out the doorway when Cynthia walked in.

She stopped to brush the snow from her coat and her hat. Her face was flushed from the cold, and strands of damp hair clung to her cheeks. She shook her head and the hair fell straight. At the table, she picked up a plate and started to join the women who sat behind the table with the kids. But Dill called out to her.

"Hey," he said, "come over here. We got worlds of room."

He slid over to make space on the straw bale beside him, and when Cynthia sat down he swung an arm up around her shoulders.

"I thought you were comin' down to the chute to help us out," he said.

"Just got here. I had school this morning. Dolly asked me to come lend a hand."

"Well that's all right, then," Dill said, grinning. He gave her a pat on the sleeve and stood up. "Well," he said, "some of us have got to work for a livin'." He looked down at Cynthia. "Come on down when you finish your dinner. I'll put you to work."

"Okay," Cynthia said. But her dad shot a look at her. He shook his head. It was such a slight movement Roddy didn't think anyone else caught it. But Cynthia did. She ducked her head and stared down at her plate while the men stood up, stretching and complaining. Roddy stopped at the doorway and glanced back. Cynthia sat staring at the stove, a stunned expression on her face. She seemed more surprised than hurt, like a small kid who's been slapped for no reason.

Roddy walked back toward the chute with the other men, wondering what Earl Dustin's look meant. His daughter was not to work at the chute, that was clear. There were one or two wives, and an old-time rancher, Millie Baxter, who worked along with the men, but it could be that Earl disapproved.

Roddy relieved Earl at the head of the chute, where he didn't have much time to think of Cynthia. In the back of his mind, he hoped she might turn up, but whatever Earl's reasons were, they kept her away. It was only early afternoon, Roddy guessed just half past three, but the light was already fading when they ran the last cow through.

The vet packed his kit and drove away, and the kids cleaned up around the chute, picking up empty syringes and vials of serum. They threw the sawed-off horns over the fence for the dogs. Dill wiped his dehorning saw and wrapped it carefully in its towel. He tucked it under his arm, and they all walked down to watch the cattle truck pull out. They reached the loading chute just as the driver switched on his headlights. The long twin beams shot out in yellow shafts, filled with white, twirling snowflakes.

Inside the truck, the calves stamped and bawled. Across the corrals, their mothers' frantic voices answered, low and hoarse, like someone leaning on an antique car horn. Some mourned in long, plaintive cries. But others were demanding. They ordered the calves to come back — as if the calves had only strayed under a fence wire where the mothers couldn't reach them. It would be a day or two before they stopped bawling. By then the calves and the old or dry cows would have been trucked as far as feed-lots in Missouri. The men lit cigarettes or pinched chews of tobacco and leaned against the corral rails. They raised their voices to be heard over the bawling cattle.

Roddy was always relieved when the truck pulled out and the cries of the cattle stopped. With an expulsion of air, the driver released the brakes and the truck ground into gear. The forty-foot trailer swayed down the rutted dirt lane, pulled up with a squeal of brakes, and lumbered onto the hardtop.

Roddy had expected Cynthia to be at the loading chute. He thought of looking for her at the house, but he didn't want to get held up. If he was going to ride home, he needed to get started before it got any darker. He walked with the other men back to where they'd tethered their horses.

Just inside the barn, it occurred to him that Cynthia would be loading her horse. He broke off and cut over toward the trucks and trailers. He found Cynthia there, coaxing her horse into a brick-colored gooseneck trailer. He watched while she tied the mare and backed out around her.

"Hi," he said.

Cynthia started and spun around to face him. But she recovered right away.

"Hello," she said, almost swallowing the word. She cradled a bridle in one hand, looping the reins up over the headstall with the other, and gazed at him in total calm, as if she had all day to stand there. She looked at him as if he might begin to show her vacuum cleaners, or sell her a subscription. Roddy glanced away.

"I didn't see you at the chute," he said. "Just wondered how you were doing."

"Fine," she said.

Roddy let his gaze swing back. Snow was falling. Large, wet flakes, floating down like apple blossoms. They touched her hair and stayed whole for a moment. It seemed warmer now than it had all day.

"Why didn't you come down to help?"

"My dad," she said.

"What did he mean by that look?"

Cynthia swallowed. She stared at something in the distance, past his shoulder.

"What do you think it meant?" Her voice was sarcastic. But then she seemed to change her mind. "I don't know, exactly," she said. "He didn't want me down at the chute. It's unladylike. It's okay for women to work cows at home, but not in public. I don't know. He doesn't tell me the rules. He expects me to know what they are."

"It was okay when you were a kid," Roddy said, remembering her out roping calves.

"It was okay for a long time," she said. "Then one day, it wasn't."

She studied Roddy's face to see if he understood. He still didn't really understand, but he tried to look sympathetic. He felt sympathetic.

"Doesn't matter," she said. She slumped, her posture so resigned she seemed years older.

"Do you think," he said, "your dad would let you take that ride with me? Promised you a ride, as I remember."

"No," she said.

"Would you do it anyway?"

"No."

"Could you give me a break here?"

She said no, but her lips tightened to hold back a grin, and Roddy laughed. "Jesus, it's cold," he said. The snow had let up, and the gray light around them had lost its warmth. Behind the mass of clouds covering the mountains the sun must have gone down. "I'd better get the hell out of here." He explained that he'd ridden down from the ranch. The ride home wouldn't be long, but it would be cold and miserable.

In the last reflected light, the color seemed drained from her face. He thought he'd better let her put her tack away and get up to the house.

"Take it easy," he said, and turned to go.

He had passed the last of the trailers before he heard her call his name. He stopped and saw her come around the hood of a white pickup truck.

"Hey," she called.

Roddy stood and waited for her to reach him. When she did, she seemed for the first time nervous.

"I lied," she said and paused for a moment. "My dad likes you."

"Why?"

"Football fan, I guess." She smiled.

"No, I meant why did you lie?"

She stopped smiling. She looked down at her boots, caked with manure and sprinkled white with snow. Her hair swung over one eye.

"I didn't want you to know." She tipped her chin up at a defiant angle and looked right at him.

"Know what?"

"That I want to." She swallowed hard, but her eyes never left his face. "That I want to go for that ride."

Roddy smiled. "Great," he said. He could have reached out and touched her smooth, pale hair, but he only nodded.

"Okay," he said. "I'll call you."

"Okay."

He turned and walked away through the snow toward the barn. He felt her standing by the trailer, watching him. He stopped to look at her again.

"Tomorrow," he yelled.

"Tomorrow *what?*"

"I'll take you for that ride."

Only half of the trucks and trailers had pulled out of the yard. Roddy could have borrowed a lift from any of the ranchers, for him and for the horse, but he wanted to ride back.

He led his horse from the barn, swung up in the saddle, and turned down through the field the way he'd come that morning. Snow swirled around him, sticking on the pommel of his saddle and to the horse's mane. The mountains before him in the east seemed to glow faintly pink. He topped the knoll and looked back at the McReynolds place.

Through the pale curtain of falling white, the windows of the ranch house glowed with a liquid, amber light. He saw a pair of headlights sweep the sagebrush as a car curved slowly down the lane before he reined his horse toward home. The snow on the ground was collecting in drifts, small mountains and gullies, but in the flat light he couldn't tell the difference. There was no wind. The snow seemed to fall, weightless, in a circle all around him. He could actually hear the snow falling — a shifting, ticking sound — so faint he hardly heard it over his own breath.

Until today, each snowfall had whitened the mountains and bared off in the valley. But some instinct or memory made him think that this one would stick. These same drifts would be on the ground in April. From now until spring the mountains and the valley would be entirely white. The world would seem to grow larger under the vast expanses of snow. But it would also seem smaller. If he stuck around, he would see old friends he hadn't seen all summer. Ranchers would stop in to visit around the stove in the bunkhouse. Or Roddy would catch them in the afternoons playing cards at the grain mill.

He had to stick around a little longer to brand and wean his own stock, but it was almost time for him to go. If he stayed much longer, he'd miss too many rodeos and never qualify. He turned his horse and squinted into the blue light ahead. He caught sight of a line of willows and red-twig dogwoods curving along the creek. All he had to do was follow, and the creek would guide him home.

12

The sky was dark, the mountains weighted under a blanket of black and purple clouds, when the rodeo team bus turned off the highway and down a lane between two lines of barbed-wire fence, the top wire gleaming like a filament of silver in the last light. At the gate, a wooden sign branded with the name "Scullie's Horse Palace" hung stretched across the road. The bus swung around in an arc and stopped in front of a large white trailer house. Beside the trailer, a new horse barn backed up against a stand of trees. Farm lights beamed down from high poles, dropping a circle of brightness in the yard. Kenny climbed last off the bus and stepped onto a thick carpet of damp sawdust. The glare of the lights and the smell of the red sawdust made him feel like he'd stepped down into a rodeo arena.

The other boys shouldered their riggin' bags and ropes and wandered through the wide door of the barn. Kenny followed behind. Inside, green metal panels circled the barn to make an arena, and at the far end, old boards and poles made up holding pens and chutes. In one of the pens, a dozen brindle calves had squeezed up to the gate. A cutting horse stood saddled and ready, his reins hanging loose to the ground, in the center of the barn. Kenny didn't see any other stock.

A small, red-haired man, his barrel torso longer than his legs, limped toward them across the arena. Mr. Gallagher met him halfway and leaned down to speak. The short man nodded, glanced at the boys, nodded again. The two walked together toward the rail, one towering over the other.

"All set," Gallagher said. "Dump your gear."

The boys piled their bags and jackets near the wall and climbed up on a low set of bleachers.

"This is Rud Scullie," Mr. Gallagher said, introducing the short man. "Mr. Scullie to you. Get ready to listen and learn."

"Evenin'," Rud Scullie said. He held a mashed-up hat in his hand. His hair was the color of canned yams and flattened with sweat to his head as if he'd been working all day. He wore a faded denim shirt, black at the edges of the cuffs, and leather chaps worn so thin his jeans showed through in places. He settled the hat down tight, turned, and walked to the cutting horse. Kenny wondered what was going on. Rud Scullie was too short to ride a cutting horse. But he scooped up the reins in his left hand and in one motion was on the horse. Barely shifting his weight, he turned the horse and trotted him back to the holding pens, where he leaned down to speak to someone. He backed the horse aside, and the brindle calves staggered, confused at first, out the gate. Kenny heard a whoop and yell, and the calves bunched up, jogging out into the arena. When they saw the boys, they scrambled to turn and tried to race back to the pen. But Mr. Scullie was there. More rightly, the horse was there.

The man sat in the saddle, upright and still, his short legs resting in the stirrups and the reins lifted in one hand. They hung in a long, loose loop. The horse was on his own. The calves stopped still. They braced their legs stiff, facing the cutting horse. The horse lowered his head, set his front legs, and swung over to cut out a calf. The rider never moved. Sitting perfectly still above the horse, he seemed to float from side to side. Then the horse swung back to pick up another calf. It was a beautiful thing to watch. Kenny leaned forward on the bench, breathing in the damp, raw smell of sawdust and horses and manure. If he could have had anything he wanted right then, it would have been to see the cutting horse go on cutting.

Scullie reined the horse aside and let the calves run through. After they trotted past him and crowded up against the holding pen, he swung off the horse and led him to the rail where the boys were watching.

"What you want to do here," Scullie said, "is try not to upset the horse."

His voice was so low Kenny had to strain forward to hear him. The boys laughed, and Scullie went on, speaking to them as if he were trying to calm an animal. From time to time he reached up and scratched the horse under the chin strap.

"You keep your behind in the saddle, the horse'll do the job. Just try and keep aboard. Keep your eye on the cow. Get the feel of the thing.

"Rodeo's the only sport we got comes out of work. Show respect for the working man and his animal." He nodded to the last boy on the end.

The boy climbed over the rail. Scullie spoke to him in his low voice while the kid swung up in the saddle, then handed him the reins. He moved around, lengthening the stirrups, and gave the boy a nod.

The horse loped down toward the chutes, and the boy backed him aside while the calves shot out. Then he tried to cut out a single calf. The horse did all the work. The hard part, Kenny knew, was feeling the horse move. His dad used to say, "Just think like a cow, only faster." You had to relax, sort of let your legs and your butt do the thinking.

None of the boys on the team handled the calves as well as Rud. While Kenny watched, everyone lost his calf, and time after time the horse slid right out from under his rider. Left him hanging sideways off the saddle or flat on his elbows in the sawdust. Mr. Gallagher hollered, and Rud strode out to reach down a hand

and help the boy up. When a rider fell, the horse stopped dead, his reins hanging loose, his head down, as if he'd been turned off by a switch. Kenny felt almost hypnotized. Until he heard a deep voice yell, "That a boy!" he didn't notice a crowd of men had collected along the rail.

After the last boy, Rud led the horse out of the arena, and everybody walked back to the chutes. They all seemed to know what was going on. Kenny didn't know, but he followed the others to the rear of the barn, where a man in a shaggy vest put his shoulder to the heavy door and rolled it aside. Behind the door, a narrow chute connected to another barn. Two men from the crowd stepped in to help Scullie haze the calves out.

The pens near the door were high and permanent, built of splintering, rough-sawn lumber. Kenny climbed up on the boards to watch the long, dusty backs of horses shoot through the door. One by one they scrambled into the holding pen. They ran full tilt until they met the far side, then swiveled, and the whole herd started circling all in one direction. From where he sat, Kenny could look down into the holding pens on one side, two bucking chutes on the other. Mr. Gallagher and Rud stood together in the arena, their eyes on the ground.

In the pens, two men worked the broncs. One slipped through the gate into the pen, flicking a long-handled whip over his head. It took only seconds for one gate to swing open, another to shut — and a horse was in the chute. Mr. Gallagher called a name, Bart Hoskins, and a big, dark-haired kid appeared beside him in the arena.

"Get up there and set your rigging," Mr. Gallagher said.

Bart climbed above the chute and set his rigging on the bronc. Rud and Gallagher hooked and tied the cinch and made adjustments. When they were in agreement, Bart braced his boots on either side of the chute and lowered himself down on the horse, talking to himself. "Hoa, boy, whoa." He tightened his resined glove with his teeth and took a hold. Then he nodded, and the gate swung open.

The horse wheeled out into the sawdust, pivoting on his hind legs. He reared, his front hooves huge and hairy, drawn up tight to his chest, and came down with a jolt that snapped Bart's head back so hard everybody heard the bones crack. Bart rolled his spurs up and forward, where they were supposed to be, but he didn't work his knees. He was laid back almost flat on the rump. Then he was off in the dirt. He stood up, dusting off his jeans with hard slaps. Two pickup men on horseback cornered the loose horse, released the bucking strap, and hazed him out. Mr. Gallagher shouted at the boys, "Okay, clear it out. Swanson, get your butt up there and help. We got no time and ten rides. Let's go."

The next kid climbed the chute, and Gallagher gripped his shoulder, talking into his ear. Kenny hunched over in front of the rider, a foot braced on either side of the chute, helping set the rigging. Gallagher's words were low and fast. "Spur him out, keep your shoulders square, jerk your knees." The kid frowned, his forehead gone white under his eyebrows. He couldn't nod. He worked his hand snug under the handhold, but Kenny saw the muscles in his neck tense up like cables.

Then the horse was gone, and another one was in the chute. A gray, mottled horse the color of a dirty tennis shoe. His eye was wild, with pink skin showing around it, and the minute he was settled in, he reared. He twisted sideways and crashed into the boards, slipped, and went down. Kenny jumped clear, landing square on both feet in the narrow space behind the chute, but a manure-caked hoof came through the boards. It struck him on the shin just below the knee. It felt like a rusty knife cutting into the bone. Kenny winced when the pain shot up his leg, turning to nausea in his stomach. He set his jaw against the pain and saw the hoof wedged between the boards. He knew better than to reach a hand down there, but if he didn't do something, the horse would tear himself to pieces, break the leg. Without thinking, Kenny waited for the struggling horse to straighten the foot. Then he knelt and braced a thigh against the hoof and pushed the leg back through the boards. It happened fast, and nobody saw. Then the horse was up, stamping and wheezing, and the boys were strapping on the rigging.

Kenny took his time climbing back up over the chutes. The bronc stood ready, but Mr. Gallagher had called the rider down to the arena. He had his arm around the kid's shoulder, his head bent, talking. You couldn't blame the boy for being scared, the bronc could have gone down with him aboard.

Rud straddled the chute and tried to soothe the horse. The wide, mottled back nearly filled the narrow space. He leaned his weight against the boards, and Kenny heard the wood groan. Rud whispered under his breath, "Take it easy, easy." The horse jerked his head up hard and flattened his ears. Rud settled him back down. He kept a grip on one of the long ears, but he looked down in the arena, then at Kenny.

"Take a seat, boy," he said. "This one ain't waitin' for the conference to disperse."

Kenny hesitated. The horse jerked away from Rud's grip.

"Take a seat, boy." He jerked off his own glove and when Kenny had it on said, *"Move!"*

Kenny moved. He slipped down over the wide back, fit his palm under the leather handhold, and without trying to set his mind to it, nodded. Rud yelled, the arena cleared, and the gate swung open.

Kenny couldn't spur the bronc out. He didn't have his spurs on. Not even boots. But the habit of it flowed through his body, his knees began to pump, his heels up on the withers of the horse. The big bronc twisted in a spiral, but Kenny stayed with him. They were tossed by a hard, jolting buck that took them both across the arena. All Kenny felt was the thrill of being up high, moving fast. The blood pumped in his face. But his body caught the rhythm of the ride, and for a second, he and the horse were one crazy, jolting thing.

Then, out of the corner of his eye, he saw the blur of the pickup man. He reached out with his free hand, let go, and dove — both arms stretched out. He got hold of the saddle and let the pickup horse drag him off the bronc. Then he was standing alone in the dirt and sawdust, his legs trembling so hard he didn't know if he could walk. He started toward the chutes, but the joints in his knees gave with every step, as if he were walking on a mattress.

The men on the rail whooped, and Kenny looked up to see everybody standing at the chute. He grinned. Then they all found something to do and only Mr. Gallagher was there. He spoke to the boys.

"You kids hold tight," he said. He turned to look at Kenny. "Swanson, I'll see you out at the bus."

Kenny stopped walking.

"Now!" Mr. Gallagher barked.

Kenny turned on his heel, dizzy and confused, and walked past the men on the bleachers.

"Good job," one said. They were climbing down, walking back to the chutes to help out. Kenny picked up his jacket and walked out the barn door into the circle of white light. A snowflake filtered down and melted on his hand. He shrugged into his jacket and stood in the shadow of the bus.

Mr. Gallagher swung around the bus, walked up close, and grabbed him by the shoulder. His fingers pressed into the muscle, and a needle of pain shot up Kenny's neck. Mr. Gallagher pushed him up against the metal siding of the bus.

"That hurt?" Gallagher said.

Kenny didn't answer.

"Does it?"

"Yes, sir."

Gallagher loosened his grip, but his face was dark and tight. A vein pumped in his neck. His next words squeezed out between his teeth in a whisper.

"No," he said, "it doesn't. But you ever pull that again, you'll know what hurt is. That clear?"

"Yes, sir."

Gallagher let go of his shoulder and stepped back.

"What the hell did you think you were doing?"

Kenny wanted to explain — to tell Gallagher how Rud had urged him. But he knew better. Gallagher would only think he was making excuses.

"I won't do it again."

"That's right. You won't." Gallagher looked at him with disgust, slapped his clipboard down on his hip, and nodded at the bus.

"Get on the bus and stay there," he said. "Don't move until we're back at school."

Kenny stepped up on the metal stair.

"Wait," Gallagher said. He ripped a sheet from under the notes on his clipboard and held it out. Kenny took it and glanced down at the paper. It was a permission slip.

Kenny started to say he couldn't, but Mr. Gallagher walked away.

He folded the sheet in two and climbed on the bus. He walked to the rear and sat down. The plastic seat was brittle with cold.

He slid over to the window, the backs of his thighs beginning to numb. His shin throbbed where the horse had kicked him, but Kenny hardly felt it. He looked at the white sheet of paper in his hand. If he'd had something to write with, he would have signed the thing himself, right then.

13

Warm steam clouded on the surface of the water and thinned in the icy air. A full moon drifting above turned pearly pink and pale blue. Where the steam thinned and drifted, Roddy located a few stars glittering through. His shoulders and head were cold, but the smooth, black surface of the water covered his chest. In daylight, the water was clear enough that he could count the small, round river stones that cushioned his feet. He felt the swirl of water around his ankle, the movement of a fish. He took large slow-motion steps and heaved himself up on a rock.

Cynthia sat just in front of him, the moon pale on her shoulders, her wet hair dark in the mist. There were others at the spring. Their voices carried, bouncing off a sheer wall of rock above, but he couldn't see them. The black water lay like a smooth blanket across his knees.

They were waiting for the train, but he hadn't told her. He'd only said that at the end of the car ride, something would happen, a surprise.

"When?" She didn't whisper, but her voice was very low.

"Soon," he said.

He wanted to reach out and touch her. It seemed like such an easy thing to do. The mist made everything so close and quiet.

He'd brought girls here before, but none of them acted the way she did. Some laughed, embarrassed, or wouldn't take their clothes off and get in. Sometimes they were awed, smiling all the time, their faces pale and sweaty with the heat. But Cynthia had folded her clothes without turning away or speaking. She stood long enough for him to see the lift of her breasts, their soft upward curve, before she slipped into the water.

Her face, when he saw it, was serious. Not frowning or laughing or excited by the place. Just there, like a profile in white marble.

He heard a voice at the far end of the pool, and a beam of light glanced off the mountain above, brief, like a flash of lightning. He heard the far rumble of the train, and the light, blinding white, exploded in the mist rising high above them. The whole pool shook, the water quivering against his skin.

"Come on," he said, and slipped into the water. Cynthia lowered herself off the rock. The air itself seemed to glow iridescent, shimmering, like the northern lights. The train blared a warning and roared over their heads, the sound pulsing through him as a physical thing. He opened his mouth and yelled, and couldn't hear or feel his own voice. He put his hand on Cynthia's shoulder to steady himself. Vibrations jolted through his palm. The light vanished, and he could only hear the clank and rattle of the couplings on the long freight train, invisible on the track carved out of the rock above them.

When Cynthia turned to him this time, he thought she was smiling. "Hey," she said, and he could hear laughter behind the one word.

"Hey," he said.

When he kissed her, her lips trembled and went soft.

PART II

Winter

14

Lenna stepped out of the courthouse into air so dry and cold it took her breath away and seemed to freeze the membranes in her nose. As she walked to the post office, her view included the entire length of Main Street, already in shadow, and two or three parked cars. They looked abandoned, huddled like turtles under layered banks of snow. Everything seemed softened by whiteness. No one else was out, but scratchy Christmas music blared across the snow from loudspeakers on the roof of the fire station, and lighted plastic snowmen swung from the streetlights. They had been hung by the neck, like effigies. It made her laugh. She loved Christmas. When her boot slid on the ice, she flattened each foot and walked stiffly across the street.

Two blocks farther on, she pushed open the glass door to the post office. While she waited for the one customer ahead of her at the window, she felt soothed by the warmth of the small room, by the neon lights and clean counters. But she was anxious to get home. Kenny would have built up the fire by now and started dinner.

"You've been working hard, Mrs. Swanson." The postmistress, Doris Blumely, smiled behind her pale plastic glasses and took the bundles of county mail from Lenna, placing them side by side in a long tray. Lenna returned her smile and said good night.

She walked around the corner to the wall of shining brass post office boxes and turned the key in the lock of her own box, on the top row. Standing on her toes, she swung open the door — like the door of a tiny bank vault — and looked inside, hoping for a card or letter. But the box held only bills, which she wedged out of sight in her handbag. She was nearly out the door before she realized the postmistress was waving a letter and calling her name.

"I'm sorry," she said, "I almost forgot. This came in at four o'clock. I usually would wait and put a notice in your box in the morning, but it looks important."

"Thank you," Lenna said and took the letter in her hand. It was a government letter, embossed with thick blue printing. She stared at it, puzzled at first, and then afraid. Doris leaned over the counter, her posture full of concern and curiosity.

"Thank you," Lenna said again and began to leave.

"Wait," Doris called. "You have to sign."

Pressing down hard to keep her hand from trembling, Lenna signed her full name, "Lenora Swanson," in even, slanting letters. Doris took the receipt and Lenna tried again to go.

"Is everything all right?" Doris asked, and Lenna turned back, making herself smile. "Fine," she said. "Everything's fine." She waved and pushed open the door to the icy night outside.

Remembering to keep her feet flat on the slippery pavement, Lenna walked back to her car across from the courthouse. She opened the door and wrapped her coat close around her thighs to slide behind the wheel. For a long moment she sat there, feeling her heart pound. Then she switched on the dome light and stared again at the letter. She'd had letters like this before; always they brought bad news. She dreaded these blue-and-white envelopes the way she dreaded the letters that came from Kenneth Swanson's lawyer.

She tore the end carefully off the envelope, to preserve it intact, and unfolded the letter against the steering wheel. Slowly she read each word. Kenny's father was dead, in a "routine test flight over the Gulf of Mexico." The air force had conducted a search for three days before they located the wreckage. There were no survivors.

"Oh . . . no . . . ," Lenna spoke aloud. Her whole body convulsed, as if it could physically push out this hard thing wedged in her chest. She swallowed, but the pain, like a dull bone caught sideways in her windpipe, would not go down. Her mind rushed toward this — Kenny's father alone in the water — then pushed it away. She saw him alive, standing in the doorway, wearing a white T-shirt and looking like a boy. A "routine test flight"? Ken Swanson thought of airplanes the way most people think of cars. He'd flown dozens of missions in the war. She read the letter again, read, "no survivors," and the pain thrust up, scraped out of her throat in a sob.

Kenny had never seen her cry; she never cried in front of him, but she cried now. She pressed her forehead into the brittle-cold ribs on the steering wheel and let the tears jerk out. What would she tell Kenny? Would she tell him? Did he have to know? Only a few minutes ago she had been standing in the warm post office looking forward to dinner. Before the letter, Kenneth Swanson was alive.

She knew she should stop crying — pull herself together — but she couldn't move. She slumped in the car, staring out at the empty street, the pathetic Christmas decorations swinging from the lampposts, her tears blurring the white lights into long stars, the points on the stars stretching and receding. Her mind would not stop working, and pictures, like the pictures that come on a night of insomnia, followed, one after another. She saw Ken in his flight suit, treading water. Waiting for search planes that never came. Then she thought about Kenny, who seemed by some miracle unhurt by the things his father had done, who loved his dad.

"I hate you," she said aloud, as if Ken Swanson were there, right in front of her. Hate curled her fingers into fists. "I hate you," she said again, and thought, Even when I found out you had another woman in another town, I never hated you. Even when you took Kenny with you, and he saw your suitcase by her bed . . .

She started to sob silently. Deep inside, she'd always thought she would win a fight with Kenneth Swanson, she would make him see, and he would change. He would take care of Kenny. Even after he remarried, there had been time, she thought, for things to come out right.

Why hadn't his wife had the decency to phone her? Lenna was not his next of kin, but Kenny was. There would be more letters. Official documents. But why hadn't someone phoned?

As she sat in the car, not thinking to start the engine or the heater, her breath frosted the windows, and her fingers and toes were beginning to ache and grow numb from the cold. She had to start the car and drive home.

Instead, she got out and began to walk, shoving her hands deep in her pockets to warm them. If she could just walk up and down a few times, let the tears freeze on her cheeks, maybe the raw air would shock her back to normal.

Twice she passed the mirrored windows of the Ralston Hotel before she convinced herself that what she needed was a drink. She'd never been in the bar before; it was not a place where women went alone. But she couldn't go home.

The café was empty. She passed down the hall and pushed open the padded door into the bar. She sat down at the first table she came to, set against the front wall of a wide, low-ceilinged room, darkened by smoke and stained paneling. The bar stools were crowded with men in dark shirts and grease-black work clothes, but Lenna was afraid to look at them beyond a quick glance. She stared down at the rings left by wet glasses on the table until an overweight young woman in tight jeans bent to take her order. She wanted something strong and quick, but she couldn't think of the names of drinks. She ordered whiskey.

When the drink came she took a swallow and let it melt into her limbs before she looked around. A pool table stood in the center of the room, and two young men took turns leaning over their shots. At two or three tables, couples sat drinking and talking. She didn't fit here, a single woman wrapped in her good office coat. Her eyes must be rimmed with red and smudged with dark mascara, but no one seemed to notice her. A man pushed a quarter into the jukebox, and he and his wife — she thought it was his wife — got up to dance, folded close into each other.

Lenna felt herself sink into the music, a sad country song with Hawaiian guitars. She had never cared for country music, not only because the twangy voices brought back the poverty of her own background, but because it lied. It made believe that things like divorce and drinking and being alone were romantic, and she knew it wasn't true. But tonight, she wanted to hear lies.

She knew she should ask if they had a phone, go and call Kenny, but she ordered another drink instead and waited for the next song. Kenny would be doing his homework now. He would have gone ahead and eaten the meat loaf she'd mixed up last night and left for him to put in the oven. She sipped her second whiskey and began to watch the pool game — not paying attention to it, just watching. One of the young men moved around in an easy rhythm, clearing the table of pool balls one after the other. She looked at his dark hair, falling long against his cheek, and thought about Kenny. Would he ever look so strong and self-contained as that? Would she look at him someday — across a room like this — and see a stranger? Then she recognized the pool player, Roddy Moyers, because Kenny had pointed him out. When he glanced up from his game and saw her, she was embarrassed.

A new song came on the jukebox, another slow, mournful song. It made her want to cry again. She had to admit that having an ex-husband had been a comfort. It had allowed her to feel less helpless, less alone. She hadn't been crying for Kenny, who had no father. Or for Ken Swanson. Only his new wife was allowed to cry for him.

She was crying for herself. Because she was alone — and shut out, even from his dying. She turned her face to the wall and felt the tears well up over her bottom eyelids again. She was ashamed. She saw her own self-pity, but she couldn't stop. She cried with her eyes open, seeing nothing.

She was startled by a tap on her shoulder. She turned and looked up at Roddy Moyers, who stood above her, unsmiling.

"A dance?" he said.

"No, no, thank you," Lenna began to say, and then she stopped herself.

"Yes," she said, and stood up. Roddy Moyers led the way past the pool table, into the darkness at the back of the room. He placed a broad, warm hand low on her back, and slowly began to move in small, close circles. She leaned her face against his shoulder and let him guide her to the music, but she didn't listen to the verses of the song.

15

As Kenny started down the metal steps of the plane, the stewardess said something. He stopped, blocking the people behind him.

"What?"

"Watch your step," she said, and turned mechanically to repeat it to the next passenger.

Kenny watched his step, angling down the stairs slowly, his duffel bag turned sideways and banging hard against his knee.

The flight had seemed so unreal to him, so quiet and outside of time that his ears felt stuffed with cotton, as if he had a cold. When he stepped on the runway, a ragged wind cut across his cheek, and his boots crunched on broken ice.

His mother waved at him from behind the glass wall of the terminal. When they met, she hesitated, kissing him on the side of the head, as if she'd aimed for his cheek and missed. The two of them strode down the cool linoleum corridor and out the doors.

Though they were out below, in the broad river plains and at the lower elevation, it was very cold. He and his mom sat in the car for a minute, waiting for the engine to heat up, the heater to come on.

When they left the airport, the streets in Bonneville Falls were glistening black with melted snow, and he could hear the cars pushing through the slush. His mom drove under a brick railway arch and turned onto the highway toward home.

"Well?" his mother said. She smiled at him, but there was worry in her voice.

"Well," he said, "I made it."

"How was it?"

"Not too bad," he said, "for a *funeral*." He laughed, despite himself. He was so glad to be going home, where he could laugh.

His mother laughed, too.

"It was okay," Kenny said. "Just a service at the chapel on the base. Sort of bare, you know." His mother nodded. He had the sense she did know. "That was the hardest part. Dad wasn't there. It's hard to believe somebody's dead. I didn't want to see him. But I sort of wanted to."

His mother nodded again.

Snow gleamed blue in the fields beside the road. Florida had been hot. In Louise's house, everything smelled stale; the air-conditioning was always on, and the cool air smelled like heat, rotting things, and old cigarette smoke.

Even the airport, when he landed, had that smell. Louise was there to meet him, and when they finally stepped outside, the air itself was thick with heat and smells. Everything he saw struck him as too white and too small. His father and Louise had lived in a low, concrete blockhouse enclosed by a jungle of vines and banana trees. He remembered walking under a green plastic carport and into the dark, cool house.

The first thing Louise did was take him out and show him tangerines and grapefruit growing on the trees. Real bananas. But the bananas weren't ripe, and she couldn't believe Kenny had never eaten a grapefruit.

At the service he was hot. The wool collar of his suit scratched him right through his shirt, and sweat ran down the sides of his face.

They had driven a long time without talking, but his mother seemed to be there, inside his thoughts.

"What's she like, Louise?"

"I don't know. She was nice."

"But what was she like in general?"

"Ordinary."

"Ordinary how?"

"What's that mean, 'ordinary how'?"

Kenny felt the car slowing down.

"You're slowing down," he said.

His mother glanced at the speedometer and pressed on the gas. "Was she ordinary big, ordinary small, ordinary young . . . ? Give me a clue."

Kenny didn't know. He tried to think why. "I guess," he said, "I was kind of afraid to look at her. Her other husband crashed, too. Did you know that?"

"Yes," his mother said. She was slowing down again.

"Mom" — Kenny felt a laugh coming up in his voice — "I'd like to get home sometime this week."

She laughed and sped up. Somehow he knew his mother didn't want to know what Louise was like. She was small, hardly taller than Kenny, and had short, curly hair and green eyes. Her little girl, Corey, had those eyes, too. And Louise smelled good. She had been nice to him at the funeral, but too polite.

His mother didn't ask him any more questions. He switched on the radio. The moon came up in the east and lighted the rolling hills of snow. The yellow-green gauges on the dash made the car seem very private and safe. He liked the smell of dust blowing in with the warm air from the heater.

An hour later, they pulled in behind the house, where the snowplow had carved out a narrow parking space. Kenny hoisted his duffel bag and they high-stepped through the deep snow to the back door. Inside, his mother turned the stove dial and opened the oven. "Just leave your coat on for a minute," she said. "I've got a fire built. I just need to light it."

Kenny sat down in the kitchen and worked his wet shoes off. Tomorrow he would shovel a path to the car for his mom. He pulled his coat tight around his chest and rested his elbows on the table. He was shivering.

"I'll make us something hot to drink." His mother poured milk in a saucepan and set it on the burner. Slowly, heat radiated from the woodstove, and they carried their chairs up close to the fire. In the corner, a fir tree, full at the bottom but twisted and bare at the top, was hung with colored lights and Christmas balls. He was shocked that his mom would decorate the tree without him.

"It's almost Christmas," she said. "Did you know that?"

"Yeah."

"You aren't excited?"

Kenny didn't know what to say. He wasn't excited. Inside him, a pool of something had gathered, something sharp and alive, almost like excitement. But it wasn't excitement.

"I feel sad, you know," he said. "There won't be anything from Dad. He never sent me anything much. But I always thought, someday, he would."

His dad had sent him something, in a way. Louise had given him his dad's pilot's wings and his medals from the war. Just before he left, she'd handed them to him, not in a case or anything, but in a paper bag.

She acted like it was something special. But Kenny wondered about the goat's head and the hide. His dad's guns and saddle. He hadn't seen them at Louise's, and the time never felt right to ask.

He woke up early in the morning, loaded the woodstove, and made coffee. Then he went out and shoveled a clean path to the car. The snow clung, wet and heavy, to the shovel, and the sky was overcast. But it was warm, the clouds holding in the heat of the sun. By the time he finished, he was sweating hard. His mom had told him that he didn't have to go to school until he was ready since it was so close to Christmas vacation. He had looked ahead to that vacation for so long, but now he couldn't think what to do with even one day alone. He wanted to go downtown and buy a present for his mother, but he didn't have much money.

In the kitchen, his mother was dressed for work, finishing her coffee. Kenny fixed a bowl of cereal and sat down at the table. She went in the bathroom to put on her lipstick and came back out, looking for her purse.

"You be okay?" she said.

"Sure." He looked up and smiled to give her the idea.

"I might be a little late," she said.

"Okay," Kenny said. His mom looked so worried about him, as if a funeral changed someone. But he couldn't think of anything to say to calm her. "I wish you could have gone with me, on the plane," he said.

"Me, too," she said. Then she was gone.

Kenny put the milk away and set his bowl in the sink. He climbed the stairs and fished the paper bag out of his duffel. He arranged the medals in two rows on his bed, fingering the metal and the ribbons. The striped ribbons felt substantial, almost greasy. Some, he knew, were given to every flyer, but others, the ones from Vietnam, were special. He scooped them back in the bag, crumpled it into a ball, and carried it downstairs. He tucked the bag in his jacket, and all the way to town he could feel it there, the warm heat of the medals against his chest. They felt to him like the residue of a dream, a dream he didn't want to wake from. He could never recall the dream, but all day he'd feel the pull, the warmth of it.

At the pawn and gun store, he stood for a long time looking in the windows. The glass was grimy with steam and dirt, the greenish-yellow of crankcase oil. Behind the glass, the window was filled with dull, dusty items. Gold rings and watches. A statue of a bulldog with a rag in its mouth, a mangy stuffed coyote, and a snaking row of red pipe wrenches, ranged in order from giant-size to very small.

He pushed through the door. A fat woman with dull gray hair flattened close to her head sat behind the counter, so low he could just see her chest and head. She looked up at him and went on counting to herself, writing on something he couldn't see. He waited for her to look up again and walked to the counter, his hand on the soft paper of the bag.

"I wondered —"

"What you got?" He shook the contents of the bag onto a felt pad in front of her, but it seemed to him she never glanced over.

"Quarter," she said.

"Each?"

"Yeah, each."

Kenny looked at the medals. There were ten. $2.50. He picked them up one at a time and put them back in the bag. He folded it over and placed it back inside his jacket. "Thanks," he said. His hand was shaking.

He walked out onto the covered boardwalk and looked to see if anyone had noticed him, but the street was empty. In the shade of the overhang, he was cold. He walked along toward the café. At the door, he worked his hand into the pocket of his jeans and counted his change. He didn't have enough to buy lunch, but he could get a donut.

The café was warm. He asked for a cinnamon twist to go, and carried it back outside. At the end of the boardwalk, he crouched down on the steps.

Across the street, he saw his mother stride out the door of the courthouse. Good, he thought, we can get some lunch. He stood and threw his arm up in a wave. "Mom!" he hollered.

Just then, he saw Roddy Moyers climb out of a pickup by the curb. He walked around the hood and opened the passenger door. Kenny crouched back down. His mother carried a roll of maps in one hand and her white snow boots in the other. She climbed into the truck and tugged her coat hem after her. The last thing Kenny saw before Roddy shut the door was the way his mother leaned toward him, then bowed her head, laughing at something Moyers must have said.

16

Roddy flipped the heater fan to high and turned the radio up higher. Christmas music. He switched it off and went on pounding the heel of his hand against the wheel to a rhythm he couldn't hear.

To the west, a cloud bank had lowered and rolled over the mountains in a dark mass, but to the east and overhead the clouds thinned to reveal high patches of blue. The road was bare of ice and slush. It was enough for him to feel it was a clear day. He let up a little on the gas and shifted in the seat.

Lenna sat upright, looking out the windshield. She wore the same blue coat she'd worn that first night, in the bar, and stockings and high heels. She was the only woman he could think of, other than his mother, who seemed to belong in high heels.

He thought about the first night, watching Lenna come into the hotel bar. She seemed out of place. She was beautiful, that much was true. But she came in with the expression of someone who'd just seen an accident. Later, when he looked over, she still seemed beautiful, but bruised. Like a girl whose lip is soft and swollen from too much kissing.

He watched her for almost an hour, through one pool game, then another. He finished a beer and switched to whiskey, and his pool game improved. Shots he normally took time to set up he knocked in hard without thinking. She couldn't even see the table — but he had to be good. He kept telling himself to go over, talk to her, but each time he racked up another game.

When he finally quit and approached her table, he had no idea what he was going to say. He thought she'd think he was coming on, just tell him to get lost. But she stood up and took his hand. He couldn't believe how it felt, how easy it was. She closed her eyes and leaned her cheek on his shoulder as if she'd known him all her life.

They danced that slow dance and the next one. Sometime later, when the music stopped, she blinked and took a small step back. Roddy ran a thumb over a smudge on her cheek. Her eyelashes were long and dark, gathered by tears into stars. When he touched her she looked up, suddenly alarmed, as if she were surprised to see him there.

Outside, Lenna shook with cold. He couldn't touch her now, but he could hear the tremor in her voice. He wanted to drive her home, but her own car was parked right there. He had to let her go. It was only later that he learned how shaken she was, and ashamed. He'd felt guilty himself, though he didn't know why he should. It had to do with trading on somebody else's sadness.

He looked over at Lenna. The girls he knew would have slid over to the middle of the seat, but Lenna sat close to the door. He drove faster. He always drove fast, but the wet black road with no snow made him drive fast enough to turn the white fields into blurs. He watched to see if Lenna would reach for something to hold on to, but she sat still.

At the ski hill road, he braked abruptly and turned off the highway. Lenna could have moved closer then, but she didn't. He could feel the space between them like a solid thing. He took another turn, onto the Forest Service road, and pushed through deep-rutted snow where the road twisted through high timber. At the crest of the hill, he pulled up with the hood of the truck facing out over the valley and set the brake.

Lenna slipped off her shoes and bent down to pull on her snow boots. He came around to hold open her door and stood beside her looking down at the valley.

"There," Roddy said, making sure she followed his gaze. He pointed out the ranch house, the slant roof of the barn, and equipment sheds. The barn was the oldest log building in the valley, what was left of the original homestead. From this distance, the ranch was a scene for a model train set, the dark log buildings gathered close together, the rail fences, a forest of leafless aspen trees inserted like twigs in the snow.

"It's beautiful," Lenna said. "How can your father want to sell it?"

"That's what he does for a living. Buys and sells. Real estate. But he's not selling the whole thing." Roddy pointed to a spot where section lines met at crossing fences. "Just that piece. It's no good for the ranch. It's all rock bar and sagebrush."

"But you'll have houses there, and neighbors."

Roddy wanted to tell her he didn't care. The land wouldn't be subdivided and built on for years, and he had no idea where he'd be by then. He'd grown up mostly on the ranch, gone to school in the valley, but he didn't feel bound to stay. "Things change," he said. "There's not so much you can do about it."

Lenna rolled an aerial map out on the truck fender, smoothed it with the edge of her glove, and held it flat. She asked him questions about the land, when it was surveyed, where the stakes and markers were. She checked creeks and fence lines against the map. Afterward, he backed the truck out and drove down to the ranch. They came in along an alley between barbed-wire fences, skidded up over a stretch of clear ice, and circled in front of the main house.

"It's like a hotel," Lenna said, standing in the entry, looking down into the sunken living room. Roddy tried to see it through her eyes. The room was furnished with oversize leather sofas and Navajo blankets and rugs. At one end a broad stone fireplace stood empty, and at the other end a black grand piano gleamed in the shadows. He showed Lenna where the wings of the house branched from the main room.

"This all came from real estate?" Lenna asked.

Roddy laughed. "Well, some of the real estate had oil under it. My granddad was a rock picker — a geologist."

"You live here?" She looked at Roddy.

"No," he said, "this way." He pushed through a swinging door into the kitchen.

"This is the kitchen," he said.

"Oh, really?" Lenna said.

"Yes," he said solemnly.

Lenna stood in her coat in the center of the room, looking around. He couldn't tell if she was impressed or disapproving. "It's like a kitchen for a restaurant."

"Hay crew," he said. "In the summer, they feed the hay crew out of here."

"I helped cook for hay crews when I was a girl," Lenna said. "In a kitchen the size of your icebox."

"They don't hire cooks like you. We get somebody's grandmother. One year we had a buck sergeant. I think he cooked in World War Two." Roddy swung open the refrigerator and reached for a beer. "You want anything? Beer? Coffee?" Lenna shook her head. He uncapped the beer and took a long drink.

He led her out the back door and along a wooden boardwalk to a low building.

"Bunkhouse," he said, holding open the door to a bare log barracks, long and narrow, with one crooked window at each end and iron cots with thin, rolled-up mattresses in rows down each wall. The farthest one was his. He'd made it that morning by throwing a green army blanket over the sheets. His shirts, an extra jacket, and his duffel hung on fencing spikes hammered into the log wall. He motioned for Lenna to go ahead down the aisle to where the fire had gone out in the potbellied stove.

"You sleep here?" Lenna asked.

"Yes, ma'am."

"Why don't you move into the house?"

Roddy shrugged. "Too hard to heat." They stood in the aisle. Lenna folded her arms across her chest, holding her coat close. Shifting to keep warm, they seemed stuck in the center of the room, circling each other.

"You want to see the barn?"

Lenna glanced down at her white boots. "I don't know. What do you think?"

"Don't worry. I'll get you something. Wait here." He went back to the kitchen and rummaged in the back closet where the cook kept odds and ends and returned with a pair of rubber irrigation boots. He sorted through the clean laundry at the bottom of his duffel bag and handed Lenna a pair of thick socks.

Lenna pulled on the socks and boots, and he helped her into his canvas jacket. It sat stiff up over her shoulders and hung past her knees. Roddy laughed. "You look like a fireman," he said. "A midget fireman." But that's not how she looked to him. She looked so small under the coat that she seemed naked. He could sense the shape of her shoulders and white arms.

He took her outside. They walked together along a path of tramped-down snow. When they passed the foreman's trailer, Lenna stopped, afraid.

"You said nobody was here."

"He's not," Roddy said. "Gone to his daughter's for Christmas."

"Aren't you going somewhere for Christmas?"

"No. Somebody has to stay and feed. Come on, I'll show you the barn."

The barn was not much used now. A loft of rough beams tilted low over the dirt floor, and the empty stalls were hung with shredding burlap sacks and scraps of stiff black harness. It smelled of rotting hay and dry manure. In the last stalls, two dark draft horses stood sleeping on their feet.

"Hey, big guy," Roddy said, and reached up to grab an ear. The big horse pulled back, then lowered his face to be scratched. Roddy scrubbed at the huge Roman nose with the stiff edge of his glove until heat moved through the leather to his hand. Lenna leaned against the half door.

"They have feet like dinner plates. They wouldn't fit in gallon cans."

"You should see them standing out in the field. Sometimes I just go watch them. Go out and holler at 'em."

"What are their names?"

"This one's Don," he said. "And that one's Chub. Chub and Don." Roddy laughed. "I didn't name 'em. We don't use them much unless there's a blizzard, or the tractor breaks down."

"How can you tell them apart?" Lenna asked.

"Chub's a girl."

Inside the bunkhouse, Roddy told Lenna to sit on the bed, and he helped her pull off the black rubber boots. He cracked some kindling and stuffed it in the woodstove. The bunkhouse was heated, but barely. He used the stove at night. In a few minutes he had a hot fire going. He turned back to Lenna, where she sat on the edge of the bed in his jacket.

"Sure you don't want a beer? Coffee? I could make you some coffee."

"No, a beer's all right."

Roddy brought six beers back from the kitchen. He worked four bottles down into the snow outside and carried two in with him.

He opened one and handed it to Lenna. She had taken off the big jacket and sat there on the bed in her blue skirt and sweater. She was flushed from the cold, her hair curled in wisps around her face. She looked at him and glanced away. For the first time that afternoon, he saw she was embarrassed. Her hand, holding the beer, was unsteady.

Roddy flipped down the mattress on the next cot and sat on it, his knees nearly touching hers. This time, she didn't look away. He set his beer on the floor, then hers, and lifted her up. He pulled her tight against his chest, enclosed her in his arms, and held her. He felt the heat of her body, the solid feel of a body, calm him, like a homing signal. Her breathing caught, and stopped. She kissed him on the mouth.

Her eyes were open, softly staring at him, and he knew something was happening to him that had not happened before. He slipped his hands under the soft sweater, and lifted it over her head. When he touched her breast, the tip of his rough finger outlining the lace edge of her bra, she looked at him as if she might blow away, like petals held out on his palm, but she held very still, wanting him to know how his hands felt to her.

She stood and stepped out of her skirt, and when he lay down next to her, they moved like one living thing, all skin and tears. This was a thing he didn't know about — grief and rage and shame. For a moment, he wanted to use his hands to soothe her, as he would an injured bird, but her body was stronger than his. She drew him in, and he followed, tracing an endless silver thread that disappeared into darkness. When he thought he couldn't go on any longer, go any farther, he did. He raised himself on both arms to see her face, to make sure she was separate and there. Her eyes were open, looking back at him, her hair tangled and dark with sweat. She let him watch her, unashamed.

When finally they were exhausted, he turned sideways and held the curve of her back against him, his hand on the softness of her breast. It seemed so surprising to him, the rough ends of his fingers pressed into her skin. He could feel her heart beating hard, then slower, under his palm.

He had been to Lenna's house when Kenny was in Florida. He had waited two days after they met, then walked into the courthouse and asked her where she lived, if he could come to see her. Except for Lenna, the offices were empty, but he still had an eerie feeling there could be people upstairs who might overhear. Lenna must have felt that, too. She put him off, said people would talk. But finally, to get him to leave, he thought, she asked him to help her with a Christmas tree, a surprise for Kenny. Roddy had parked the ranch truck downtown and walked over. He told himself he did this not to avoid gossip but because there was no sense in upsetting people, but he knew better. He knew there would be talk.

But that time had not been like this. Lenna had been tense, and when it was over, crying.

"I can't do this," she had told him. "It's wrong."

"It's not wrong," Roddy said. "Why do you say that?"

"I have to help Kenny. I have to do this right. Be a mom for Kenny. You can't understand." Her voice broke. "I feel like I've been a mother so long." Roddy put his arms around her, listened to her cry. When she stopped, she said, "I need to be sad. I want to grieve for Ken, and I can't. I'm so glad to be alive myself."

Roddy remembered kissing her where her cheek was damp with tears. He had tightened his arms around her and whispered,

"It's not wrong. It's fine. Just have fun. These things don't come along that often."

She'd looked up, surprised. "Not even for you?"

Roddy laughed, wondering what she thought his life was like. "Not even for me," he said.

Roddy left the cot to make coffee and stoke up the fire in the woodstove. When he returned, they sat up together on the cot, wrapped in blankets.

"I have to go," Lenna said.

Though it was nearly dark, Roddy didn't want her to go.

"Kenny thinks I'm at work. The office thinks I'm looking at the ranch."

"You wish you hadn't come?"

"No. But you don't know how lonely it is to be the divorcée, how ugly people can get."

He could tell it took some struggle for her to admit it when she said, "I'm scared.

"Roddy," she said, narrowing her eyes as if she could force him to understand just by the heat of her feelings, "I've never done anything like this before. I've never felt like this before."

"Felt like what?"

"I don't know. Sad. And wrong. Guilty somehow. Ken was such a bully — so *right* all the time. But when I had to file for divorce he acted like a little kid. He was so hurt. That's how I think of him now. Waiting for a rescue plane — just a boy out there in the water by himself."

"You might be wrong," Roddy said. "It might have been different. He was trained for that, wasn't he?"

"Yes."

"Well, think of something terrible he did."

"I do that, too. I hate him. I really hate him. I think of things he said — and I can't sleep at night. He lied. He saw other women. He spent all the money. I'd go to town to buy something, and they wouldn't take Ken's checks. Once, I was standing at the checkout stand with a cart filled with groceries. I felt I should have put them all back, but I couldn't . . ."

She stopped and looked at Roddy. "I don't want to tell those things. I never wanted anyone to know. At the end, he told me he'd bet his co-pilot two hundred dollars that I couldn't get a job. Couldn't raise a boy."

"Didn't he send money?"

"Child support. Not much and never on time."

"Won't you get insurance money?"

"No. He signed it over to his new wife."

"Jesus," Roddy said. "No wonder you're mad." He kissed her on the edge of her mouth so softly they nearly lay down again. She pulled away.

"I have to get home."

"Not right now."

17

He's *dining* with me again," Cynthia said.

"The boy?" Dill grinned.

Cynthia grinned back at him. "Kenny Swanson," she said.

Dill lit a cigarette and coughed. She wanted to ask him for one, but she didn't dare. She thought about Kenny Swanson, the new kid. She joked about the boy "dining" with her, but he was disturbing. Early in the year, she'd seen him most days leaning on the wall outside some class.

Before vacation started, he'd been following her outside to a bench on the snow-packed lawn, no matter how bad the weather. He sat just near enough to hear her if she spoke. When she looked up, he lowered his eyes. She felt odd when he did this; it was odd for a ninth-grader to hang around a senior. It was partly that he followed her, but it might have been the way he looked. He had fine reddish hair, pushed out of his eyes, and long eyelashes. He was so pretty it embarrassed her.

"How do you come to be down this way?" Dill asked her. "You ride down on Goldie?"

"She's outside."

"Didn't even hear you comin'," Dill said.

"You must be getting old."

"Not so old as that horse. Your dad know you're here?"

When she left the ranch, her dad had been out feeding. While she saddled the mare, she kept watch on her father and the hired man far down in the field pitching hay from the sled, the cattle trailing behind like sleepwalkers. From a distance, the dark red cattle in the snow looked like a crooked line of stitches in a blanket. They seemed so small and far away. She could remember how big and menacing they seemed when she was small and her dad had packed her out on the sled with him every morning.

She'd ridden Goldie out across the fields, down to the river, and along the old swamp road until she came to the dump. Dill had strung the chain across the entrance, but smoke rose from his trailer, and his rusty Dodge pickup, overflowing with cans and scrap iron and rolls of chicken wire, was parked in front. She'd put up her horse in the shed and knocked on the door.

Now she looked to see if he was paying attention. "Dill," she said, "I might get a scholarship."

"Well, that beats all," he said. "You goin' out below?"

Cynthia didn't answer. The small room was hot; a trickle of sweat ran down her temples. She shifted her hair behind her ear. Dill reached back and opened the silver door. She could smell the acrid black smoke from tires burning in the dump.

"You tell your dad?"

She shook her head.

"You tell your dad about that school. He won't find out from me. But he'll find out. He pays the bills."

"I know," she said.

"You tell him, then. He'll surprise you. Your dad'll be proud."

"Proud?" Cynthia didn't believe it.

"If it was like when him and I were kids, if you'd stay here in the valley, he could watch over you. He doesn't know about this music thing. But he's proud of you. He told me that."

She looked at Dill with suspicion. What he said made her throat contract, as if she were going to cry, even though it made no sense. It didn't have the feel of truth; it didn't fit anything she knew about her father.

She sat back against the wall, a wave of anger tightening her jaw.

"Not going for music," she said. "It's a science scholarship."

Dill blinked at her. He looked surprised, and a look of sadness came into his eyes. He reached out and groped for her hand. She looked down at his hand, the creases black with grease, and her own white fingers.

He held her hand a long time, and when she said nothing more, he let it drop to her knee and carried his cup to the sink.

"I need to head out and get that machine runnin'. Got customers today."

He moved around in the small space of the kitchen, his shoulders slightly bent so he could walk upright.

Cynthia felt overwhelmed with shame. She couldn't stand for him to feel sorry for her. She couldn't tell him how for music you had to go away for an audition. You had to have better teachers than she had. He'd never understand.

He jerked on a heavy canvas coat. "Stay as long as you want," he said. "Maybe we can get some cards together later."

"Dill?" she said.

He turned slowly around. "What is it, sweetheart?"

"I need to ask you a favor. On the form for the scholarship, on the papers, they want an address."

"You've got one, haven't you?"

"I want to put your box number down."

"I can't go along with that."

Cynthia felt trapped. Nobody was going to help her. She had asked. She couldn't ask again.

"Fine," she said. She picked up her own coat and stood up. Dill was blocking the doorway. She'd figured it all out, applied to the one place that didn't want her dad's income and signature. She'd rent a box at the post office herself.

She pulled on her coat and stood only a foot away from Dill. A network of wrinkles, like creeks branching into rivers, was carved in the red skin of his neck.

Before she knew what had happened, Dill grabbed at her. He twisted, and shoved her out the door. She tripped on the stairs and landed hard, on her feet, but tripping off balance. Dill gave her another shove from behind, his hand in the middle of her back.

"Fine," he said, imitating her. *"Fine."* He pushed her along toward the equipment shed. "Ain't fine," he said. "I know it ain't fine. You know it ain't fine. What were you thinking to do? Never visit me again 'cause things don't go your way?"

He shoved her up to the bulldozer, gripping the seat of her pants as if she were a kid, and climbed up after her. He kept yelling, but when he started the engine, it was so loud she couldn't hear. He backed the huge machine out of the shed. At the edge of the dump, he lowered the heavy blade. He pushed back as far as he could in the seat, took her elbow, and dragged her onto his lap. He shoved her feet down on the brake pedals and throttled up. Cynthia felt the heavy power of the Cat, and heard the crack and tumbling crunch of boards and dirt, rolling and breaking. Slowly she pushed the debris ahead, the vibration shaking in her arms and legs, until it began to shift and tumble over the edge of the pit. Dill shoved on her knees to force her to brake, raised the blade, and threw the lever for reverse.

"Back 'er up," he yelled.

She craned her neck to see, but Dill's shoulder was there, his rust-stained jacket.

"Nothin' comin' but a Greyhound," he said. "Just hold her steady, push straight back."

She let up slowly on the brakes, and she heard the *ding, ding, ding,* and the huge yellow Cat lurched backward, knocking her forward. Dill took a grip on her shoulder, and yanked her back. He hauled on levers, lowered the blade, and let her steer the huge bulldozer until the front tires hung on the edge of the pit.

When they reversed again, he set the brake, and his arm came around her arms and chest. He pinned her against himself. The throb of machinery rattled her teeth. Up high in the cab, the wind blew the stench of the dump away, and she was able to see over the trees and willows to where the river made a flat, silver ribbon, winding away to the north.

18

On the day of Christmas Eve, Kenny watched the snow begin to fall, wet, heavy flakes dropping straight down. By afternoon, half-moon drifts covered the front room windows. Kenny elbowed his way through the back doorway with an armful of logs so high he had to arch his neck to see where he was going. The dark room seemed to slope underground, like a bunker. He dropped the wood on the hearth, swung open the stove, and wedged in another log. When he closed the heavy door, he could hear the air and wood burst into flame. The sudden rush of heat beat like wings up the stovepipe and set the iron doors shuddering. He turned the damper down.

In the kitchen, his mother was whistling a song. Her whistle was thin, liquid like a bird song, riding up and down the notes. He loved to hear her whistle and tried to talk her into doing it more. But she said that at one of the schools she'd been sent to, the nuns had slapped her hand and told her, "Whistling girls, like cackling hens, all will come to no good ends." His mother laughed about it now, but she never whistled except when she was by herself.

The steamy, warm smell of turkey in the oven made juices spurt in the back of his mouth, under his tongue, but he didn't feel like it was Christmas. Someone in his mother's office had given them an old couch, a chair, and a small three-legged table that had to have a matchbook wedged under one leg. His mother had bought a used TV and sewed curtains. But the room still seemed empty to him, as if they were moving in or out. He switched on the lamp and closed the curtains to shut out the snow.

He drifted into the kitchen and stood close behind his mother, leaning over to watch her chopping apples for salad. He smelled the clean shampooed smell of her hair and reached around her to steal a pale cube of green apple. He hadn't eaten anything all day.

"Quit it," she said.

"I'm starving."

"Good."

He reached for another piece, and she swatted at his hand.

"Why don't you do something useful?" she said. She turned around, and Kenny stepped back. "Bring in some wood."

"I already did."

"Go shovel snow."

"Did that, too."

His mother turned back to the sink, swept up the apples, and dumped them in a bowl. She wiped her hands on her apron and stretched up to reach into the cupboard. She brought down three china plates, and held them out to Kenny. "Set the table."

Kenny looked at the plates. "We only need two," he started to say, then took the plates, glancing at his mother. He swallowed and pushed down the stab of alarm in his stomach. "Mom?" he said. "You gave me three plates."

"I know."

"Why?"

"I invited a guest."

Kenny was so relieved at first, he didn't know what to say. He had thought his mother was setting a place for his dad. Since the trip to Bonneville Falls, his mother had been doing funny things. She'd been staying late at the courthouse, and more and more when he came down to the kitchen in the morning, she was already there, sitting by herself with the oven on, drinking coffee. Neither one of them had mentioned rodeo lately.

Kenny spaced the dishes around the table and laid silverware at each place. He folded three nubby paper napkins and weighted them down with the forks.

When he was finished, his mother stared for a long time at the table. She straightened a knife and stood back. "Maybe we should use the other napkins."

"What other napkins?"

His mother disappeared into her room. He heard a drawer slide open and closed. She returned with three white napkins draped over her hand. Moving around the table, she slipped the paper napkins out, laying the cloth ones softly at each place.

"We can use these tomorrow," she said, and put the paper napkins away.

"Who's coming?" Kenny asked. It all seemed so strange to him. It still seemed like his mother expected his dad. She didn't know anybody in town. Unless it was a person from work.

"Somebody you know."

"Who?"

"Roddy Moyers."

"What?"

He stared at his mother, but she wouldn't meet his look. Instead, she pulled out her chair and sat down. "I thought you'd be pleased."

"Mom, I don't *know* Roddy Moyers." Somehow, his mom had gotten the wrong idea. "I just talked to him once. Why is he coming here?"

His mother hesitated. "Well, he didn't have anyplace else to go. So I asked him if he wanted to come here."

"Why didn't you tell me? Why didn't you tell me he was coming?"

"I thought you'd like it. You can talk rodeo."

"But why didn't you tell me?"

"Sit down," his mother said. Kenny pulled out a chair and sat at his place. He wanted to put his elbows on the table, but the plate was there, and he felt awkward with his hands in his lap. His mother was looking at him as if she were the one who'd asked a question. She was waiting for an answer. But Kenny had asked the question.

"I'm sorry," his mother said. "I should have told you. I met Roddy Moyers." She picked up the plate in front of her and set it aside. She pinched at a crease in the tablecloth, lifted the fabric into a small tent, and tried to smooth it flat. "While you were gone, in Florida."

"I saw you."

"What?"

"I saw you get in his truck."

His mother turned pale. The color faded out of her face almost in a line. "How?" she said. "You were watching me?"

"No," Kenny said. "No. I was just there."

"Where?"

"Across from the courthouse."

"Why didn't you say anything?"

"Why didn't you?"

He glared at his mother. Her eyes were wide and blue. She blinked. She was the one who looked away, but her voice when she spoke was cold.

"I don't have to tell you everything I do. Every place I go," she said.

"Then I don't either."

Kenny scraped back his chair, shoved it into the table so hard the dishes jumped in place, and walked away.

"Yes, you do." His mother was yelling. He heard her get up, heard her footsteps behind him. He started up the stairs.

"Kenny — come back down here. Come back."

Kenny closed the door of his room and sat down on the bed, his shoulders tensed for the sound of steps coming up. But his mother didn't follow him. He heard the bedsprings pinch underneath him, then the faint sound of his mother running water in the sink. He sat still for a long time finishing the argument. Why didn't she tell him? Why was it his fault now? He hadn't done anything.

But he knew why she hadn't told him. Not in words. But he knew. He sensed something wrong, something his mother had done wrong. Suddenly his mother was someone he didn't quite know. He stood up and walked under the low roof to the window. It had stopped snowing, and the world seemed laid out flat in the snow. Houses and barns he couldn't see in the summer sat square and neat like Monopoly pieces. But he wouldn't have been able to walk to them. The snow was so deep he couldn't walk anywhere now but down the middle of the street. He stood up too fast and struck his forehead on the slanting eave. "Shit," he said, and sat down. He didn't wince or reach up to rub the swelling lump. He let the pain break in his skull and burn hot. When it subsided, he reached over to the bureau and lifted the package he'd bought for his mother. He'd planned to wake up early and hide it under the tree. His mother always wrapped a dozen presents for him so the tree wouldn't look so bare, but only one was his real present, a sweater or a new jacket. Last year she'd given him a new clock radio to help him get up in the morning, but they kept it downstairs. The other packages were socks and cans of salted peanuts, presents from the grocery store.

When the girl at the counter wrapped the box, Kenny hadn't even looked at the red-and-green wrapping, Christmas trees and red banners that said "Merry Christmas" over and over. He lifted the folded ends of the paper, felt the tape peel away, and slid the box out. Inside, a short string of blue beads, the chalky blue of jawbreakers, had rolled into the corner. The center bead was the largest, and the rest grew smaller up to the clasp.

Kenny had walked around the store until his feet began to hurt. The girl at the counter asked him twice if he needed any help, but he didn't know what he wanted. When he finally decided, the girl started to wrap the beads in a small white box, but Kenny asked her for a big box. He wanted to surprise his mother.

He laid the beads back in the box, but they looked wrong, cheap, like something from the drugstore. He crumpled up the tissue paper in a nest, but when he put the lid on, he could feel the beads roll heavy to the corner, and the box tipped in his hand. He pried off the lid and arranged the beads again, but he saw he'd have to try to find more tissue paper. He set the open box on the floor and stretched out on the bed. It was cold, but he didn't get under the covers. He stared at the wallpaper on the ceiling, at the picture postcards, the long tear of paper falling from the slope. The smell of roasting turkey drifted up the stairs and felt more like smoke in his nostrils. It kept him awake for some time, as if it were a noise or music playing on the radio. His mother began to whistle.

He woke with a start when he heard her climbing the stairs. She knocked and shoved the door open. Kenny sat up. His mother had taken off her apron and changed her clothes. She wore her pink dress, even though it was winter.

"Roddy should be here," she said, "any minute." Her voice was light. Offhand. "Why don't you change clothes and come down?"

Kenny wanted to forgive her, to go along with her and pretend nothing was wrong, but something stopped him. He wanted everything to be all right, but he couldn't help himself.

"I bought some eggnog," his mother said. "Why don't you come down?"

"Okay," he said. But she didn't leave. She stood in the doorway, waiting for him to make some move. "In a minute."

"Try and look nice," she said.

"Okay."

He sat on the edge of the bed and listened to his mother's steps on the stairs. When he finally stood up, he saw the box of tissue and the beads exposed, where he'd pushed them into the middle of the room.

Kenny thought he heard voices downstairs, then he was sure a deeper voice was talking to his mother. He pictured Roddy Moyers sitting at the kitchen table, his mother moving around. The radio came on in the front room, playing Christmas music. He wished he'd been downstairs when Roddy Moyers got there. Now he would have to walk in, say something. He moved as quietly as he could down to the hall and slipped through the bathroom door, glancing quickly into the kitchen. Moyers wasn't at the table. He was standing up, his back against the counter.

Kenny splashed cold water on his face until he almost couldn't breathe, then flung his head back. He used a towel to dry his hair and combed it. He hadn't changed his clothes; his jeans were so dirty they'd stretched another size and hung low on his hips, and there was a stiff spot of dried egg on his sweater. He rubbed at it with the corner of the towel. But he wasn't going to dress up like a kid going to his grandmother's for Christmas, not for Roddy Moyers.

He flushed the toilet, walked out, and stood in the doorway.

"Hey," Moyers said.

"Kenny," his mother said, glancing at his clothes, then at Moyers. She introduced him as her son.

"Hi," Kenny said.

He dreaded the moment when Moyers would talk about their meeting at the rodeo grounds and connect him with his mother. He flushed with embarrassment, but Moyers didn't say anything. His mother reached into the refrigerator and brought out a green-and-red carton of eggnog. She poured three glasses and handed them around.

His mother thought he liked eggnog, because she wanted him to drink it. She thought it would help him put on weight. But it was so thick and sweet he felt like he was drinking condensed milk from the can. His mother lifted her glass.

"Merry Christmas," she said.

"Merry Christmas," they repeated. Kenny watched Moyers take a sip from his glass and set it down on the counter.

"You don't like eggnog?" his mother said. She wiped her hands on her dress as if she still had an apron on.

But Moyers only grinned. "You got something to put in it?"

Kenny knew they didn't.

"I'm sorry," his mother said. "I should have thought."

"Hang on," Moyers said. He went out the back door without his jacket and came back with a whiskey bottle in a Christmas box. He pulled the bottle out and unscrewed the cap.

"You shouldn't have to drink your own whiskey." His mother was upset.

"It's okay. I get a lot of these," Moyers said. "Christmas cheer."

He held the bottle over his mother's glass. "Say when," he said, but she stopped him after just a drop. He took a spoon from the table and handed it to her, then turned to Kenny.

Kenny waited for his mother to say no, but she didn't say anything while Roddy poured the whiskey into his eggnog. She handed him the spoon. "It's Christmas," she said, laughing in a funny way. Kenny had never seen his mother like this. She was nervous, he could tell, but excited.

She told them to go in the front room; there must be a ball game on the television.

"Rather keep you company," Roddy said. He glanced at Kenny, who shrugged as if it didn't matter to him.

"Then you can help. We're almost ready."

Moyers helped her lift the turkey out of the oven and onto a platter, and she gave Kenny the potatoes to mash while she made gravy in the bottom of the roaster. Last year she'd made him learn to carve, because his dad was gone and it was a job for the man of the house. For a minute, he was afraid she would ask Moyers to do it. But she spooned out the dressing and carved the turkey herself. Finally they sat down around the table.

They ate in silence. Kenny could never believe how good turkey was. And he was always disappointed to be full so soon. How could the dinner take so long to make and be over so fast? He and Roddy both took second helpings and thirds. Then his mother stood up and brought over the pies.

"I can't eat any more," Kenny said.

"You want to take a break?"

"Yes." Kenny and Roddy spoke at the same time, and his mother laughed.

"Okay."

His mother started to pick up the dirty dishes, three steps back and forth between the table and the sink. Kenny reached for the dishes around him, handing them up to her. He knew he should get up and start washing. Washing the dishes was his job. But he waited for his mother to ask, to give him a look. When she finally turned back to the table she only asked him to go turn on the Christmas tree lights.

The front room was dark. He plugged in the lights, and the room was suddenly pretty. The spindly tree glowed in the corner, blinking slowly on and off. He switched on the overhead light and bent to look in the stove. The fire had burned down to red coals, but they radiated so much heat he felt as if his skin were burning.

He pulled on his jacket and went out for more wood. When he elbowed his way back in, he set the logs by the door. He could hear his mother and Roddy Moyers talking in the front room. The house seemed very warm, the air thick with heat and the smell of turkey. The whiskey bottle stood on the drain board beside the carton of eggnog. Kenny glanced into the other room. His mother was sitting on the couch and Moyers had pulled Kenny's rocker over to sit across from her. Someone had turned up the radio.

He poured himself a half glass of eggnog and, checking to see that his mother wasn't coming, filled it with whiskey. He had to stir a long time before the clear amber-colored liquid disappeared. When he dumped the new logs by the stove, his mother and Moyers stopped talking.

He had to get his drink from the kitchen, and it felt awkward walking back into the front room. What were they going to do now? He wished he could turn on the TV.

"Sit," his mother said. She indicated the couch next to her. He sat at the end, both feet on the floor, leaning out over his knees with his glass in both hands.

Moyers's glass was dark with whiskey.

"You play football?" He rocked forward and addressed Kenny.

"No."

"Ought to go out next fall."

Kenny saw Moyers was trying to make conversation. He shrugged.

"You know the coach?" Moyers asked.

"Sure," Kenny said. "Nice guy."

Moyers laughed, and Lenna asked what they meant.

"Coach," Moyers said. "I guess you could say he's got a temper. One time in gym he was going to teach us boxing. He was standing out on the mat with the gloves on, asking for volunteers. Nobody volunteered. So, finally I went up with him, and he knocked me out cold. One punch."

"That's terrible," his mother said.

Moyers shrugged. "That's just the way he was."

"Still is," Kenny said. He sipped his drink. In the first one, he could hardly taste the whiskey. But this one burned his throat. He looked over to make sure his mother hadn't seen him wince.

The radio voice announced an hour of oldies with no commercials. The first song was "Rockin' Around the Christmas Tree."

"I used to love this song," his mother said.

"You want to dance?" Roddy said. He tilted forward on the runners of his chair.

"No," his mother said. "There's no room." Kenny thought she was going to giggle.

Roddy lifted his chair with one hand and swung it back out of the way.

"Sure, there is." He stood in the middle of the floor. "Come on."

His mother shook her head, smiling, but Roddy reached down and took her hand. He pulled her up into his arms, and slowly she began to move with the music. They did a slow kind of swing, with Roddy twirling his mother under his arm, then the two of them rocking side to side together. They were good.

The next song came on, a little faster, and Kenny watched them make up new steps. His mother looked like a girl. Her face was flushed pink. When the music paused, she stood back, laughing. Roddy sank down on the couch beside Kenny and threw his head back.

"Take over," he said.

Kenny's heart jumped.

"Come on," his mother said. "Get on up here."

"I don't know how."

"There's no 'how' to it," Roddy said. "You just get up and move around."

"Come on," his mother pleaded. "I'll show you."

"What," Moyers said, "you afraid of the coach?"

Kenny stood up, grinning, and at first felt a wave of weakness in his stomach.

His mother took his hand.

"It's all in the wrist," she said.

"That's what they always say."

"No, really. Just use your wrist and arm. Pull me in."

Kenny pulled, and his mother jerked toward him.

"With the music," she said. "Now push."

He gave a small push and his mother spun away, her whirling skirt billowing with air.

"That's the way."

Slowly, Kenny started to get the hang of it. When the music stopped, his mother showed him how to raise his arm and let her duck under, and on the next song he moved around the room, twirling his mother farther and farther out to the end of his grasp. Roddy sat on the couch, leaning back to clap his hands together when they made a tricky move. On the next song, he cut in, and Kenny sat on the couch. He leaned over and took a sip of Roddy's drink. He'd never seen his mother so happy. He felt giddy himself. Roddy Moyers was okay, he thought. But the oddness of it hadn't gone away. Why was Moyers in their house on Christmas? Something wasn't right about that.

When the song finished, his mother stood breathing hard in the middle of the room, Roddy's arm around her waist. The fire had died down, but still it was hot.

"Let's go downtown," Roddy said. "We can look at the lights. Go see the manger."

"Oh, no," his mother said. "I'm done." She pushed her hair back from her face with the heel of her hand.

Roddy looked from Kenny to his mother. "It's early," he said.

Kenny stood up, thinking he would check the fire. But the room darkened, and he felt a second wave of sickness rise in his stomach. He sat back down.

"Why don't you guys go?"

"No," his mother said. "It's Christmas. I'm not going to leave you here alone."

"I'll be okay," Kenny said. "Christmas isn't 'til tomorrow."

"Have you ever seen the manger scene?" Roddy said. "It's great. The Four-H kids trailer in their sheep and donkeys. And the Elks Club gets dressed up — you see a lot of bathrobes. Last year Joseph got so drunk we almost lost him."

"Go on," Kenny said. "I'm going to bed." If he stayed up any longer, he was going to be sick.

After his mother was gone, Kenny walked out to the kitchen.

His mother had put the leftovers away, but the dishes were piled up in the sink, greasy with bones and leftover bits of soggy lettuce. He started to scrape the dishes, but he had to stop suddenly and go lie down.

He lay on the couch with his eyes open. When he closed them, the room turned black and spun around. He didn't think he could make it up the stairs. The radio was playing the Mormon Tabernacle Choir, but the music seemed to swell and churn inside his head. In the corner, the Christmas tree lights blinked on and off, a faint twinkle in the corner of his eye, pale pink and yellow and blue and green.

When he awoke, he knew it was much later. He had been dreaming of his dad. Another Christmas when his dad had been away from home. The tree lights were still blinking, but the radio station had gone off the air and the room was filled with a static buzz. It was very cold, and he was alone in the house.

19

Cynthia overheard her parents in the kitchen, and she hung back on the stairs. She was supposed to play in the Christmas service at church, but if they didn't leave soon, they'd be late.

"Cynthia can deliver the poor boxes," her mother said.

"No," her dad said, "I can't trust her." He paused for a moment and continued. "Not in this snow."

His first words hurt so much that Cynthia kept hearing them, as if he hadn't said the second part, the part about the weather. She knew why her parents were arguing. Her dad was lined up to drop off boxes of food after the service. But his shoulder was giving him trouble. He didn't like to admit it, but Cynthia had seen him wince getting up from the dinner table.

"She'll have one of the boys along."

"Now, *that's* a comfort," her dad said.

"Well, I'm a little concerned," her mother spoke softly. "You can't afford to be laid up."

Cynthia stepped around the door frame. Her dad stood up, and before he saw her, she saw his jaw tighten with pain. His face was damp and gray. She couldn't stand to see him hurting.

"We can do it," she said.

Her dad gave her a sharp look. She was wearing wool slacks and a sweater.

"That what you're wearing to church?"

"I'll keep my coat on."

"God can't see under your coat?"

"God doesn't care about the outside."

"You don't know what God cares about. Go up and change."

"We'll be late."

"Cynthia," her mother said. "Don't talk back. Go on upstairs."

Cynthia turned and went up the stairs. She felt hollow, as if her body were only a thin shell around her, and getting up in front of everyone to play at church seemed impossible. Sometimes she hated her mother, who cared only about how things *looked.* There was a false note in her mother's pretense toward religion, but Cynthia was so used to it it never occurred to her to argue or complain.

On the drive into town, Cynthia watched the snow come down, hypnotic; it seemed like the car was standing still and the snowflakes were shooting at them. Her mother and father were quiet in the silence of the snowfall.

In town, the lights glowed faint, and people drove slowly, with an odd politeness, like dreamers. Her dad pulled up and parked behind the church.

Cynthia's piece was short, but it came at the end of the service, giving her more time to be nervous. She settled into the pew, her coat pulled tight around her even though the church was brightly lit and overheated. She could hear the furnace kick on in the basement. At the end of the sermon, she slipped outside, came in through the side door, and stood in the doorway off the entrance to the altar.

The congregation was sparse, scattered in the long, empty pews. They were mostly old people. The church seemed so much bigger from the altar. Cynthia always thought the minister liked it because he could look down on everyone. She only wanted the service to be over.

When it was time to play, she forced herself to walk across to the piano. For a moment, she wasn't sure she could make the notes. But when it came, the music flowed on its own, and while her hands were on the keys she felt better.

After the benediction, she followed her parents downstairs into the basement and ate a dry cookie cut in the shape of a Christmas tree. Her father joined the men in the back, dragging heavy cartons of canned goods across the linoleum toward the door. She went to stand beside her mother, who never took her eyes off Earl. He was breathing hard, and his white shirt clung damp between his shoulder blades. When all the boxes were stacked, her mother made up her mind. "He can't go out in his condition," she said. She set off toward the circle of men resting by the door. "I'll have the men speak to him."

Harold Cray, the saddle maker, had been in the choir. He helped Cynthia carry boxes to the car and load them in the trunk. She could hear the men arguing, her dad's voice rising, and the other men lowering their voices to remonstrate with him. She heard her father grumble Harold's name. If he heard Earl, Harold paid no attention. He finished loading the boxes and closed the trunk. Only his strange eyes showed between his hat brim and his muffler. He waited on the other side of the car, slapping his green wool gloves together to stay warm.

Standing beside the car, Cynthia felt the snowflakes touch lightly on her face and melt. She slipped in behind the wheel, but she waited for her mother to come to the window before she turned the key. Harold lowered himself into the passenger seat and slammed the door.

"Harold," her mother said. "Get done and get her home. It's Christmas Eve. We should all be home."

Her father glared at Harold as if he wanted him to disappear.

"Ten," her father said. "No later." He reached up and swept a glove across the snowy windshield. "Turn your defrost on."

Cynthia watched her parents walk over to the neighbors' car, her father looking back, his mouth tight with anger, and climb in the backseat before she turned on the windshield wipers and the defrost fan. When the other car had driven away, she backed slowly out of the parking lot into the wide street.

She drove and Harold delivered the boxes. She kept the heater running and watched him lumber up to the doors and ring the bells. He wore army surplus camouflage and a dull green cowboy hat. When somebody opened the door, he mumbled "Merry Christmas," shoved the carton into their arms, and loped back to the car. Sometimes an old person opened the door, looking bewildered, and Harold had to carry the box inside. At the last house, the people weren't home. Harold walked back to the car, set the box down in the snow, and leaned in the window.

"Nobody home."

Cynthia shrugged. "Just leave it."

"Dogs'll get it," Harold said.

"It's just cans," she said.

"No, this one's got boxes." He bent down out of sight. "And beer."

"Just leave it," Cynthia said.

Harold shook his head. He came around the car and held the carton of bottles up to the window.

"Take it," he said.

She set the beer on the seat beside her, and Harold ran the box back up to the porch. She remembered her dad saying something about Harold staying off the booze. When he got back in the car, they both sat there, not looking at the beer on the seat, and Cynthia burst out laughing. She couldn't believe it. Somebody from *church* had buried beer in the bottom of the Christmas box.

"What are we going to do with it?" Harold said, his voice so blank and innocent that they both heard it and laughed out loud. Harold's laugh surprised her. It was low and masculine and musical.

Cynthia gunned the motor and let the big car fishtail across the road. With one hand, she spun the wheel with the skid and straightened out.

"Jesus," she said. "I guess we'll have to get rid of the evidence."

"We got no opener."

"We'll just have to get one."

Cynthia pulled in behind the city hall. She lifted two bottles. They were cold and beaded with water. She climbed out and walked behind the car. She'd seen men pop bottles open on rear bumpers. She didn't know exactly how to do it, but she hooked the crinkled beer cap on the sharp edge, hit it with her gloved fist, and it popped off. Beer foamed up and crawled down the bottle, onto her glove. She set the bottle in the snow and opened the other one.

Back in the car, she handed one bottle to Harold, turned up the radio, and took a long swallow from her own beer. She could feel the cold slide down her throat and drop into her stomach. Harold tossed his wet hat in the backseat. He took a drink, and she heard him sigh.

"Let's go," he said.

Cynthia gripped the neck of the bottle between her glove and the steering wheel and drove out onto Main Street. She wished she could drive faster, but she could feel the road slide out from under the wheels.

"Where to?" she said.

"Not here," Harold answered.

"Where?" Cynthia took another swallow of beer.

Harold signaled with his bottle. "I know a place," he said. "Go straight."

Cynthia headed out onto the highway. They rolled down the windows and let the snow fall on their arms. Light specks of ice flew in and danced around the car like sparks. She sped up, following the yellow line on her left. The night ahead was blank and white, and wraiths of snow streamed in sheets across the pavement. It felt like driving up above the clouds.

They sang, throwing their heads back and pitching harmonies against the voices on the radio. Harold sang tenor parts in the choir, but in the darkness his voice hit bass notes that made her laugh so hard she almost had to stop the car.

They pulled over to open the other four beers, and back inside the car she and Harold began to sing the *Messiah* — the Easter part — in a voice so low and country, so twangy, Cynthia had to reach behind the seat, fishing for a box of tissues.

All we like sheep
da da da da
All we like sheep
da da da da
Have gone astray

After the choir director had admonished them one year by saying, "No, this is not the cowboy's lament," nobody in the back row ever sang it right. "All we, like sheep, have gone astray."

She felt so good. A sweet euphoria, as if nothing could go wrong, as if she could drive forever, came over her, and the low car sailed down the highway. The moon had come up somewhere behind the clouds, and the snow falling all around them glowed as if each flake held a tiny drop of light. Her coat sleeve was caked in slushy snow, but she didn't care. Harold's cheeks glowed pink, as if he'd been out sledding.

They pulled up at a tavern on the county line. The lot was filled with cars, their windshields and windows blanked out by snow. They could hear heavy music thumping inside. Cynthia parked, and they sat watching the smudged blue neon signs in the window blink on and off.

Harold found his hat in the backseat and rocked it low over his eyes.

"They won't let me in," she said.

"What're they going to do?" he said. "Kick us out?"

"Yup."

"On *Christmas?*"

Cynthia could hardly talk for laughing. "No," she said, "on our butts."

When she recovered, she combed her wet hair back, parted on the side and slicked down like a boy's.

"Let me wear the hat," she said.

She handed Harold the keys. "In the trunk," she said. "Coveralls."

Harold threw her dad's padded coveralls through the window and stood in the snow while she struggled to pull them on over her clothes. Outside, she tried to stuff her skirt down into the legs. Harold pretended he was on guard duty. When he looked at her, another laugh came from down low in his chest.

"No," he said. "Never."

But they walked arm in arm to the door and shoved it open.

Inside, the bar was so dark and full of people she had to hold on to Harold to keep from losing him. He was trying to say something to her, but the band was so loud she couldn't catch the words. Somehow, he found a small table in the back and they sat down. He leaned close to her ear.

"Money," he said. "You got any money?"

"Shit," she said. "In the car." He didn't hear her. "In the car." She yelled over the noise. He rose to go, but she pushed him down. "I'll go."

She stood up and started making her way through the crowd, twisting around arms and shoulders. Somebody gave her a shove, and for a minute she was too dizzy to walk. But the music, the excitement in the bar, kept her going — the night seemed full of possibility. She walked along the edge of the dance floor, feeling tall and easy on her feet.

Outside, the snow fell thick, and the car was covered with white. When she opened the door, a thick sheet of snow fell whole from the driver's window. She found her wallet in the glove compartment and shoved it deep in her pocket.

She hadn't realized that now she'd have to go back in the bar by herself. It was so cool outside, the music from the dance floor muffled by the snow. But the quiet made her head spin. She pushed open the door and stepped into the crowd. Nobody stopped her. She headed back toward the edge of the dance floor, the only clear path through the room. The band was playing a fast two-step, the dancers reeling in a circle around the floor. An older woman, her gold hair teased up in a swirl, stumbled. She reached out and grabbed on to Cynthia's arm. Her partner swept her up into the music again, but she turned and gave Cynthia a wink. The kind of wink she'd give a young cowboy. Cynthia could just barely keep from laughing.

She couldn't wait to get back to the table to tell Harold. She felt like some kind of warrior, returning to camp with great news. Harold sat tapping his foot to the music, lost in some thought of his own. She slid into a seat close beside him.

"Some lady winked at me." She leaned in close to his ear.

"Why?" Harold said.

"I'm so cute," Cynthia said, her eyes wide. She pressed her lips together hard, and let out a snort, almost a loud nicker. It sounded so funny that tears stung her eyes.

Harold reached up and sank the brim of her hat down over her eyes.

"Police up your act. Give me the money," he said.

Cynthia pried the hat brim up and saw the waitress making her way toward them, her tray balanced high over the crowd.

She had a ten-dollar bill in her wallet. She managed to get it out and hand it to Harold. Then she bent down, as if she were looking for something on the floor.

"Bud," Harold said. "Two."

The waitress hesitated long enough for Cynthia to stiffen, but then she said, "Two Buds," and moved away.

Cynthia unbent to sit up in her chair. Harold flattened the bill on the table and weighted it down with an ashtray. "You pay when you get it," he said. He looked around the room and leaned back hard enough to make his chair creak. "So far, so good," he said.

"Not so good," Cynthia said.

Harold frowned.

"I have to pee," she said.

"No sweat." Harold jerked his thumb toward the door. "Just go outside. In the snow."

"Don't make me laugh." Cynthia tightened her jaw and rocked in her chair.

"Then hold it," Harold said. "Until the beer comes."

"I can't."

"You have to."

"Shit." She gritted the word out through her teeth, fighting not to laugh. "I got to go. Now."

"Wait till the beer comes. Once we got it, you can go to the women's. You go now, it's the men's."

"It's the men's," she said and stood up carefully.

Harold picked up the ten and moved in front of her, blocking a path through the crowd. She kept her head down, her eyes on the heels of Harold's wet boots.

He shoved open the door marked "Bucks," and she followed him in. The room was dark, and a pool of water had spread like melting ice across the floor. The wet floor was black with boot marks and littered with pieces of sodden toilet paper. She saw two booths, and against the wall, a broad plaid back at the urinal. Harold stepped up and shoved on the door of a booth. It was empty.

Cynthia sat in the booth, the flesh-pink partition scrawled with graffiti, the straps of her coveralls tied in front of her to keep them off the dirty floor. She wanted to get out. The smell of urine and rotting wood was making her ill. But she heard the door swing open and the sound of men's voices. Somebody pushed hard on the wooden door of the booth and she started with fear.

She worked up her nerve and stood up. She stuffed her skirt lower down in the legs of the coveralls, buckled the straps, and pulled the hat down low. She pushed out through the door, head down, but she couldn't resist looking up before she reached the door.

Roddy leaned against the wall beside the door. She met his eye for just a second, long enough to catch him take in what he saw, and she felt the wildness rise in her again — the knife-edge of a secret. She winked.

Outside, she couldn't imagine what he thought. She had him. A high hit-and-run energy moved her through the crowd. She couldn't wait to tell Harold.

But Roddy came behind her. She felt a touch on her shoulder and turned so fast, they collided. She threw her arms around Roddy's neck, her hat tipping off onto the floor, and collapsed against him. She laughed so hard she could barely stand, but Roddy held her up.

"Hey, I don't usually dance with boys," he said.

"I do," she said.

He gripped her under the armpits and looked at her. She focused on the corners of his mouth while he tried to decide between surprise and laughter.

"Come on," she said. "Let's dance." She was so glad to see him.

"You're drunk." He said it as if he couldn't believe it. "You're drunk."

She leaned forward and kissed him, letting her whole weight, almost her whole being, subside into his arms.

20

At the bar, Lenna shifted on her stool. As soon as Roddy had moved away to go to the men's room, a friend of his — she thought he'd said his name was Chip, or Chuck — had leaned in close to her. He had one arm braced on the bar, his face in front of hers.

"I don't say this to too many ladies," he said, "but you're very pretty."

His voice wavered a little and drifted off too much at the end of the sentence. He leaned closer, and Lenna craned her neck away. He was sweating, his glasses sliding down his nose. When he pushed the frames back up, his eyes seemed very large, pale blue, but in the light reflected from behind the bar the thick lenses seemed greasy — not as if they were dirty, but as if they were out of focus, even for him.

"That's a nice thing to say," she said. She tried to be polite, but she clutched her purse against her chest. His thigh pressed against her leg. It was getting hard to breathe, and she was a little drunk herself.

"Excuse me," she said, and tried to duck out from under his arm, but the arm didn't give. She tried to remember his name, as if that would help. But she'd met so many people in the bar that the names all ran together, and she was embarrassed. She searched the crowd pressed up to the bar for Roddy. The man leaned close to say something else.

"I'm with someone," she said.

The drunk blinked. "Oh, oh," he said. He released her from the trap, his hands coming up in front of him, palms out. "No offense," he said. "No offense." His eyes seemed lost for a moment, looking out over the crowd.

Lenna twisted off the stool and moved away, not looking back. She wanted to get outside, get some air. She started toward the rest room, looking for Roddy. It was time to go home. The mood in the tavern had grown sour. She noticed for the first time how the music had gotten heavier, more frenzied, and the dancers on the floor seemed out of control, couples colliding, backing accidentally into each other. And the air smelled like stale beer and someone being sick.

She hadn't wanted the night to be over so soon, but she remembered how it went. At first liquor made her happy, made it easier to talk to people, smile at strangers. She and Roddy had danced every dance for an hour. She almost turned back to the bar to order another drink, then thought no. She was too tired to get that kind of feeling back.

She moved on around the edge of the dance floor. Near the rest rooms, she spotted Roddy, or thought she did. His back was turned slightly, and he was kissing a girl. Lenna could see her arms draped around his neck, and white-blond hair.

She took a few steps closer and stopped. The kiss went on, and there was something intimate about it, some way Roddy's head was tipped, the girl's long arm around his neck. Lenna moved forward, as if drawn to a car wreck, though she didn't want to see it. When the girl stood back, Lenna saw she was young. She couldn't be much older than Kenny. Lenna felt a hot blush move up her neck, pulsing in her cheeks. She wanted to get her coat and leave. If she'd had her car, she would have been in it now, and on her way home. But she stepped up close enough to hear and stood behind a thin man in a black satin shirt.

She saw Harold the saddle maker shoulder a path through the crowd, stoop beside the girl, and hand her a hat. He took hold of her forearm.

"No problem," he said to Roddy. "I got her."

"Quit," the girl said. She shook off his hand and straightened her shoulders. "I'm okay," she said.

Lenna could feel some kind of real trouble. The people at surrounding tables had stopped talking and were staring. The girl raised a hand. "It's okay," she said. "Tend your own business." Then she smiled at Roddy. "We got a table," she said. "Come on." She started to walk, stopped, and steadied herself. This time she let Harold take her arm. "I think I better go sit down," she said.

Lenna pushed around the black shirt and stood beside Roddy, moving close, but not touching, the way a child sometimes tries to stand near a larger person. Lenna thought the girl was leaving, but she turned and saw her standing with Roddy. She shook loose from Harold and came back.

The girl just stood still, not speaking, and stared at Lenna. The pressure in the room seemed to drop, like the air before a storm. Lenna heard the music pounding in her ears, but the tables around them grew quiet. She could feel people staring. She glanced up at Roddy.

"Lenna Swanson — Cynthia Dustin," he said, introducing them. "Everybody knows Harold." Harold nodded at Lenna. "Come on," he said to Cynthia, "let's get you some coffee."

Cynthia didn't move. She kept staring at Lenna.

Two can play this game, Lenna thought. She kept her gaze steady on Cynthia, thoughts moving fast in her mind. Who was she? What was going on here? Then she remembered the way

Roddy had kissed the girl. Her heart pounded once, pulsed in her throat, and she knew — something was going on here. She dropped her eyes.

The girl didn't move or speak. Roddy shifted his weight, and Harold looked away.

"Let's get some coffee," Roddy said again to Cynthia, who turned to stare at him.

"You said you were going to somebody's house for dinner," she said.

Lenna looked down and saw the girl's hands were trembling.

"Well," Roddy answered, "that's true."

The girl turned slowly and stared at Lenna until she felt forced to meet her look.

"Was he at your house?"

Lenna wanted to lie, to somehow get them out of this, but she couldn't. She nodded yes.

"Did you know about me?" the girl said.

Lenna couldn't answer. Everything in her told her to say no, to tell the girl the truth, that she was innocent. She didn't know anything about Roddy's life away from her. But she knew she was not innocent. She felt sick with shame, over being in the bar at all, over finding herself in some country song. Sick for being so stupid. Roddy had made a fool of her.

"No," she said.

The girl turned on her heel, knocking down an empty chair, and walked steadily toward the door. Harold went back for his jacket, and Lenna saw him lift an abandoned whiskey bottle off an empty table without slowing down and follow her out.

Most of the tables were empty now. Some couples were still dancing, but the majority had gone home. The people who'd been staring went back to their drinks. Lenna looked up at

Roddy. He brushed his hair back with his fingers, and sweat glistened at his temple. A slow grin started at the corner of his mouth. Her hand flew out to slap him, hard, but he grabbed her wrist and pulled her into his body — the way a fighter moves in close to ward off blows.

21

Cynthia started the motor and revved the engine. She shoved the gear lever into reverse and jerked the brake release. The car shot backward, fishtailed in the snow, and spun around. She stomped on the brake, and the car slid sideways. When it came to a stop, Harold threw open the door, jumped in, and let the door slam on its own. Cynthia stepped lightly on the gas and felt the tires grab. She turned onto the highway.

Her hands shook, and she had trouble holding the wheel steady. She felt cold, the muscles in her neck and chest clenched tight, her teeth chattering so loudly she knew Howard could hear. Without gloves, her hands were dead white.

Harold passed her his bottle of whiskey, and she tipped it to her mouth, the cold glass clinking on her teeth. When he reached over and took the bottle back, she pressed on the gas and watched the speedometer needle quiver and swing up to sixty.

It had stopped snowing and the moon cast a cold blue light above the clouds. The road ahead was packed with snow, glistening damp in the headlights where tires had worn smooth tracks. Harold switched on the heater.

She tried to see again what happened in the bar, but it came to her in odd, short pictures. She couldn't remember what the woman looked like. She couldn't call up Roddy's face.

The dashboard glowed green in the darkness. She was going seventy. She glanced over at Harold. He slumped in his seat, the bottle between his legs, leaning his head back.

Then she heard the tires hit a drift, the sound like hitting a dog on the road. The wheel jumped in her hand, and the snow took the car. She stomped on the gas to push the big car through the drift and slithered sideways onto the other side. She pulled over on the side of the road. From one side to the other of the highway long fingers of snow tapered across the road, one following another on into the darkness.

Cynthia climbed out of the car. The wind had blown the road in earlier. Now, it only lifted veils of snow from the tops of the drifts, as they rolled into the distance, wave after wave. It was as if there had never been a road at all.

She walked out in the field on a thin crust. At any time, the ground could give way to deep snow. But she went on walking. The wind had drifted smooth white hills and ridges across the field in some places and blown it nearly bare in others. Only the tips of sagebrush, plastered with snow on one side, were visible up ahead. Suddenly, her knees weakened and she sat down. She didn't hear Harold come up behind her. She felt him kneel beside her, his presence near her almost like a source of heat.

"You can't sit out here," he said.

She didn't answer.

The sky was enormous and black, the stars burning white. The dipper loomed huge on the horizon, as if it were suspended in an endless, flat, black space. As if at any moment, it could slip and fall behind the white edge of the earth.

"Cynthia?" Harold's voice was rough in the darkness. "Can't stay here."

She could feel how she herself could fall, like the dipper of stars, off the world and into the vast space beyond the field.

"We have to go," Harold said.

"What?" She couldn't think what they could do. She didn't care. The car wasn't going anywhere.

"Might be I can back the car," Harold said.

"I don't think so," she said.

"Please," Harold said. When she looked up, he shoved his huge hands under her arms, lifting her whole body at once, and held her against him as if she were a doll. He began to walk her back in the direction of the car. She realized, wading through the drifts, how cold it was.

They sat in the car and ran the heater until their faces stopped stinging and their toes and fingers throbbed with pain. She couldn't turn the car around, and reverse would only get them stuck much worse. If they ran out of gas, they would die. She looked at Harold.

"We'll just sit tight," he said.

A gleam of gold caught and refracted in the windshield glass. Far up the road, they saw the plow, then heard it. Its yellow emergency light spun around, lighting the drifts in brief, sporadic bursts, and the huge iron blade sent waves of glistening snow up over the banks and off the road.

Almost an hour later, Cynthia pulled up in front of Harold's shack.

"What time is it?" she asked him.

Harold folded back his jacket sleeve and tried to read his watch. He held his arm up to the window, where the light off the snow seemed like twilight.

"Oh-two-hundred," he said. "Two A.M."

"It's Christmas morning," she said.

"Merry Christmas."

She looked over at him. He watched her as if she might bite him. Then he laughed. He'd been waiting until it seemed safe to laugh. "Shit," he said, "she sure didn't want to tangle with you."

Cynthia wanted to laugh, but, sober now, she was ashamed of what she'd done.

"You in trouble?" he said.

"I hope not."

He glanced at his small, dark house. "Good luck with Earl," he said. "Earl's okay." He opened the door and climbed out.

"Merry Christmas," she said.

He slammed the door and she watched him jog through the snow to his house.

She drove slowly through town and up the gravel road past the dump. She tried to stay in the deep ruts, gunning the motor through the drifts, but she could hear snow scraping on the underside of the carriage. She prayed not to get stuck again.

At the house, she parked in the yard and stepped out into deep snow. Behind the car, she climbed out of the coveralls and folded them on top of the toolbox in the trunk and tried to lower the lid softly. It latched with a small click, but the sound carried sharp in the air. Her skirt had bunched up under the coveralls and clung around her waist in sharp folds. She tried to smooth it down, but the creases remained. She stuffed her arms into her coat and tried to button it. Her fingers were so cold they couldn't find the holes. A light flicked on in the kitchen.

There was nothing else to do. She made herself numb, empty inside, and walked into the house.

Her father was sitting at the table, the bright overhead light gleaming off the Formica. He wore long underwear and his ranch coat, the arms patched with red canvas where he'd snagged it on barbed wire. He looked up, his eyes gray and watery, his jaw set hard.

She knew what she looked like, her skirt crumpled, her hair in her eyes.

"We went off the road," she said.

"That's a lie," he said.

"I had to get the coveralls. From the trunk."

"It's three o'clock in the morning."

"The road was blown in."

She was telling the truth, but lying about why she was late. The lie burned like shiny coal, sharp and faceted, inside her stomach. And her father knew. He had a way of knowing. She could feel the charge of his anger in the room. But the lie made her strong.

"Call Harold," she said.

"Come here," her father said.

She didn't move.

"Now," he said. "Move."

"No."

He was around the table before she could flinch. His hand struck her face so hard her cheek burned as if he'd hit her with the flat bottom of an iron. Tears stood in her eyes, but she didn't cry. Her hand came up, involuntary, to her cheek, but she stared back at her father.

They stood there, locked in some kind of tunnel, as if the room around them had disappeared. She could feel the cold wall behind her. Her father glared hatred at her, his eyes hard. Fear locked them together. She thought he could kill her.

"You're a whore," he said.

The word hit her like another slap, and the heat of shame shot up, burning in her throat, in her face.

She turned and ran, her heart knocking so hard that all she wanted was to escape it. She got out the door and flung it closed, but she could feel her father right behind her. She plowed out toward the barn, running hard, until the drifts caught at her knees and threw her down in the snow. She spun around and looked behind her. There was no one there.

22

Kenny sat up. A dull pain thudded low in the back of his skull, and the bones in his neck seemed to grate against each other. He felt for the lump on his head where he'd banged into the ceiling. The air in the room was almost crystalline, and his breath blew out in a mist. He stood up slowly, so cold he felt invisible, and walked over to switch off the radio. In the kitchen, he turned the oven dial, listened for the hiss of gas, and levered the door open. He lifted his coat off the hook. It was so stiff with cold it held the shape of a hanged man until he shook it out and pulled it on.

He looked at the clock. It was Christmas morning. He was hungry. His stomach felt concave with pain. He ate a slice of pumpkin pie, the filling half frozen and gritty. But the pain didn't go away. It stretched taut and hard inside him.

He didn't light the fire in the woodstove or open the curtains. He sat for a while on the couch, trying to find some warm place inside his body. Quiet seemed to pulse in the room.

The lights on the tree blinked on and off, each bulb casting a thin light. There was only a bunched-up white bedsheet under the tree. But there must presents somewhere, he thought. He stood and walked through the kitchen into his mother's room.

The bed was made with a faded pink spread, and the perfume bottles on the dresser stood in a circle on a painted tin tray. It looked too clean, like a motel room. He opened the closet door. Inside, the clothes hung neatly on the rod, and a sweet smell, almost like warmth, the smell of his mother's wool coat, came from them. The hook on the inside of the door was draped with too many dresses and scarves. A thin white belt had dropped on the floor and uncurled.

He reached up on the shelf and felt under the folded sweaters for something like a box. But he found nothing. He thought he might go get a chair. But there were other places to look first.

He knelt down and flipped the hanging spread up over the bed. Deep in the shadows, he saw something. He had to lie down flat on his stomach, his shoulder caught by the frame, and reach with his whole arm. His fingers touched the square corner of a box. It seemed weighted, like a box of books, and at first he only pushed it farther away. He managed to turn it slightly and get a grip on the edge. He pulled slowly with the bent tips of his fingers, sat back on his knees, and slid the heavy box out.

The box was brown cardboard, sealed with wide paper tape. It was addressed to him in blue ink, and the return address said Swanson. At first, he couldn't understand. It seemed so mysterious, as if he'd sent a package to himself. Then he thought no, it was a package from his father. It scared him, then. He lifted the box up onto the bed and went to the kitchen for a knife.

He used a serrated steak knife, sawing along the seam of tape. A sick feeling made him want to stop, slide the box back under the bed, but he cut through the tape and spread open the cardboard flaps.

A sheet of stationery floated on top of crumpled newspapers. He picked it up.

"Kenny," it said. "These are some things of your dad's I thought you might want." It was signed "Merry Christmas from Louise." Her writing was small, the letters curved tight into each other. It made her seem so far away. A person with a whole life, separate, and safer than his.

Under the newspaper, he found a pair of Tony Lama boots, so

old the toes had accordioned back in deep creases. They were made of something bumpy, like ostrich skin or alligator, something expensive, but they were mildewed dusty green on one side. Kenny scraped at the dust with his fingernail and the green came off. He had no memory of his dad ever wearing these boots. He didn't think they even belonged to him.

In the bottom of the box he found a fly rod, broken down and packed into a long, brown case. And there was a gun. Not his dad's new rifle, but the old one, the shotgun. Kenny wondered what had happened to the Winchester. He hadn't seen it at Louise's house. The trophy of the goat wasn't there either. And his dad had never sent him the fleece. It was as if these things, the hunting trip, had never existed. As if Kenny had dreamed them, and then woke up.

He picked up the big box. It was light now, almost weightless, but he dumped the newspaper out on the bed, just in case there was something he had missed.

In the pile of paper, wrapped in layers of white handkerchiefs, he found a silver-and-gold rodeo buckle. It said, "Best All Around Cowboy, Fargo, North Dakota," and a date. The date was before he'd been born, in a time he knew only from photographs.

He sat down on the edge of the bed, slipped the rod case apart, and drew out the pieces, wrapped in an old, soft curtain. The pieces rolled under the cloth, narrow and jointed. Gently, he lifted them out and fitted them together. The rod was made of bamboo, with tiny green varnished bands painted at the joints. It gleamed, a rich golden color that had always made him think of pheasants. It was heavy, heavier than the rod he had now, and Louise hadn't sent him the reel.

Suddenly his back seemed to fold inward, as if his ribs were hinged to his spine, and a hard knot of tears tightened in his chest. He looked at the rod. I bet she doesn't know — he thought, and sobs broke through the tightness. I bet she doesn't know how much a handmade rod like this would cost now. He bent over his lap, the sobs choking in his throat. He felt as if his ribs were cracking.

Louise didn't know anything about his dad. God, he wished his mother were home. She would know. She would understand how he'd always treasured the bamboo rod.

He looked up at the window where deep blue light had begun to glisten through the frost. His head throbbed.

He fished one of the handkerchiefs out of the paper on the bed and blew his nose hard. The handkerchief smelled of dampness and mildew, closed-up houses. It smelled like Louise's house, and he never wanted to smell that smell again. He wadded it up and aimed it at the oval plastic wastebasket, sucked in air, and stood up.

With care, he broke the fly rod down, wrapped it, and slid it into the case. Then he went upstairs and dug his duffel bag from the bottom of the closet. He reached under the clothes in his bottom drawer and felt the shotgun shells roll toward the back. He got his fist around them, their red paper jackets like rolls of quarters, and stuffed them in the bottom of the canvas gear bag. Downstairs, he fitted the boots in, then the buckle. Last, he stuck the end of the fly case in. He zipped the bag closed, the rod case sticking out of the corner, and slung it over his shoulder. He wrapped the gun in a towel and cradled it over his arm.

It was nearly dawn outside, the snow giving off a faint glow of blue. He kicked through the drifts, sinking sometimes to his knees, and walked out on the road. The plow hadn't come yet, but a car had been down the road.

In town, he walked down the center of the street, the snow

squeaking like cornstarch under his boots. The sound of his footsteps was the only sound he heard. The stores were closed.

He saw the glow of headlights far down the road and turned
away, following the ruts behind the buildings, the way he walked
to school. Here, a truck had driven through, somebody feeding
cattle, or the milk truck, and the ground was bare.

He headed toward the river. The trees on both sides of the narrow road were frosted white with ice. Ahead, he was faced with a
wall of mist. He walked into it, the white blindness like a touch
along his cheeks. He took shorter and shorter steps, the slow
panic of not being able to see urging him to run. But he knew the
mist could be thick all the way to the river. He forced the panic
down and swam into the brightness.

Salt tears had frozen on his cheeks and crusted in the corners
of his eyes. The only sound was the crunching of his boots on the
snow. This is where his dad was, he thought, someplace where
the clouds pass right through you.

He noticed willows glistening damp beside the road, and suddenly the mist was gone. The trees up ahead stood out sharp and
clear. He walked on. Then the mists came and went. Every time a
trickling stream crossed under the road, running to the river, the
mist floated over the water and drifted like steam across the
road.

He saw the painted sign for the dump and without thinking
turned into the drive. The ruts had filled during the night with
snow, perfectly smooth and rounded, begging for tracks. He
waded into the drifts, circling wide around the caretaker's trailer,
where a thin line of gray smoke drifted from the stovepipe. With
effort, he worked his way to the far side of the deepest pit and
stepped out to where he thought the rim was. Below him, the
cascaded garbage was buried in white drifts, but here and there

fires smoldered, and he could make out a table with the laminated surface ripped away, the rusted shell of a washing machine, black tires. And movement. He looked closer. Where a load of lumber had been dumped, the boards stuck out like pickup sticks and made caves in the snow. Huddled along a gray board were three cats. Then another, and up the slope another. A raven cawed in the cottonwoods at the edge of the dump, and his eyes jerked toward the sound. The sky was lightening above the tall, brittle trees.

He laid the rifle down at his feet and unzipped the canvas bag. First he took out the rodeo buckle. It was an oval of silver with a raised gold vine of tiny leaves and flowers circling the edge. The silver was worn down to brass on the back side, and the front was dull with scratches. Kenny could remember his dad wearing the buckle. But he couldn't wear it. You couldn't wear somebody else's prize. The buckle seemed to him like a dead person's eyeglasses, or false teeth — no good for anything. He tugged off his glove and cradled the icy metal in his hand. Then he hooked his index finger around the edge and snapped it sideways, like a stone, out into the pit. He threw it so hard the tendon in his elbow ached.

The boots were more awkward. The first one landed on the slope, bounced, and skidded a few feet. He didn't care. Nobody was going to climb down there for one boot. He walked along the rim and heaved the second one so far it struck near the bottom of the pit and disappeared.

He aimed the rod case at the cats. It sailed out over the quarry, floating for a moment like an arrow, the back end dipping lower than the front. Two cats shrank back, but an old tom, his ears flat to his head, only blinked.

He tried to dry his sweating hands on the cloth wrapping the shotgun. He lifted it and broke it open, thumbing in the shells. When he touched the cold gray barrel, it stuck to his wet skin like a metal ice tray. He jerked his hand away.

They had all lied to him. "We're never going fishing again," he said to the cat. "And I'm never going to learn to fly." Sobs broke up through his chest. He opened his eyes and stared out over the dump. The ravens glistened black in the trees. One gave out a sharp, scolding caw and glided, indifferent, to a lower branch. He felt almost boneless. His father was dead, and nobody cared. Not Louise. Not his mother. He could sit there all day waiting for his mother, waiting for anybody. But he knew no one was coming.

He didn't want his father's old stuff, not even the rod. He wanted them all to know — they couldn't buy him off with these things. He planted his feet in the snow, raised the rifle, and took careful aim. The old cat twitched an ear. He fired both barrels, the kick like a baseball thrown hard at his shoulder joint. The tomcat spun in place and shot back in the cave, and the ravens flapped, squawking, into the air. Kenny rammed two more shells in the gun, swung the barrels up, and blasted into the trees.

23

Cynthia dreamed the cool touch on her bare feet was the smoothness of her own sheets. She stretched and opened her eyes. This wasn't her bed. She was in Dill's trailer, and the sun was up.

"Mornin'," Dill said. He hunched down on a stool, his back only inches from the stove. The air in the trailer was thick with the smell of split pine stacked too close to the stove, a smell like scorched ironing. And coffee.

Dill stood, his back unbending slowly, and poured her a mug from his percolator. He waited while she sat up before he handed it to her. She wrapped her palm around the hot coffee and didn't feel the burn until the thick mug dropped from her hand. It thudded onto the floor and bounced. Scalding coffee splashed on her leg, on the cot, and in a wet brown wedge across the floor. She jumped up, fanning her skirt away from her thighs.

"It's okay. I got it," Dill said. He grabbed for a towel on the sink.

He pushed her back down with one hand, lifted her skirt, and folded the towel under the clinging fabric.

"Let me know when you wake up," he said. "I'll give it another try."

It hurt to turn her eyes to look at him, and her head ached. She looked down at the wet stain on the floor and let her hair swing over her face.

"Is Goldie okay?" she asked him. "Where is she?"

"She's not taking any harm. She's got plenty of feed and water."

"Thanks."

Dill moved, his head bent to walk upright in the trailer, and ducked into the bathroom.

Cynthia thought back to the night before, pushing Goldie through drifts so deep her stirrups dragged in the snow, following her own tire tracks back down the swamp road. She remembered unrelenting cold. Her fingers burned like dry ice until she couldn't feel the reins in her hand. Finally, she dropped the hard leather and hunched down on Goldie's neck. She closed her hands into fists under Goldie's warm mane and spoke to her, urging her on, begging the old horse to keep moving. When Dill pulled her out of the saddle, she couldn't walk. He had to carry her inside.

She remembered the heat of the trailer, a cup of coffee. Thin needles of pain shooting through her fingers and toes as they thawed, as she tried to tell Dill what had happened.

Now, it all seemed dark and far away, like something that had happened a long time ago. She heard the toilet flush, and in a moment Dill reappeared.

"I can't go home," she said.

"We'll see," Dill said. "You get yourself into the bathroom. Put these on."

He handed her a limp pair of jeans and a flannel shirt.

"Go on."

The bathroom in the trailer was so tiny she had to squeeze between the sink and toilet. The old carpet was black with stains, and the sink was copper green with oxidation around the drain. But Dill's comb and brush, his nail clippers, and scissors were arranged in a neat row on a damp wooden shelf. She splashed cold water on her face and reached for a towel hung up on a nail by the mirror. It was so stiff it scratched her cheek, and the sweet, souring smell of mildew clung to her hands and her face.

When she slid open the door, the smell of burning bacon fat filled the trailer and a gray haze of smoke hung in the air. Dill had opened the outer door. She sat down on the cot and looked out. The snow was smooth and white, and the sky, dry and blue, surprised her. It seemed too sharp and clear.

Dill closed the door and motioned her to the table, a shelf that hinged down from the wall. She ate the bacon and eggs on her plate and drank another cup of coffee. The eggs were bubbled and laced crisp around the edges, and the bacon charred black. But the weight of food in her stomach made the coffee taste good.

She smiled at Dill.

"Merry Christmas," he said.

His eyes twinkled, shadowed by the brim of his wool cap. She realized she never looked at Dill. She noticed how gray his skin seemed, and networks of tiny red veins had crabbed in patches under his eyes.

"I don't want to go home, Dill," she said.

"I know, sweetheart. But you got to."

It was hot now in the trailer. Cynthia felt her eyelids grow heavy, as if she could go back to sleep.

"Cissy." Dill's voice changed. She could feel a seriousness in it. "I want to tell you something about your dad."

Nobody had called her Cissy since she was a very little girl, and the very sound of the word seemed musty to her, like a book she'd loved when she was small.

"Your dad," Dill said, "is going to feel worse than you do."

Cynthia didn't believe him.

"Now listen." Dill's voice was sharp with anger. "Pay attention. What I'm telling is important." He looked right into her eyes.

"Your dad is going to feel real bad — and that's goin' to make him dangerous. You understand me?"

She did. She didn't understand the words exactly, but she knew that Dill was right.

"You got to give him time."

Cynthia nodded, her eyes wide and fixed on Dill's face.

"Here's what you do," he said. "You just go home and go about your business."

He got up and refilled their coffee cups.

"We'll sit tight a little bit here — wait for the plow to go through. I got a few chores I need to get to. Then I'll ride you up in the truck."

"What about . . ."

"She'll keep all right here. I'll bring her up this evening."

"Okay."

Cynthia felt her breathing calm to normal, her heartbeat slowing down. She moved over to the cot and sat cross-legged, holding the warm cup of coffee in both hands. She leaned back against the curved trailer wall and closed her eyes. This place gave her a sense of safety. Now Dill would drive her home. They had a plan. She searched inside herself for a calm, steady place. Far off, she'd heard the dull echoing pop of gunfire, the sound of duck hunters on the river. Then the sound came again, closer.

Dill was on his feet faster than she thought he was able. He motioned her to stay put. She sat up and watched him step outside.

Before she could get up, Dill was back. He shook his head and grinned.

"It's your boyfriend," he said. "Out there hunting tin cans with a bird gun."

"Who?"

"That Swanson boy." Dill winked. "How many boyfriends you got?"

Cynthia flushed.

"Sorry," Dill said, "I wasn't thinkin' of the other one." He gave her arm a pat, reached up to the rack by the door, and pulled down a jacket. "I'm going to get the big Cat runnin', push some snow out of here. You want to ride along?"

"No," she said.

"Sure?"

Cynthia nodded.

"Suit yourself," he said and ducked out the door.

Cynthia pulled on her coat. The heavy wool was stiff from drying by the fire, and the lining had ripped out along the hem. Her mother would shake her head over that. She borrowed thick socks and a pair of black rubber boots from Dill and went outside.

The sun shone bright on the snow, but the icy air rasped in her lungs. She was wide awake now. She stomped a path out to the edge of the biggest pit. The garbage was almost completely hidden under hills and valleys of snow; she might have been looking down into a crater filled with fallen trees and boulders, except that here and there smoke steamed from a smoldering tractor tire and the smell of rotten meat hung in the air. When she spotted Kenny, she sat down on a rusted oil drum, where he couldn't see her from the pit.

He wasn't shooting at tin cans. He stood straight-backed, sighted carefully, and shot at a raven high in a leafless cottonwood at the edge of the dump. He missed and reloaded. Then he stood very still and waited. In the silence, a single raven gave a sharp, barking caw. Cynthia waited as well, and in the quiet, with the sun glaring on the snow, she felt assaulted by the kitchen garbage stink of the dump.

Another slick raven glided onto the rim of a tire and tilted like a mechanical bird to peck at an item inside. It stepped back and cocked its head. Even from where she sat, Cynthia saw clearly the oil-slick gloss of its feathers, its beak like wrinkled black leather. She watched Kenny aim again, miss, and with his feet braced far apart, reload and fire both barrels at the bird. This time she heard the flat impact of the bird shot and saw broken feathers. The raven squawked and struggled to fly on a wing torn at right angles and hanging from its body. Kenny went after the bird, and Cynthia stood up. She scrambled down the slope of the pit.

When she reached the tire where the bird had been, Kenny was lower in the pit, bending, awkward and frantic, trying to catch the raven. It escaped him, screaming and cawing. Finally he straightened up and shot the bird again, and this time he shot its head away, leaving a raw red neck and a live, thrashing confusion of feathers. He dropped the shotgun and caught the bird, grabbed it up against his chest and tried to hold its beating wings still. Cynthia was afraid to move, afraid he'd turn around and see her there. She felt as if she'd stumbled on some obscene private act. But Kenny stood where he was, hunched around the bloody feathers. She wanted to run, but before she could turn, he looked up and started coming in her direction, swinging the huge bird by its feet.

He wasn't pretty now. He looked as if he had been running hard and had slowed only to catch his breath. His hair hung in his eyes, and his face was pale except for red, transparent blotches along his cheeks. She thought he would stop, but he kept coming.

He swung the mess of bloody feathers at her face. It was the smell of blood, more than fear, that made her stomach buckle.

She screamed and pushed at him, flailing out with both arms, but he swung again. Through her own screams, she heard him sob. She closed her eyes and struck out blind, not knowing where he was until he came within her reach and she grabbed for him. His head only reached her chin, but he was strong, sharp knees and elbows struggling. She could barely hold him. She clenched her teeth and grasped her own wrist with her other hand behind his back. All she thought about was making a vise against his thrashing — as if pure thought could make her strong enough. He butted her chest and kicked, but she held on.

When finally he stopped fighting, both of them were breathing hard and soaked with sweat. She could feel his heartbeat through her coat. She held on to him, exhausted, and for a moment she could feel a flow of heat, a warmth like being clung to by a sweaty child. Then Kenny broke away.

He stepped back and looked at her. He wasn't crying, but his fists were knotted hard, and the skin around his eyes was white. Sweat stood out in beads on his forehead. She knew he could do anything. A word, "oh," came out of her mouth. She heard her own tears in her voice. "I'm sorry." She tripped, turning in the snow to get away.

She ran back to the trailer, stumbling in the snow. She slammed the door shut and stood in the middle of the tiny room. She'd had no right to spy on him. He had to feel exposed, like a hunter caught leaving behind a wounded, gut-shot deer. She had witnessed a person turning inside out, and what she saw was raw and ugly. What could he do but strike out at her? And she had run away.

She swung the door open so hard it crashed against the outside of the trailer. She walked back out to the pit, the winter sun on her face. Kenny was gone. The shotgun barrel glinted blue where he'd dropped it on the ground, and a pool of red blood and feathers had started to freeze, frothy and pink at the edges.

She made her way around the trailer to Dill's shed. Inside, Goldie stood dozing, her head hanging so low her breath had blown the hay chaff away from the floor and cleaned a smooth, round circle in the dirt. Cynthia smoothed a hand along her flank, fitted on the bridle, and heaved the blanket and saddle into place. She swung up, struggling with her long coat, and turned Goldie's head down the lane.

On the road, she saw Kenny far ahead. He stumbled forward, his steps uneven, his arms close to his body. She didn't hurry. She knew he could hear her — Goldie's hooves made squeaking noises in the dry snow — but he didn't turn to look. When she rode up beside him, he picked up his pace, but when she reined Goldie up, he stopped. She leaned down from the saddle and offered him her hand. He looked at her for a long moment before he grasped her wrist and let her swing him up behind her saddle.

24

Lenna let the house overheat until it was so warm that steam clouded the windows and dripped in runnels down the glass. She filled the kitchen sink with scalding water and slowly, taking a long time with each plate and glass and fork, washed the dishes.

Then she went to the bathroom and looked at herself in the mirror. Her mascara had smudged black smears under her eyes, and her skin felt dry enough to crack. She scrubbed her face and combed her hair. At the hall closet she removed, one by one, all the towels and blankets, making a stack on the floor. She lifted out Kenny's Christmas presents, carried them into the front room, and laid the packages under the blinking tree. She looked under the bed for the box that had come from Kenny's stepmother. It was gone.

She went back into the kitchen and sat down at the table. The box was gone. And Kenny was gone.

She didn't know what to do. A voice, like a shrill bell inside her, said to call the sheriff. To call somebody. To do something. But another voice kept telling her to wait. It was Christmas. If she could just make things normal, Kenny would come home. He was on foot. She tried to imagine where he might have gone; she pictured him out in the dark by himself. His bed hadn't been slept in at all, and his present for her was just where she had pretended not to see it the night before. Christmas Eve. The box was open, left stranded in the center of his room. The whole terrible night came back to her. What on earth had she done? It had all seemed so easy, so innocent. Then suddenly it wasn't. The storm came back to her, snow falling in thick blankets, the world muffled and white despite the darkness. Now the morning sun outlined the bare limbs of the cottonwood trees and glistened on the snow. But the night, so vast and black, was still with her like the dread of a long winter.

"Oh please, Kenny," she said. "Please come home."

She stood up and walked around the table. She went into the living room, wiped the condensation from the glass, and looked out the front window. Then she carried Kenny's rocker back into the kitchen.

She kept thinking she ought to call the sheriff. What if Kenny was hurt, lying in some snowbank? She stood quickly and went to the phone. She dialed the number for the hospital, heard the number ring, and hung up. If she didn't call, Kenny would be all right.

She thought about Roddy Moyers. She hadn't wanted him to touch her. They drove back to the ranch in silence. When finally she felt able to speak, Roddy couldn't understand why she felt so angry and humiliated. She would never forget the girl who stared her down, how young she was. How that look of pure hatred burned. It struck a part of herself she'd never seen before, the place of genuine terror, of immediate fear for her life. It amazed her how Roddy couldn't understand what he had done.

They drank a pot of coffee together, but Lenna knew that everything was changed. She saw how all the charm, all the excitement, had come from Roddy, not from her. He had treated her as if she were beautiful, as if everything she said had special meaning, like a story. And so she had told him about her life, the grandparents who had raised her on a ranch in Nebraska, about Kenny, and Kenneth Swanson.

She understood who she really was. A woman too old for Roddy. Sitting in the ranch kitchen, she knew the fluorescent lights showed her swollen eyes and every wrinkle on her face. She felt exposed and exhausted and gave in to the urge of laying her cheek on the table and burying her head in her arms.

In the truck, Roddy had told her about Cynthia Dustin as well as other women he knew. He kept repeating how he never meant to hurt her. To hurt anybody. As he talked, she began to feel as if she were his mother, not his lover, and though she wanted to believe him, she couldn't find in herself any sympathy. Finally, she suspected that she'd never been in love with Roddy. She'd been in love with being in love.

In her own kitchen, she felt hungover, groggy as if from some kind of drug. The world seemed flat and dull. But she had Kenny. If he'd only come home, she promised herself, she'd never leave him again.

She had to call the sheriff's office. She didn't want Jeff to know, to know she'd left her son home alone on Christmas. It made her feel trashy and ashamed. But she had to do it. She went to the phone and dialed the numbers.

She reached the dispatcher and then, after a long wait, heard the buzzing, intermittent sound of Jeff's voice on the radio. He was at the scene of a car crash, with urgent voices and sirens in the background. She told him what had happened, that Kenny was gone, though she couldn't be sure he could hear her. The line crackled and his voice broke into fragments. Finally, she heard him say it would be an hour, maybe more, before he could get back to town.

She didn't know anyone else who could help her. She couldn't call Roddy. And she didn't know anyone else very well.

She stood up suddenly, dizzy, unsteady for a moment, and pulled on her coat. She wrapped a wool scarf over her head and tied the ends behind. Then she pulled on her snow boots and grabbed her purse and gloves.

The least she could do was go look for Kenny herself. She struggled out through the snow to the car. It was buried up to the wheel wells, and the track behind it had filled with snow. She tossed her purse in the front seat and waded over to the shed to get the shovel.

She started behind the front wheels, lifting away shovelfuls of soft, flaky snow. But then the snow got harder. The wide shovel sliced away slabs of snow, and it took all her strength to bend and heave them back behind her. Sweat trickled down her sides underneath her sweater. She finished the wheels and started shoveling the track. But the snow was deeper than she'd thought. It was like shoveling a beach away. She saw that even if she could get the car out, the road was snowed in. She began to cry, in anger and frustration, but she went on shoveling, her arms and legs trembling, and the muscles low in her back burning like torn tendons.

She stood up and leaned on the shovel. She heard the slow thud of a horse's hooves, the sound muffled by the snow. And the horse appeared, a dark gold horse, damp with sweat, its mane hanging thick in its eyes. It carried two people. Cynthia Dustin and Kenny.

The horse turned into the yard, taking jerking hops through the deep drift at the curb, and halted by the back door. Lenna waded up to the horse's head. Cynthia looked at her without speaking, but there was a sadness in her face, a sense of resignation. Kenny slid off.

He looked up at Cynthia as if to say thank you, but he didn't speak. She reined the horse around and followed her own post-hole tracks through the snow.

Lenna took her son in her arms and held him tight.

"Oh, Kenny," she said, "I'm sorry. I'm so sorry."

He stood very still, his arms hanging loose at his sides. There was dark, dried blood in his hair and on his face. "It's okay," he said. "I'm okay."

His voice was tired and without anger or hurt, without accusation. He reached around her with both arms and hugged her back. But his chin cut into the ridge of her shoulder. Their bodies didn't seem to fit together anymore.

25

Roddy swung his hay hook into a top bale on the stack, yanked, and pivoted aside while the heavy bale thudded onto the sled. He lifted it by a strand of twine and heaved it in the back. His next swing brought the whole top layer down, the bales frozen together. He threw up an arm, and tried to twist out of the way. But the bales knocked him sideways off the sled.

He picked himself up and brushed the snow from his chaps. He could feel a deep bruise swelling on his forearm. He stood staring out over the snow. He shook his head to clear it.

The sun had come up hours before, but the air was brittle with cold. His eyes watered and he wiped at his nose with the back of his glove. White with snow, the granite peaks in the west seemed smaller, dwarfed and flattened by the smooth, white fields.

Chub and Dan stood quiet beside the stack. Chub shifted her weight and snorted, her breath thick and white in the cold. There was no wind, and aside from the horses and his own breathing there was no sound. He'd always liked that silence, so quiet he might as well be deaf. He should have gotten up and fed the cattle first thing in the morning.

He climbed back on the sled. The hay had been baled too loose, and the heavy bales bowed on the orange twine when he heaved them up on his thigh and stacked them. Sweat broke out on his forehead. It smelled like whiskey and stale cigarette smoke. He hooked the bales down and stacked them faster and higher, working the sweet, sour smell out of his skin. When he finished, he lifted the reins and drove out to the feed ground.

The team moved slowly on its own in a wide circle while he stood on the back cutting bales with his jackknife and kicking the split bales off into the snow.

The cows had sheltered down in the willows in the storm, but slowly they came, first one, then another, until a long line of white-faced cattle trailed toward the sled. Roddy swung the team back for another load.

By the time he drove into the darkness of the barn and fed the horses, it was noon. At the kitchen door, he kicked his heavy work boots in the corner. The cuffs of his wet jeans had filled with hay chaff. He skinned them off so he wouldn't track hay through the house. In the kitchen, he put on the kettle for coffee and went, barefooted, through the house to the guest room. He hadn't made it to the bunkhouse last night. He closed the drapes to shut out the light and looked at the rumpled bed. His bare thighs, pale with cold, felt clammy. Even his underwear was wet. He felt a strong pull to crawl back in the bed, as if the sheets might still be warm.

Instead, he picked up his town boots and carried them back to the kitchen. He drank a cup of black coffee, so hot it burned and numbed his tongue, and made a few calls. The foreman had gone out below for Christmas, but he could get Al to come up and feed. He took a long, scalding shower in his mother's bathroom, put on a bathrobe he found folded in the closet. He pulled his boots on over his damp feet and walked out to the bunkhouse.

His muscles convulsed with cold while he pulled on clean clothes and threw his gear in a bag. He thought he'd get the truck started, the heater going, while he closed up the house. But the truck wouldn't start because he hadn't plugged in the block heater. He never thought it would get this cold.

He pushed the truck out where the sun would hit it, put a charge on the battery, and went back in the house. At least the storm had blown the road clear.

He walked through the house, turning the heat down, the lights off. He didn't lock up, even though his mother had told him to. Nobody ever broke in. He left a check for the girl who came to clean and stood in the living room. He liked the house this way, dead quiet. He walked over to the piano and looked in at the strings. As a kid, he'd been fascinated by the strings, so taut and new. He'd once poured a glass of milk in there. Now he lowered the lid to keep the dust out.

On the road, he kept the heater and the radio off. The silence of the morning, the house, the field, the barn, not a sound anywhere, stuck with him. He wanted to keep it that way.

In town, the snowmen were still lighted, hanging pathetically from the lampposts, and everything was shut up tight except the hotel and café. It had been a big storm; the plough had scraped up shoulders of snow so high you couldn't see the storefront windows.

If he drove straight through, he could make it to Denver while it was still Christmas. He thought he might stay through the stock show, then drive down into the backcountry through Arizona to L.A.

PART III

Spring

26

It wasn't until March that the hardened drifts of snow began to melt. The sun shone hot on the fields, and in the daytime, pools of water stood in the hollows. They froze slick at night, in wide sheets of blue ice, and melted again the next day.

Lenna woke up early and brought inside split logs that left bark and sawdust all down the front of her bathrobe and skinned her palms. Kneeling, she built a fire over the coals. She wanted the house to be warm when Kenny came down.

She poured a cup of coffee and went to stand out on the porch. The day was damp, with gray clouds, like mist, hovering low. The brown grass around the back door looked shredded, as if mice had nested in it, and wet wood chips littered the frozen ground. The house and the trees and the fences looked raw and shabby.

It looks like a mining camp — in Alaska, she thought, but there wasn't anything she could do to clean it up. Kenny spread woodstove ashes on the ice outside the back door, and when it honeycombed to slush, he shoveled it away. But the next melt-and-freeze brought the ice back. She'd fallen twice now, her arms filled with grocery bags.

Often now she found tears pooling but not spilling over. When it happened at work, she went into the bathroom and washed her face.

For weeks, she'd sat in the kitchen in the morning, the things that needed to be done swarming in on her. The washing machine was broken and the drains backed up. The car made disturbing sounds when she shifted gears. They were running out of wood.

She was covered by health insurance now, but she put off telling Kenny. In bed at night, she curled up and pretended that she was only sick, that the cold or flu would go away soon.

Then she would pick everything up, get organized. She saw she was only feeling sorry for herself. Kenny wasn't home very much. He'd finally become involved in things at school, and she was glad for that. When he was home, he spent hours in his room, claiming to be reading and doing his homework. He asked her not to go up there, but she did. She had to put his clean socks away or find some lost thing in the attic.

That morning she heard Kenny moving upstairs. He always sounded as if he were reeling, stomping the floor and thumping into furniture. She could never figure out what he was doing that made so much noise, but she was always relieved to see him come down the stairs, still half-asleep but unharmed. She smiled thinking about his rumpled hair, his pajamas buttoned wrong.

He reminded her more now of his uncle Jack than of his father, and she felt for Kenneth's parents, who had lost two sons. Though he was the older, Jack seemed like the younger one, diffident and clumsy. Just running into Jack used to make her happy, as if she were swimming in an icy lake and suddenly felt her bare legs find a hidden pool of warmer water. When Jack died in Vietnam, they all said, "He was just too good to live." Even though she was an air force wife, his death had made her furious.

Kenny stumbled down the stairs without glancing into the kitchen, and she heard water running in the bathroom, the faucet turned on full, splashing in the sink. She wanted to go to the door, remind him that the thawing snow was filling up the septic tank, the drains would be backed up all day. But all she did was nag at him now. She would just skip a shower herself. She finished her coffee and went into her room to dress for work.

When she came out, Kenny was at the table, spooning cereal out of a mixing bowl.

"I'm late," she said. "Anything you want me to pick up after work?"

"Six pack of beer, some chew," he said, his mouth full of food.

Lenna laughed. "What time will you be home?"

"Don't know."

"If it's after five, I could pick you up?"

Kenny waved her away. "Go. You're gonna be late."

She'd been late to work several times in the last few weeks. She didn't know what it was. She woke up early and was dressed and ready on time, but something always came up. She couldn't find her purse or her checkbook. Or she found herself drifting around the house, looking for her lipstick or something she'd promised to bring to work. Or one morning the car refused to start.

"Don't *you* be late," she said to Kenny. "It's almost eight o'clock."

"Don't worry," he said. "I'm done." To prove it, he stood up and carried his bowl to the sink.

Lenna pulled on her coat and went out the door. She stepped carefully on the ice and made her way out to the car.

After she was gone, Kenny sat back down. He wasn't in any hurry. He wasn't going to school.

He waited for Cynthia on the corner. When the big car pulled into sight, he jogged to meet it. Inside, the heat was thick, and he rolled down the window.

Cynthia drove without talking, up the highway, turning finally onto the ski hill road. They parked above the Moyers place on the Forest Service road and slipped down the path on wet fallen leaves.

Formations of geese, great squadrons of geese, passed overhead — some heading north, some flying south. Kenny and Cynthia stopped at the foot of the path and listened to the racket overhead.

"You know why," Kenny asked, "geese fly in formation, one off the wing of the other?"

Cynthia looked at him, suspicious. "No, why?" she said.

"They're drafting off each other, like race cars. The one in front makes a vacuum — makes it easier for the one behind. My dad explained it to me."

"If you say so," Cynthia said.

"You know why in a formation of geese, one side of the *V* is always longer than the other?"

"No," she said, "why?"

"There's more geese on that side." Kenny let loose laughing. Cynthia boxed him on the arm, but she laughed, too. They walked on to the ranch house.

Inside, the living room was bigger than any place he'd ever been. On one side, there was a fireplace you could stand up in. At the other end, a black grand piano.

Cynthia threw her books down on the couch and tugged sheet music from a brown satchel. She set it up on the piano and turned back the cover from the keys, but she didn't start to play.

Kenny sat behind her on the couch, watching how she stretched and flexed her shoulders, her shoulder blades pinching close together underneath her shirt.

"You look like a chicken," he said.

She stuck out her elbows, flapped, and gave a *"balk, balk, balk."* She swiveled around on the piano bench, and imitating an announcer on the radio, she said, "And now, the chicken concerto . . . in D major, by Johann Sebastian Balk."

Kenny liked to stretch out on the couch and listen to her play. At first, all the music had sounded pretty much alike to him. He never listened to this kind of music. When it came on the radio, it made him feel sleepy. Old and sleepy, and he switched to something else.

But the real piano had a different sound. The last time Cynthia brought him here, he sat beside her on the bench, and she taught him how to count the notes and measures, how to turn the music sheets for her.

It took him a while to get over being afraid someone would catch them inside the big house. But Cynthia had permission. Roddy had given her permission to come play his mother's piano. His mother had arthritis now and couldn't play. The foreman only showed up early every morning to feed.

It was hard for Kenny to stay inside and watch the weather turn, warming up. The air itself seemed to draw him. He sat as long as he could, listening to Cynthia play, but after a while his legs would start to twitch. A muscle in one leg would jump, and he would have to stand and walk around the room. The soft carpets were woven in strange designs that, if he stared at them too long, began to give him the creeps.

He wanted to go out and see the colts. Roddy raised roughstock. Bucking horses, just for fun. He never sold them to a stockbreeder or concession, not as far as Kenny knew. But he kept a dozen green colts just to see how they would go. See if he could teach them to buck.

At lunchtime, they walked out the back door and down the

alley to the empty barn. They made nests in the hay and ate whatever they had packed to take to school. They talked. Kenny had never said so much in his whole life. He just opened his mouth, and words came out.

Cynthia told him how, after the night at the bar, Dill left Goldie in his shed and drove her home. On Christmas Day.

"We pulled into the yard," she said, "and it felt like somebody else's yard. The dog woke up and she went to Dill instead of me. Sat down on his boot and looked up at him. My dad came out on the porch.

" 'Brought your girl,' Dill said.

"My dad didn't say anything. I think he was ashamed to have Dill there. I didn't tell Dill my father had hit me the night before. But Earl must have thought I did.

"My dad stepped off the porch and made room for me to go past him, inside. 'Go on' — that's all he said. I went up to my room and sat on the bed. I just sat there for a long time, thinking my mother would come up and ask me where I'd been. I kept thinking she'd be upset I tore the coat.

"Finally, I hung it up in the back of the closet. It's still there. Then I just stayed in my room the rest of the day. It didn't feel like Christmas. I used to get excited, wondering what I'd get. From my mother. From Aunt Helen. But I didn't this year. Did Roddy give your mom a present?"

"No," Kenny said. "Not that I could see."

"I don't know what happened to the presents," Cynthia said. "The next day, the Christmas tree was gone and there weren't any packages. Even the ones I got for my folks were gone. I think my dad took them all to church. It feels worse not to care than not to have presents.

"Sometimes," she said, "I wish my dad was dead. I lie awake at night, and I want to shoot him, with a gun. I have a picture in my mind of a revolver. A silver, metal gun. But the picture always ends up with the gun pointed at me. Right at my head."

When Cynthia talked like that, it scared him. He half believed her and half didn't. Other times, she talked about how much she wanted to get out of there. How all her life she dreamed about going to New York to live with her aunt Helen. But now she didn't want to live with anybody. She wanted to be on her own.

"Do you ever feel that way?" she asked him. "Like you want to get up in the night and walk around — go anywhere you want. I think there are places where everybody stays up late. They're going dancing, or out to hear music."

Kenny took in the damp green smell of the hay. He smelled Cynthia, a clean, sweaty smell. They sat in the hay, their backs against old milking stanchions, and looked out the wide door of the barn. Most of the time, he didn't know what she was talking about. But he told her no. It didn't feel good not to have a dad. He told her how once, after his parents divorced, one of the popular kids had befriended him. The boy and his dad had invited him to go out to a lake, to go out fishing. But he and the boy had ended up racing, swimming to a slippery raft out in the water. He remembered the deep mud at the shore, and how they dove in to get past it without sinking to their ankles in black sludge.

By lunch it was cold, and they stood shivering in their wet swim trunks while the dad made a fire and roasted hot dogs. The dad asked him, "How's your mom?" Kenny didn't know the man even knew his mom, and he felt embarrassed that he did.

"She's fine," he said.

"Don't you have a dad?" the boy asked.

His father shut him up, angry, as if the boy had said something dirty. "Of course he does," he said. "Everybody has a dad."

Now he told Cynthia, "Not everybody has a dad. Don't wish your dad was dead."

He leaned back and thought about the weeks of spring and summer ahead. He thought he could talk her into coming to the ranch again and helping him catch one of Roddy's horses. They wouldn't even have to cut school. Next week the spring vacation would begin.

"My dad used to always say, 'Call if you need anything.' I don't know how I knew, but I knew he didn't mean it. It got to feel like a bad joke. But now, I wish I'd called him anyway."

27

The foreman had turned the colts out in the south pasture to forage on their own. As the sun went down, the grass began to stiffen and freeze, but rivulets of water ran in streams underneath. The fence lines curved into a sharp corner, where a thicket of willows grew.

Kenny and Cynthia stepped apart, moving slowly, pushing the colts into the corner.

"Don't spook 'em," Cynthia said. "Go slow."

She hated catching horses, and they hardly had a chance in hell of catching one of these. Kenny held a rope behind his back where the colts wouldn't see it. Cynthia carried a bucket of grain, but she didn't shake it. These colts wouldn't come to grain. But at least her dad wasn't there, waiting to see her mess up.

The layers of frozen swamp grass had a give and spring under her boots, as if she were walking on a floating island, but where the ground had thawed, her boots sank in watery black mud. She tried to move without making sounds, but she knew the colts were watching their approach.

Despite their winter coats, the colts glistened in the dirty golden light, the muscles in their chests rounded in curves above their long, straight legs.

She signaled Kenny and they moved up closer. One of the horses, a black two-year-old with white socks, lifted his head and turned to watch them. He arched his neck, pivoted on his back legs, and snorted. The other colts milled around each other. It made her uneasy, moving up on the horses in the dim light. She could see, but yet she couldn't.

They were close now, but too far apart to stop the horses if they charged. She knew one would hit the corner, see the trap, and come galloping out past them. She and Kenny stopped at the same time, to let the horses settle down, go back to feeding. What they should have done was saddle up another horse and drive the colts into the corral. They resumed their slow steps forward.

The black colt spun out of the corner and made a break. He came straight at Cynthia, his head held high. Any second the other colts would shoot apart and run.

"Whoa!" She held her arms wide and shifted sideways to head off the first colt. "Whoa!" She ran at him, waving her arms to turn him back into the fence. But he kept on coming.

"Move!" she heard Kenny holler, but she knew the colt would cut aside if she stood her ground. She flapped her arms and yelled. Her hair fell in her eyes, and she could only hear the hooves thudding through mud. She whooped at the colt and ran right at him.

He pivoted, turned, and galloped back up the field. "You shit," she said. She bent over and braced her hands on her knees, breathing hard. She'd done just what her dad would have wanted — the right thing, the thing she hardly ever did when he was watching.

They wouldn't ever catch the black colt now. Once one got started like that, he never quit. She motioned for Kenny to move up. Kenny held his loop down by his side, hefted it in his palm, and grasped the end of the rope in his other hand. They were close now, the horses almost in between them. She wanted to squeeze them a little closer toward Kenny, so if they bolted he could get out a loop.

A big gray colt jigged along the fence, first one way, then the other. He lifted his head and began to trot out between them. He would speed up suddenly, she knew. Even if Kenny got a loop out, he wouldn't be able to hold him. But Kenny made his throw, and she heard the rope slap down. Kenny took a wrap on his end, and dug his heels into the mud, ready for the colt to take off. But the colt stopped dead, fear showing white in his eyes. Kenny didn't wait. He closed in hand over hand, twisted a hackamore over the colt's nose, and threw his leg over. He was up.

The horse didn't buck. Instead, it ran at Cynthia. Terror hit her cold, and she felt the blow like a hundred-pound sack of grain. It hurt. Right away it hurt — all down her arm, and her hip, and her leg, a dull pain like she'd never felt before. She was on the ground, her elbow twisted in the mud. But she got up fast. She ran for the fence, climbed over, and sat down.

The colt was far down in the field, heading back, a glimmer of white in the dusk. She couldn't see what Kenny was doing, but he was still on. Then his left arm was in the air and waving. He was spurring the damn thing, trying to get his ride. But the colt wouldn't buck. It did every other thing — ran him into the willows, stopped, and reared and spun around. The next thing he'd do was go down, roll Kenny off, and break his leg, or his back.

Kenny was pulling too high on the rope. The colt couldn't get his head down, Cynthia thought, and then Kenny did, too. He loosened the rope, and the colt lowered his head, arched his back and started bucking. Kenny's whole body flopped, but he stayed on.

Cynthia could tell he'd had enough. He tried to yank the colt's head back up — let him run it off — but all he did was lose his concentration. He went off backward over the rump, landed hard on his shoulder blades, and rolled. The colt took a run down the field, a dim silver glow in the distance, like the gleam of a coin underwater.

She walked down the field toward Kenny. He was sitting up, his legs stretched out in front of him. He looked up at her, but his eyes weren't right, he didn't seem to see her.

"You all right?" he said. He remembered the colt knocking her flat.

"I wouldn't go that far," she said.

Kenny laughed and stood up. Then he sat back down.

"I'll be okay," he said. "Give me a second." A black smear of mud across his face made one eye seem startlingly white when he opened it. He was shivering. They retrieved his rope and started walking back.

In the house, she guided him through the dark to the bathroom. She didn't dare to turn on any lights, but the big bathroom had no windows. She flipped on the light, the fan, and the heat lamp, and sat Kenny on the closed lid of the toilet.

She twisted on both faucets in the big tub and let them blast. In the red light, she saw Kenny's lashes were caked thick with mud. She marveled how he missed getting it in his eye.

"Give me your clothes," she said. "You can't go home like that." His jeans were black with mud up to the knees and a smear of green manure cut across the shoulders of his jacket. He shrugged out of the jacket one arm at a time, and turned around to step out of his jeans. She hung his blue parka on the back of the door and made her way through the dark house to drop the jeans into the washer. No one would ask about her clothes, old ranch jeans she wore to do chores.

On the way back, she took a bottle of beer from the refrigerator. Kenny was in the tub when she opened the bathroom door. The room was misty and hot with steam, and it smelled like something that had been dead a while. She picked up Kenny's stiff socks and tossed them out the door into the hall. She sat down on the floor and opened the beer.

Kenny sank underwater, and when he came up his hair was slicked back dark. His face was flushed from the heat, but his forehead gleamed white. At the curve of his hairline, new, wispy hairs made him look sweet, like a small child. She reached up for his jacket and wiped at the manure with a wet washrag.

"Give me a towel," he said. She stood up and held out one of the big towels. Kenny stood up behind it, wrapped it under his armpits, and stepped out of the tub.

"You can get in," he said.

She looked in the tub. The water was nearly black. "No thanks," she said. Kenny laughed and she pulled out the plug. Kenny wrapped another towel around his shoulders and sat down on the carpet.

"It's nice here, isn't it?" he said. "I've never been in a bathroom like this."

"It's like this in hotels," she said.

"I've never been in a hotel."

"Never?"

"I was in motels, when I was little. My dad was in the air force."

Cynthia stood in the tub, peeled off her clothes behind the shower curtain, and dropped them out. She pushed the showerhead away from her, turned it on full blast, and felt for the right temperature. She craned her neck to look at her shoulder. Her arm and hip and leg were marked with mottled blue and red bruises, like deep thumbprints. Suddenly, the steam and hot water made her feel sick deep in her bowels. She thought she might throw up, or pass out. She sat down on the hard porcelain bottom of the tub, the water streaming down her face, into her nose and mouth. She reached up and turned the faucet off.

"You okay?" Kenny said.

"No." She swallowed saliva. "I need a towel."

The towel came around the curtain. She held its softness up to her face, pressing into it. She had to concentrate on not throwing up.

"What's the matter?" Kenny said. He was standing up. "You okay?"

The waves of sickness weakened. She took a deep breath, stood up slowly, and wrapped herself in the towel. She drew back the curtain. The smell of manure and beer and Kenny's socks was thick in the steam. She stepped out of the tub.

"Open the door," she said to Kenny. She stepped past him into the hall. In the cool air she could breathe. She felt it on her face, deep in her lungs.

"I have to lie down," she said, and moved toward the bedroom.

She crawled under the sheets and lay there, sweat beading on her forehead, the wet towel warm around her.

Kenny didn't know what was wrong. At first, she wouldn't talk to him, and he felt abandoned, as if she weren't any longer there.

"Please. Tell me what to do," he said.

"Just sick," she said. "I'm okay now."

But then she was quiet for a long time. Kenny stood by the bed until his eyes saw red spots in the blackness. His wet hair dripped, one cold drop, then another, down his back. He was shivering.

He went back to the bathroom and pulled on his shirt and underwear. He had no idea where his jeans were.

Cynthia still hadn't moved in the bed. He thought maybe she was sleeping. He pulled back the covers and crawled in. The sheets were freezing cold. He inched over to Cynthia, curled up on his side, and curved himself behind her back. She was wet. He could hear the slow, even pull of her breathing. Carefully, he brought the covers up over his shoulder and hers, and wrapped his arm around her. Gradually, the wetness grew warm. Cynthia slept, but Kenny stayed awake. Every inch of his skin was awake. He closed his eyes and skimmed along a shimmering surface, like a water bird, just barely touching down from time to time into the sea.

28

Lenna sat at her desk, downstairs in the courthouse, listening to the other women talking back and forth. A heavy file drawer slid open and shut.

Outside the window, she heard a bird sing, a fluttering, high string of notes up in the trees. She hadn't realized until that moment that she hadn't heard a bird all winter. Every place she'd ever lived before, birds came even in the winter. But in this high valley only scavengers, the ravens and magpies, stayed. She pushed back the urge to go to the window and look.

To her, this was the sure sign. Winter was over. She felt the warmer air like a reprieve. She felt lighter now that it was spring. She'd let Kenny stay out late. He was only fourteen, but it was so close to Easter vacation. He had been sleeping when she left for work. It amazed her how much he could sleep. For the first time since his father died, she had the sense that she was taking care of him. She swung around and rolled a printed form into her typewriter.

When her phone rang, she stopped typing and answered, her voice light and friendly. The sheriff was on the line. He asked her to step back to his office.

Over the winter, she'd come to like the sheriff and the deputy. In the last few weeks, she'd taken all the overtime she could and found herself many nights in the overheated, empty building with only Jeff and the dispatcher listening for calls on the phone or radio. After they carried food across the street from the café to feed the jail inmates, she sometimes ate her meal with them.

She walked through the hall to the back of the big building. Her heels made satisfying clicks along the polished floors. She came in the back way, through the jail and into Jeff's office.

Two elderly people stood at the counter, applying for driver's licenses, she thought. Then, past the swinging gate in the sheriff's enclosure, she saw Kenny and Cynthia. They sat side by side in wooden chairs facing the sheriff. The first thing she noticed was Kenny's jeans. They clung, wet, to his thighs as if he'd gone in swimming. And his boots were caked black with mud.

The sheriff stood and swung back the gate for her to come in. She looked at him, then at the kids. She couldn't understand what was happening. It seemed so odd to see Kenny there. She'd left him at home sleeping.

"Sit down," Jeff said, hauling a chair over. She hadn't even brought her purse. She sat down, but she kept wanting to reach for her purse and hold it in her lap.

The sheriff turned to the older couple standing at the counter.

"Mr. and Mrs. Leavitt," he said tentatively, as if he might have the name wrong. The woman nodded. "This is the boy's mother, Lenna Swanson."

She couldn't look at the old people. She looked at Kenny. His hair was whirled in a cowlick, as if he had just woken up. He wouldn't look at her. He stared down at his hands, clasped together between his knees. Cynthia glanced at her, but her eyes didn't make contact. Lenna hadn't seen her since she'd ridden Kenny home on her horse.

"What's the matter?" Lenna said. "Jeff?"

The sheriff stood up and strode over to the Leavitts. "Could I ask you to wait outside for a minute?" He indicated the door that led out to the main hall.

When they were gone he turned to Lenna, a typed report in his hand.

"The Leavitts are friends of the Moyerses'. They drove in early this morning and found the kids at the ranch. In the big house. They want to file charges." He read from the report. "Trespassing. Breaking and entering. At least unlawful entry. The kids say they didn't break in. The place was open. I have a man up there checking for damage."

He glanced at Cynthia. "Earl's on his way."

The sheriff's office seemed suddenly stark and official to Lenna. Her pulse raced, and she couldn't shake a sense of the confusion.

"Kenny," she said. He looked up at her, his eyes resigned and blank. "I thought you were home . . ."

"Apparently," the sheriff said, "they broke in last night and —"

"We didn't break in," Cynthia's voice interrupted.

The sheriff ignored her. "Broke in and spent the night."

He looked at Lenna, as if this news would hurt her. She tried to take it in. "They spent the night," the sheriff said, "in the Moyerses' bedroom."

Darkness closed around her in a black pool. At the bottom of the pool, she felt the shame of the whole town knowing, of what would happen to Kenny at school.

"What can I do?" she said. "What do we do?"

"I have a call in to Roddy's folks. They have to press the charges."

"Does he have to stay here?"

"I should keep 'em."

"No," she said, the word coming out, involuntary. She could feel the tightness in her nose and eyes, the start of tears. She blinked hard.

"No, Jeff," she said. "I need to take him home."

The sheriff reached over and laid a broad hand on her arm. She felt the heavy weight of it.

"I want to take him home."

"You're in no position," Jeff said, "to take care of this at home. A few hours in jail will do him good."

He suddenly wasn't her friend, or anyone she knew.

"What about Cynthia? Are you going to keep her here, too?" she said, struggling to keep the tears out of her voice.

The sheriff laughed.

She felt as if he'd slapped her. The meaning of it, the loud, coarse laugh, the sense that she was stupid to think they'd keep a girl in jail, stunned her. She was suddenly nowhere near crying.

"I'm taking him home," she said. "Now."

She left her chair and took a step toward Kenny. At that moment, Earl Dustin came in from the outside door. Kenny stood, then Jeff.

"Earl," the sheriff said. But Earl Dustin didn't answer. He remained in the doorway, his hat tipped low over his eyes. His narrow face was gray, his lips set hard.

He pushed open the swinging gate, walked over to Cynthia, took her by the arm, and ushered her toward the door.

The sheriff stood in front of Lenna. His black leather holster and gun seemed huge to her.

"Hold it, Earl," he said.

Earl stopped at the door, turned around, and stared back at the sheriff. "You know where I live," he said, and slammed the door.

The air in the room was charged with fear and anger. Jeff stood, red patches rising in his cheeks, staring after Earl. He glanced at Lenna and jerked his chin toward the door.

She let Kenny walk in front while she held back the urge to reach out and touch him, and let the heavy door close on its own behind her.

When they were home, she sat Kenny down in the rocker. He hadn't said a word in the car. She took clean sheets from the cupboard and made up a bed on the couch. Upstairs, she found pajamas and brought down Kenny's quilt and pillow.

She watched him struggle to pull his boots off, bending as if he were stiff or hurt. Chips of dark mud fell and broke on the floor, but she barely noticed. She went into the kitchen and put water on while Kenny undressed. She looked in once, and saw his white, narrow shoulders. And bruises. Deep purple bruises, nearly black. She swallowed hard and turned away.

She brought him a cup of hot chocolate and sat beside him while he drank it. The sun shone bright on the wooden floor, and a fly buzzed in the heat trapped on the windowsill.

"What happened?" she said softly.

"Nothin'," Kenny answered. "I got bucked off." He looked up at her, too tired to care. "We were only riding colts."

She didn't ask for more. She watched him swallow the last of the chocolate and carried the cup to the kitchen. When she came back, he had stretched out under the quilt, his head on the pillow and his eyes closed.

She sank into the rocker and turned the radio on low. Out the window, a rusty-breasted robin skittered down onto the dry grass, pecked at the ground, and flew away.

Lenna rocked back and forth. After dark, she'd go back to the office and pick up her purse and coat. Tomorrow she could call in sick.

29

The sky was clear, a soft, hazy blue, and the sun shone bright. Cynthia knew it was warm outside. She sat on her bed, staring out at the hay fields, at a mirage of green that only distance allowed her to see. Up close, the sprigs of new grass disappeared against the dark soil. Her dad was sleeping, and the house seemed closed up, stuffy. She wanted to go down and practice, her fingers almost ached with a need to work them. But her dad had been up calving heifers most of the night.

More than anything, she missed calving. It was hard to believe only two years had passed since her father decided she needed her sleep. She used to get up every four hours in the night to go check the heifers. The ground, soft with manure and old hay, sucked at her boots in the daytime, but at night it froze in a crust that crunched under her boots. She used to love walking around the heifers when they were bedded down, their breath white in her flashlight, the sound of their hard breathing making it seem as if they were all in labor. But heifers were tricky. Some never showed signs the way old mother cows did. Sometimes they calved standing up, their bags still small and round, as if they had no milk. With the old mother cows you watched for their bags to grow so heavy that the swollen pink teats didn't hang, but stuck straight out on all sides. Calving had been the only time her dad ever needed her, ever thought she was worth her keep.

Since he'd picked her up at the sheriff's office, he had hardly said a word to her. He didn't even talk about what heifers he thought were coming along. As the days went by, she began to see the new calves, sleeping folded up and tiny in some slight hollow in the field, and it was as if they belonged to some other rancher and had nothing to do with her.

It was her mother who had sat her down, talked to her, as if they were coconspirators. Cynthia tried to tell her mother what had happened. That nothing had happened. It was Kenny's mother who had called and talked to the Moyerses. Roddy had never told Cynthia she had permission to play the piano, but they never even thought of pressing charges. Still, it was all the same to her mother, to the kids at school. The minister thought it best she not sing or play at church anymore.

Cynthia didn't care about that. She was glad not to go. But judging from the weight of it — the whispers at school, the high tension when she'd first gone back — she might as well have turned up pregnant. Only Mr. Everts had acted like himself.

Her mother even suggested Cynthia take a trip, stay with her aunt Helen in New York for a while. The unfairness of it burned in her. She and her mother and the town all lived in different universes. It bound her to Kenny because they shared a secret. Only the two of them knew the night at the ranch house had been simple — a logical, simple thing.

She wondered why Roddy was somehow above it all. A football hero. Nobody had asked a single question about her dates with him. Where they'd gone or what they'd done.

She missed Roddy, missed the easy physical touch of him. The way when they made love, she knew, just knew, it was a good thing. It made a crazy kind of sense to her that the whole town stared. The world had finally come out and said what they'd thought of her all along. But they couldn't touch what she knew. Roddy had felt good to her. And that feeling could not be wrong.

Finally, spring had come, but she couldn't go out. She wasn't allowed to leave the house except for school. She couldn't even take the bus. Her mother dropped her off and picked her up.

Still, she didn't feel confined. A strange sort of power was growing inside her — as if she could tap a chair and make it slide across the floor. She knew a different world was out there. All she had to do was go and find it.

She tiptoed down the stairs. Her mother had gone shopping, and the house seemed unreal — so barren and quiet. The rooms smelled faintly dusty.

On the mud porch, she tugged on her boots and stepped out the door. The spring sun fell on her face and her arms. She thought she might just go sit in the hayloft, look down at the nursing calves in the field. Smell the steam rising from hay heating under the tin roof.

She stopped at the corral and whistled for Goldie. The old horse angled over, looking coy, but dropped her head just inside the rail where Cynthia could reach up and brush the flies away from her face. Goldie sighed while Cynthia smoothed a palm over one closed eye, then the other.

Overhead, she heard the call of sandhill cranes. She looked up into the sun-white sky, but she couldn't see them. Their calls were ratchety and long, sounding close. But when she finally saw them, the birds were circling high, higher than jet trails, it seemed. The entire flock, maybe a hundred cranes, banked in one motion, and the sun caught their wings. Like cards for sending code, their wings flashed — brown, then gray, then silver-white — until they disappeared into the light. The whole flock vanished.

She knew what she could do. The car was forbidden, but no one had forbidden her to ride. And Goldie needed exercise. The old horse was so fat Cynthia would have thought that she was pregnant if she hadn't known better. For years, her dad had tried to breed the mare, to get a colt with her dark palomino color, but Goldie never settled.

She slipped in through the rail and looped a piece of baling twine high on Goldie's neck. She glanced up at her father's window and had a sudden reckless feeling. Even if he saw her, if she moved fast, he couldn't get down in time to stop her. She trotted Goldie to the barn, slipped the bridle on, and led her out through the gate. She took a fistful of long mane at the withers, and, just the way she'd done it as a little girl, she swung up on her back trick-rider style, in one motion. She didn't take the lane. She cut across the pasture, out of sight of the house, and kicked Goldie into a lope. Goldie pulled at the bit and whinnied at the other horses in the field, who began to pace the fence, trotting back and forth, their tails high, as if they were jealous. Cynthia laughed, amazed at the old horse.

Her father didn't allow anyone to run his horses. They were working animals, he said, and unless they were chasing down cattle, he made all the hands ride at a walk. Cynthia let Goldie stretch out, galloping on the soft new grass. They pounded down the fence line. At the corner, she knew she had to pull up and open a gate to cross to the next field, but she didn't slow down. She didn't know if Goldie could make the fence anymore. Already her breathing was labored, but Cynthia didn't rein her in. She didn't care. If Goldie couldn't jump the fence, the mare would cut away at the last minute and send Cynthia headfirst over the fence.

Only feet from the wire, she felt Goldie gather herself, and she lifted into the air as Goldie jumped. They landed hard on the other side, but the old horse recovered and trotted out toward the road.

"That a *girl*," Cynthia crooned at her, and watched Goldie tip one ear back to listen.

They stayed off the road and went down through the swamps toward Dill's. At places, Goldie sank up to her knees, lunging forward out of the sucking mud. The willows were gold and deep rust colors, the leaves on the scattered aspens uncurling like tiny chartreuse roses. The streams and rivulets running into the river were thick with floating islands of watercress.

At the river, she plunged Goldie into the cold water and let her swim with the current in the deep center for a way, washing off the mud. They crossed the road and turned in toward Dill's trailer.

She slipped off and walked beside Goldie, letting her cool down, and tied her in the shed. Dill's truck was there. She knocked on the door, then pushed it open.

"Anybody home?" she said. A high delight spun in her stomach. She couldn't wait to see Dill's face. He wouldn't believe she'd had the nerve to ride down.

She stepped around the trailer and looked out toward the dump. She hadn't heard machinery. She walked out farther and saw the big yellow Cat. But it wasn't moving, and Dill wasn't in it.

She went back to the trailer and let herself in. She thought she'd wait a while. Dill might have taken a ride to town with someone. The percolator was still warm to the touch. She poured herself a cup of dark, syrupy coffee and sat down on the bed, leaving the door open wide to catch a breeze, to let Dill know she was there if he returned. She hadn't been able to talk to Dill since the morning at the sheriff's office.

She drank the coffee, but she couldn't seem to sit still. She found herself prowling around the tiny trailer, looking at Dill's stacks of old paperbacks. She often wondered why he tore the covers off, but she'd never thought to ask him. Then it occurred to her, he picked the books from the garbage.

She went to wash her coffee cup, set it in the sink. Up above, she saw a long white letter propped up on Dill's set of plastic salt and pepper shakers, the old turquoise plastic sticky with grease. The letter was addressed to her. It shocked her, as if she'd found a love letter to Dill, something private. She sat back down on the couch, the cool envelope almost weightless in her hand. She tried to unstick the flap, but the glue held tight and the envelope came open with a ragged edge.

She wanted to look, but she was afraid to. She glanced down at the first line. "We are happy to inform you . . ." She felt herself smiling. Then stood up. Suddenly, she couldn't keep still. This was it. She had the scholarship. They wanted her. "Dill," she said aloud. "Where the hell *are* you?"

She folded the letter three times and stuck it deep in her back pocket as she left the trailer. She looked around again, as if Dill must be there, someplace. She almost went to the shed and told Goldie her news.

Dill was the only person she could tell about the letter. And there were only two places he could be, down at the mill playing cards or in the café. She jumped into Dill's old truck and turned the key, which was welded into the ignition, laughing at Dill. In his time, people didn't steal things, and he could never keep track of small items like keys.

She drove north of town out to the tall granaries first, pulling up in the wide yard outside General Mills. She almost went inside, though she knew the empty lot meant the men weren't playing cards today.

She spun out through the loose gravel, bumped over the deep ruts in the dirt road, and turned back toward town. Her mother should be home by now. Cynthia thought, I should have left a note, just said, "Gone riding," and nobody would wonder. Her dad would notice Goldie gone, but if she'd left a note, they'd have thought she was on the place somewhere.

But the news, the letter in her pocket, changed everything. She rode high on the excitement of it, the strength of her own happiness obliterating everything — the way an emergency could stop time and make people forget what they'd been doing just before.

She parked in the alley behind the hotel and went in through the kitchen door. Dill wasn't at his booth in the corner. The café was nearly empty.

The waitress gave her a look, almost but not quite a wink, and Cynthia grinned at her. She seemed to know something had changed.

Back in Dill's truck, an idea came to her. It seemed urgent, like an errand you remember halfway home. She drove up the old highway, both windows rolled all the way down, the wind whipping through the truck. She couldn't get there fast enough. She knew, she suddenly knew, Kenny would be there. And she could talk to him.

She pulled in, the truck bumping and jolting across the hay field, and cut the engine. The old rodeo grounds looked deserted, but she knew Kenny was there. But for some unknown reason, she felt timid. The wide sky, the empty space around Dill's pickup, struck her as too big, the silence too huge. She was moving too fast. She walked slowly around the truck to the rail and stood there, the sun warm through her shirt. A wash of red sunburn had appeared on the curve of her forearm.

Kenny was there. He sat up on the bleachers behind the high wire fence that separated spectators from the arena. Slowly she walked over, climbed one high step at a time, the old boards bowing under her weight, and sat down beside him.

"It's dangerous up here," she said.

Kenny didn't look at her. He sat with his elbows on his knees, his hair hanging long in his eyes. Then she saw a smile break at the corner of his mouth.

"Shit," he said, "it's dangerous *everywhere.*"

Laughter, the whole pent-up excitement of everything, burst from her. Kenny laughed, too. And the boards underneath them shook and swayed.

"Hey," Kenny said. "Take it easy, you're gonna rock us off here."

Cynthia wanted to reach out and kiss him, just lay a hand on him, touch him somewhere. She wanted, more than anything, for someone to touch her.

Kenny placed a hand on her arm, his voice quiet and serious.

"You okay?" he said.

"Yeah." The word came out like a sigh, not so much a sound but a change in her whole body.

30

A wind came up and the dust rose off the arena, drifting like a single cloud of smoke over the bleachers. Roddy heard a click and snap, and the arc lights came on, murky yellow in the artificial dusk. He passed his tongue over his front teeth and glanced down at his beer can, where the rim was gritty with dirt. He wiped it with his thumb and tipped the can to his mouth. Arizona was the place to get rides in the winter, but this late in the spring the sand and dust were miserable. Roddy hitched the heels of his boots on the next seat down and propped his elbows on his knees.

Barrel racers were warming up, slowly circling the arena. He watched the rodeo queen and princesses, their satin blouses gleaming blue and red and white through the dust. At the gate earlier, they'd all looked as if they'd stepped fresh out of store windows, but now the heavy satin clung with sweat to their shoulder blades.

Dolly McReynolds heaved herself up the steps. Like most of the friends of his parents', she spent winters in Arizona and tried to follow the rodeo circuit. After she caught her breath, she gave him a broad smile. She wore khaki trousers and a man's shirt, a shapeless cowboy hat pulled down over her gray curls.

"If it ain't our Mr. Moyers," she said.

"Hey," he said.

"You goin' out there?"

He held up his card. Number 17.

"You going to win?"

"Hell, yes," Roddy said and laughed.

The rodeo queen was angling her horse over to the rail.

"Nice-lookin' girl," Dolly said.

"Takes after her grandma."

Suzy McReynolds stretched up over her saddle horn and handed her hat, the brim encircled with a tall sequined crown, to her grandmother. Dolly balanced it on her knees and offered Suzy a tissue.

Suzy blotted at her forehead, careful of her hair and makeup.

"How about a date sometime?" Roddy said. "You got any openings?"

Suzy lowered her long lashes and laughed. "Maybe next year," she said.

"Keep after her," Dolly said. "She won't be queen forever."

The bleachers across from him filled with bright shirts and cowboy hats. The color guard jostled to line up outside the gate. Tinny music blared over the loudspeakers, the gate swung wide, and the bearer of the American flag galloped into the arena. The other flags followed, then the queen and princesses. The youngest princess couldn't be more than ten, Roddy thought. She leaned over her saddle horn, and when she kicked her horse, her short legs stuck out straight, like wings. Roddy stood up and lifted his hat. He stood beside Dolly, his hat held over his heart, as the American flag went past. The riders lined up, and a scratchy recording of "The Star-Spangled Banner" blared, loud, over the arena.

The music always made him jittery. In a minute, he'd go down and help with the barrel racing and team roping. Anything to keep his mind off his ride. He'd drawn a bronc he'd ridden before, a short, ugly thing that wouldn't buck. Last time he'd gotten a reride. But his chances of getting a score weren't good.

The music scratched to a close and the arena emptied. Dolly slapped her newspaper against her thigh, sending up a vapor of dust.

"Where're your folks?" she said.

"Someplace air-conditioned," he said. "Should be at the Silver Dollar later."

"I'll look for you."

He stopped at the concessionaire to pick up a cold beer, and walked among the parked horse trailers. Riders moved lazily along the dusty road, barrel racers warming up. He circled around the trailers he recognized; he wasn't in the mood for visiting.

He rested his boot on the lowest rail of the arena, crossing his arms across the top, and watched the barrel racers, then went to help Bill Whitcome get set for team roping. Bill partnered with his son, Angel. He found the two of them near the gate. Bill was having a little trouble with his roping horse. The mare had come up lame the week before, and Bill was walking her up and down, swearing under his breath.

"We're up in a few," he said. "See how the kid's doing."

Roddy would have laughed some other time. The kid was nearly forty, a big, square-jawed man with two or three kids, all in rodeo.

Angel glanced at his dad. "He's in a mood," he said to Roddy. "Damn horse ran right into a post. Swoll her knee back up. And you can't see for the dust."

"I'll ask around," Roddy said. "Maybe borrow another ride."

Angel shrugged. "He says she's fit, but for the knee. Should hold up."

Roddy helped Angel saddle his horse and stood back and watched him coil and recoil his rope, shifting the balance in his glove.

Roddy climbed up on the rail near the chutes to watch the Whitcomes. When the tape came down, Bill was right on the steer, his rope swinging over his head, Angel right behind. Bill got a loop on the horns, and Angel went for a loop on the heels. Both horses backed up, and the ropes snapped taut for a second, then slacked. It looked good. They should be in it, Roddy thought. He turned toward the gate to see who was up next, listening for the Whitcomes' score to come over the P.A. Instead he heard a wave of noise from the crowd. He was over the rail and in the arena. Bill's horse was down. He hadn't seen it go down, and he couldn't see Bill either. The mare had her neck stretched out flat, her legs kicking. She was rocking, trying to get up. He could hear Bill screaming and Angel calling for a gun. Others were shouting, "Get the vet!"

Roddy sank to his knees in the dust. Angel was trying to push the horse up and off his dad. Trying to shove fifteen hundred pounds. Each time the horse heaved up, struggling to get to her feet, the men shoved, but each time the heavy animal fell harder, crushing Bill. There was a short pop, an echo, and the sulfur burn of gunpowder in the air. They couldn't hold the dead weight of the horse; they jumped back. Then all the men together heaved, and the paramedics slid the injured body out and lifted it on a gurney.

Bill was alive. His face was dead white, pinched in pain. Angel ran beside the paramedics, his face streaked with dirt and tears. Then they were gone, the flashing light of the ambulance spinning through the dust and out of the arena.

The announcer came on. "Cowboy's okay, folks. Let's give him a big hand." A scattering of applause drifted down from the bleachers. The voice went on, telling a story to distract the crowd from a tractor sent to drag the carcass of Bill's mare out of the arena, but Roddy could hear the siren as the ambulance turned out of the fairgrounds, the sound thinning as it took the highway into town.

Roddy walked out of the arena and talked to the tractor driver, who hoisted the mare up so Roddy could unstrap the cinch, drag the saddle out. He unbuckled the bridle and lifted it off her big head. The bit was still green with hay froth. He couldn't tell them what to do with the mare. "You'll have to wait for Angel," he said. He heaved the saddle up on his shoulder and walked back to Bill's trailer.

Somebody had brought Angel's horse from the arena and tied him up. His coat was dark with sweat and thick with dust. Roddy put the tack away and fed the horse. In the men's room, he filled the dirty sink and washed his face. The water came off brown. He was surprised to see his own face. It was white, and even after the cool water, sweat broke out on his forehead and ran down his face. "Shit," he said. "It was his own damn fault."

His own ride was coming up pretty quick. It was dark now, the lights of the arena dim. He picked up his rigging bag and walked to the chutes.

He tried to put Bill out of his mind. Get focused on the ride. He could do it. He'd seen a lot of accidents. This was nowhere near the first, nor the worst. He sat down on the planks and flexed his legs. The calm feel he could get before a ride came back to him. He let his mind go blank.

Somebody tapped him on the shoulder, nodded. He set his rigging, checked it, and climbed up on the chute. He lowered himself and took a good grip on the handhold. "Goddamn little shit," he said to the horse. "You're gonna buck." He dug his spurs in hard when the gate swung wide.

He got out clean and the bronc set up a rocking ride. Roddy caught the rhythm in the muscles of his back and stomach. He knew he'd have it if the bronc would show some fight. The buzzer sounded and the damn horse did what he should have done before — bucked sideways out of rhythm. Roddy came off hard, his back twisted and his leg crushed underneath him. He was up and on the rail when his score came. Just out of the money.

At the Silver Dollar, the music was so loud he could barely hear. His mother was asking him to go for another round of drinks. She reached into the pocket of her skirt and handed him a hundred-dollar bill. At the bar, he had to shout the order over the noise of the crowd, then make two trips back to the round table in the back. His dad was talking to Dolly McReynolds, asking after Bill Whitcome.

"Won't ride again, that's for sure," Dolly said.

His father nodded. "Man's lucky to be alive."

"Aren't we all," Dolly said, and his dad laughed.

"Well, I guess," he said.

Roddy handed his mother her Manhattan, and she looked up and smiled. She indicated the seat next to her, but Roddy gave her a signal, maybe later. His dad looked like him, except his hair was silver now. His skin tanned dark, the same sharp nose and high cheekbones. He wore a tan western suit and a Resistol. His mother never wore western clothes. He watched her for a moment from the bar. She's like a queen, he thought. She was standing to shake the hands of some young cowboy and his wife.

His mother was a little heavy, her makeup ruddy in the dim light, her hair gleaming dark with red highlights. She had on a full blue skirt shot with gold and a red low-cut blouse. She would always be a beautiful woman, more a friend to him now than a mother.

Suzy McReynolds was dancing with some cowhand. He found

a place to lean sideways into the bar and sipped at his whiskey. The music stopped, and Suzy left her partner on the floor, thanking him politely. She'd changed into skin-tight jeans and a plaid shirt.

"You did all right, I hear," she said. Her eyes were shiny and her voice just holding back a laugh.

"Not bad."

"You able to dance?"

Roddy grinned at her, but he shook his head. His back felt like somebody had run a steel cable up through his spine and given it a twist. He thought about how many drinks he'd have to drink to have some fun. Already, another cowboy stood at Suzy's shoulder. "Some other time," he said.

He made his way back to the table and pulled out the chair next to his mother. He sat down, moving slowly.

"You need to see the doctor?" His mother looked at him in the way she had when he'd run home needing a Band-Aid, when just the sound of her voice could make his boy's pain go away.

"Head doctor, I think," he said, and she laughed with him.

"Dolly needs her horses trailered home," his mother said. "Are you fit enough to drive?"

"I could be."

His mother put her hand down on the table, next to his. He was surprised to see the knuckles bent like tiny bamboo bridges, with arthritis. She still wore rings on all her fingers. She lifted her hand and placed it on his, a movement no one else would notice.

"Go on home," she said. "There will be other years."

31

Kenny knew he shouldn't do it, but he had to find Cynthia, and the only way was to walk across the valley to her house. Roddy Moyers was back. He'd parked his white sports car in front of the hotel, and Kenny had looked in the window and caught a glimpse of his dark hair and jeans. He'd jumped out of sight, not knowing exactly why. But he knew he had to warn Cynthia before she ran into Moyers by chance.

He walked west on the swamp road. It had been raining, and, up ahead, misty clouds hung in the foothills, soft and inviting, like a place in Japan. Cottonwoods along the road shimmered, black-green from the rain, but farther on, where the road seemed to narrow and grow small, the sunlight fell in white and yellow rays, glowing like a picture of the garden at Gethsemane.

Beside the road, a robin tugged at a worm in the damp earth and tried to drag it. Kenny walked right up to the bird, which was so serious about the worm it didn't fly away. It's so fat, he thought, we could make pies.

Despite the rain, the sun above the clouds was warm on his shoulders, the air like sweet steam from a loaf of warm bread. But he was nervous.

He walked past the entrance to the dump and glanced in, looking for Dill's truck. Though the air was warm, smoke rose from the stovepipe of the trailer. He thought maybe Cynthia was there, but he saw no tracks on the damp road.

At the ranch gate, he cut across the field and hiked through the alfalfa. He came in at an angle from behind the barn, feeling like an enemy soldier. Thinking he might be shot anytime.

When he reached the barn, he looked back at the house. Earl Dustin's truck was gone. He felt so relieved he almost laughed. A kind of giddiness made him feel like jumping around. But he still had no way of letting Cynthia know he was there. Maybe he could just watch from where he was. Wait to see if she might come out to feed the dog or do some other chore. Her horse was in the corral.

The old horse hung her head. The rain had darkened her coat to the color of molasses. She must have been a beauty, he thought. Now, her withers were sharp and high, her stomach wide and hanging low. She stepped away from him, and seeing her from behind, her stomach round on either side like bulging saddlebags, he realized, This horse is pregnant. He looked at her bag, swollen full with milk. She's going to foal, he thought. Not only that, but she might do it now.

As he watched the old horse, she stretched her neck to lick her flank, and looked at him, bewildered. She circled, shifting on her feet.

Cynthia had told him how hard she was to catch, but he whistled for her, softly. And she came. As if she knew he was her only hope. He opened the half door, and she swayed right through and walked herself into a stall. She lowered her head again and stood without moving, as if she were already exhausted.

He looked in the dark barn for a bucket. The least he could do was see that she had water. But the spigot was outside, between the barn and the house. He needed to tell somebody the old mare was getting ready. But he hesitated. Earl wasn't there, but Mrs. Dustin probably was. Still, what could she do? Yell at him? Call his mom?

The mare circled in her stall, and he heard her lean on the wood wall so hard it creaked and started to give way. She's trying to go down, he thought.

He suddenly felt tired of being ashamed all the time. It felt like he'd been looking at the ground for so long that he just wanted it to stop. He slid open the barn door and walked into the yard. He let his legs swing easy and made his way down to the house. When he got to the door, he stood up straight and knocked.

Mrs. Dustin opened the door. She looked at him and caught her breath. He could tell she didn't know what she should say. "Earl's gone out below," she said.

"Your mare is down," Kenny said.

Mrs. Dustin looked at him, and her hate seemed to stab into the air.

"Cynthia home?" he said.

"No," she said.

Kenny didn't know what to do then, but he stood his ground.

"Mrs. Dustin," he said. "We didn't do anything. You're wrong about me."

She looked as if he'd tried to hit her. As if just saying anything at all was a sin.

"Cynthia," she called. "That boy is here. Come here. Tell him to go." She looked behind her. "Cynthia!"

Cynthia entered the room behind her mother and walked to the door. She looked at him, confused, then at her mother. She shoved past her mother and pushed Kenny in front of her.

"He's going," she said.

To Kenny she said, "What? What are you doing here?"

"Mare's foaling."

"Which mare?"

"Goldie."

She swiveled and started running for the barn. Her mother yelled, but Cynthia kept going. Kenny followed.

In the barn, Goldie was down and heaving with contractions. With each huge shudder, she gave a wheezing groan and tried to get back on her feet.

"Sit on her head," Cynthia said. "Keep her down."

Kenny did what he was told. He straddled the mare's neck and used his whole body weight to try to keep her down. "Whoa," he said, and kept repeating it. "Whoa, girl."

"I see hooves," Cynthia said.

The mare gave a heave and threw her head so hard her skull hit him on the chin and knocked him back against the stall.

"Watch out," Cynthia yelled, and the mare was up on her feet. They saw the foal's nose, sealed in pale blue membrane, its eyes closed, as it dove out front feet first. Cynthia tried to catch the long thing in her arms, and managed just to break the fall. The two of them were down in the straw, Cynthia frantic to tear the membrane so the foal could get air.

"We got him," she said. "He's breathing."

Kenny watched the slick narrow chest move in and out. A tongue snaked out and licked. He couldn't get over it. He reached down and felt the wet, soapy hair.

Cynthia crawled out from under the foal and stood up.

"Come on," she said, backing up. "Let's let Goldie take him."

They stepped away and Goldie turned to find her foal. She pushed it with her muzzle and sniffed. Then she began to lick, hard licks that knocked the baby over. Already it was struggling to get its feet under itself.

"God," Cynthia said. "That was easy. I was afraid. We didn't breed her. She did this on her own. I wouldn't breed her at this age."

They couldn't tell from the wet foal what color it would be, but they saw it was a horse colt, not a filly. Cynthia went out to wash her hands. When she came back, she looked at herself and laughed. Her jeans and shirt were streaked with slime and manure.

They both sat down in the straw outside the stall and watched, unable to take their eyes off the foal. It shook its head, twitching, and flopped its ears from side to side.

"Looks like a mule," Kenny said, and Cynthia gave him a warning look.

"Don't talk like that about the little guy."

They watched him struggle to his legs and find the milk. Goldie seemed to heave a sigh of relief, and they laughed. They stood, and Cynthia stretched out her arms and gave Kenny a hug. The smell of her, a warm milk smell, made him want to kiss her on the neck. He hugged her back and felt her breasts push up against his chest. He pulled back, embarrassed. But Cynthia grabbed his hand and laughed.

"You better get home before Earl gets here," she said.

He felt black. Suddenly hollow again, just hearing her say Earl's name. And when he turned, Earl stood in the doorway.

"What's going on here?" he said. "Mother said that boy was here."

He came straight for Cynthia and jerked her by the arm. "How could you do that to your mother? Get in the house."

"Stop." Cynthia tried to pull away. "Stop it."

Her voice sounded so scared and also, Kenny heard, embarrassed. It was the shame he heard that made him move. Earl slapped her to her knees, and Kenny moved.

He grabbed Earl from behind. He clamped Earl's arms down, using all his strength. But Earl shook him off. The old man's neck was burning red, and his hat was gone. Kenny tried to watch his eyes, but Earl rose in front of him like a bear swinging his paws, and when he cuffed him open-handed, the blow came like a bag of nails, not like a slap. Kenny could feel broken teeth sharp against his cheek, and he tasted blood. Cynthia was yelling, "Stop, Kenny, stop!" But it was as if he just went crazy. He charged the old man. Earl hit him again, a huge fist on the bone above his eye. He couldn't see. He just kept moving in. Punching the old man, screaming, "Don't you hit her. You can't hit her." Earl threw him, and air rushed underneath. He landed on his arm, and felt his elbow go. He scrambled to get up, but he could hardly see. He stood, shaking so hard he could barely stand.

"Get the hell off of my place," Earl said. "Get the hell out."

Kenny wasn't sure what happened then. Cynthia sobbed and sucked in air. And Earl just kneeled down in the straw. His jaw tightened, and he folded down and rolled over on his side.

Cynthia was crying, "No, oh, no! Earl!" She yelled at Kenny to go get help. Call an ambulance. He ran for the house and found her mom, but she wouldn't call the ambulance. She wouldn't let him talk. Finally he just pointed to the barn and said, "Go! Earl's hurt," and she ran.

Kenny had to call the sheriff, to tell the dispatcher to send an ambulance. When he got back to the barn, Cynthia was trying to revive her dad. Breathing in his mouth. Her mom was trying to make her stop, trying to hug Earl. Kenny pulled her off and shook her, and her face seemed to fall apart, as if all the bones were gone. She grabbed on to him, as if he were Earl. And though pain shot through his arm, he held her, in much the way he'd held on to the old man.

PART IV

Summer

32

Lenna shifted her weight on the bowed and aging bleachers at the old rodeo grounds and tried not to think about Earl. When the sheriff had driven Kenny home from the hospital, he said Earl had suffered a major heart attack. That he could have another anytime. The old man had been briefly conscious, strong enough to refuse a helicopter, but a second attack would kill him.

Lenna shifted again on the uncertain boards, a combination of sorrow and fear drawing her shoulders down. From where she sat, she couldn't see Kenny's face where the bruises had begun to yellow, the purple fading to brown. But his crisp blue shirt gleamed against the overcast sky as he bent over the chute to help a younger boy get set for his ride.

In the cool air, dampness crept into her clothing, tunneling down the back of her collar in a way that seemed inescapable. When the younger boy was ready, the gate flew open and a squat black bull charged out. The boy aboard could not have been more than eight or nine, she thought. But he stuck on. His father leaned over the fence below, hollering advice. When the boy came off, the spectators seemed to stop breathing; the arena fell dead quiet. Then he was on his feet and making for the chutes. He'd managed to keep his hat on, pulled down over his ears, and he walked bowlegged, listing forward like a determined old cowboy. His dad grinned, and the spectators laughed out loud. Lenna could barely bring herself to smile.

She shifted again to balance her weight. It had been drizzling all week, and hooves had churned the arena into a slough of mud and manure. She'd thought of having a word with the coach, but she knew what he would say. "The boys won't take any harm. Need to compete in all kinds of places. Any weather."

She didn't want to watch the rodeo, but she had made a decision. If Kenny wanted to ride, she would watch. She would drive to every practice, every event, as if he were playing baseball, never letting on how terrified she was. She'd seen men disfigured and crippled by these animals. She'd seen a man die. In truth, she watched because she felt, deep inside, that if she were there, nothing bad would happen to her son.

But Kenny had six stitches over his eye, and they'd made two trips out below to see the dentist. How a grown man could do that to a boy, she didn't know. When Kenny came home that day, his face had looked like spoiled meat.

Earl remained in the hospital, and it was all she could do to let her mind even skirt around the edges of this fact. No one had known his heart was failing; he might have known it himself, but he was the kind of man who would never tell. She had dreams on the night after Kenny and Earl had fought — of the old man dying, of Kenny causing the death of this man.

She tried to disbelieve it, worrying the facts over and over, the way a person might relive a bad accident, thinking, What if I had driven the other way? She awoke drenched in sweat, believing she'd had a nightmare, then knowing that the dream was real. There would be no reprieve, no turning back the clock.

When the sun seemed to drift out of the clouds, her mood began to lift. Maybe the sun would bake the arena dry. They'd had so much rain that Kenny kept a close eye on the weather reports, worried about the Fourth of July, hoping the new arena would be ready. Despite his swollen bruises, he'd been practicing hard with the team and out on a barrel he'd strung from two trees with heavy rubber strips.

Though Kenny had been released into her custody, she heard over and over the sheriff's words. If Earl came to and stayed conscious long enough, he would probably press charges for assault, or if he could, attempted manslaughter. Upstairs in the courthouse, the district attorney had her sit in a schoolhouse chair in front of his desk while he explained what procedures would follow if Earl died. Again, she shook herself. It seemed impossible, but she had witnessed the DA press more unlikely, unfair charges. His words haunted her sleep, like contusions under her own skin. How had this happened? What had she done to expose her boy to such permanent harm?

She heard the clatter of boots and shouting. The metal-on-metal ring of spurs. The 4-H clubs had repaired most of the holding pens and railings of the arena, but the old place didn't inspire confidence. She strained to catch sight of Kenny. When she couldn't locate the blue of his shirt, she climbed down like a toddler, using both hands for balance, and walked with care over to the chutes, avoiding the worst of the mud. She thought she might stand back there for a while, look over the stock, though she didn't know which horse Kenny had drawn. Some parents had pulled their trucks close to the rail, where they could watch sheltered and dry in case it rained. None waved at her or nodded.

As she turned behind the chutes, a hollering went up, and she knew another bull was out, spinning and twisting in the mud. She stood still, glad she couldn't see, and waited for the group sigh of relief when the boy came off all right. She looked toward the mountains, where the long rays of sun shone through glistening rain, the kind of light that causes rainbows. Over her shoulder she saw movement, and when she turned, Roddy Moyers's truck was there. It rolled slowly in the mud and stopped beside her.

"Hey," Roddy said.

It shocked her to see him after so long, and she couldn't think what to say. Her face flushed with shame, and it was all she could do not to back away.

"How have you been?" he said. His face was deeply tanned, and he squinted at her, as if he might smile.

"How do you think?" She couldn't keep the brittle tone out of her voice.

"I've been gone a while," he said.

"That's true."

Another man strode up and leaned in the truck to slap Roddy on the shoulder.

"How the hell are you?"

"My girlfriend's pregnant and my wife is sick. You want to hear about it?"

"No. No, I don't think so. Things that bad, you better keep 'em to yourself."

Lenna walked away, left them to their joking. She sat side-saddle on a loading ramp, hugging a post, where she had a view through the rails to the arena. The bareback broncs were up. Roddy, she thought, had a special nature; all sorts of people, not only women, were drawn to him. She'd heard him say, "A person can live glad or live sad." He was the glad one, and despite herself, she remembered how his voice alone could feel like an arm around her shoulder, an embrace. Roddy was the sort who could make things right. She was shocked by how strongly she remembered his skin against hers.

When she was younger, she'd had stern ideas about right and wrong, and about fairness. Though her memories of harm and betrayal would never fade entirely, she now thought she understood forgiveness. With each year, events had overtaken her. People simply wore her down. She had grown too tired to hate them. She couldn't hate Earl Dustin; she knew what it would do to Cynthia if her father died. And it had been in the spring, when she'd first begun to hear birds again, ordinary robins and starlings, that she had finally stopped hating Roddy.

Suddenly Kenny was in the chute, and she jumped up when his horse lunged from the gate. She held her breath so long she saw dark spots and had to wrap her arms around the splintered post to keep from falling. She couldn't help rooting for him, standing on the toes of her boots, watching the bronc hurl and flap the boy back and forth, the way a dog might fight a rag. He didn't make his time. She saw him lose his balance early, lose his ride. He slipped off sideways and rolled.

When he stood, his blue shirt was smeared nearly black with mud and manure. He'd be mad and disappointed, but not hurt.

33

Earl remained in intensive care. One lung had collapsed, and they'd threaded a breathing tube down his throat. His eyes opened from time to time, but he couldn't speak. Though he was monitored by machines, the nurse took his pulse every hour, and the doctor stopped in twice a day.

"He could still have another," the doctor told Cynthia.

"Why?" she'd asked him. Her dad was a strong man. Why were things going so wrong?

"The body gets tired," he said. "Things wear out, just like machinery. We're not made to go on forever."

When finally Earl could breathe on his own, they moved him to a double room with a second, empty bed. Cynthia pulled the visitor's chair close to Earl's head, where sunlight filtered through the only window. The minister had driven her mother home to rest.

A nurse tiptoed in, wearing white polyester pants and a homemade print smock. "You want something to eat?" she asked Cynthia.

"No, thanks."

"You do, you come on down to the kitchen. We've got fresh pie."

Cynthia nodded. Earl had been drifting in and out of consciousness and deep sleep all day. He looked so wrong in the hospital bed. His nose jutted from his face like an escarpment, and she saw the bruised, tunneling veins rising on the backs of his freckled hands. They didn't shave him every day, and his finger-nails were grimy. Her mother kept saying she would bring his razor and nail clippers from home. But each day she forgot. Cynthia would have to do it.

She listened to his rattled breathing, the hum of the machines. Slowly he opened his eyes and gazed at the light from the window.

"What time is it?" he tried to say, but his voice slurred, and he threw out an arm in frustration, glaring at Cynthia.

"After supper," she said, although he was being fed through a tube.

He turned his head toward her, his pale eyes filled with a vague terror.

"Cissy?" she thought he tried to say. "Cissy."

Tears came; she couldn't help it. "Yes, Earl." She leaned forward and lifted his heavy hand from the sheet. "It's me, Daddy."

He threw her hand off.

She felt tears roll down her cheeks. She wiped them with the edge of her hand so he wouldn't see. But he was gone again, asleep.

She leaned back in the chair, one leg tucked beneath her. Nobody came or went, and the hospital was quiet. She listened to Earl's labored breathing. She felt as if she could sit there forever, without moving. Just sit there. While she did, she didn't have to think. She was doing something everybody thought was a good thing, an important thing to do. For the first time, *she* was the good girl. She would not be called upon for anything else.

When she heard Roddy Moyers coming down the hall, joking with another patient, she wondered if somebody new had come in, if there had been an accident. She didn't think so. But time seemed to whiten and float in here; anything might have happened outside.

The door was open and Roddy walked right in. He nodded at her, but he didn't speak. He pulled up another chair and sat down. Earl hadn't had too many visitors. The doctor discouraged it. He told people just to wait a bit. When people did come, they either whispered or they yelled. She wondered what Roddy would do if Earl woke up.

"How is he?" Roddy asked her in a normal voice.

Earl opened his eyes and glared, as if to say, "I'm right here. Don't talk like I was dead."

When he closed his eyes again, they retreated to the corridor, where Roddy asked, "How is he, really?"

"We begged him to get on the helicopter. Both Jeff and Dill told him they'd stay right by, go with him to Denver or Salt Lake, but he refused to go." She felt tears coming again and looked away.

"Can I do anything? Take you out to eat? Have you eaten yet?"

"No. Dill's bringing Mother back. Then I'll go eat with him."

Roddy grinned at her. "I could take you for a ride . . ."

She gazed at him a long time, studying his face as if for the first time before she spoke. "I don't think so," she said. "My aunt Helen will be here soon, and I'll be going back with her."

"Back east?"

"New York."

"You got that scholarship?"

Cynthia nodded. "But I might not take it."

"Why not?"

She nodded at her dad's room, but she said, "I talked to my aunt Helen. There might be a way that I can go to music school, if I wait until next year. I can't decide."

"You'll still be here for the Fourth?"

"I don't think I'll be in a party mood."

"Well. Anything. Anything at all I could do to help out. You'll let me know?"

She watched Roddy walk back down the hall, his boot heels loud on the linoleum. He grinned at the secretary at the desk and went on out. Suddenly she thought of something he could do. She ran down the corridor and caught him in the parking lot.

"There is a favor I would ask of you . . . ," she said.

"Anything."

Later that afternoon, she sat at the fold-down table in Dill's trailer, watching him fry steaks. Burn 'em, as he said. The door and all the windows were cranked wide open to let out the smoke.

"Should of done this all outdoors," he said.

"It's okay," she said. "Just don't light a cigarette, we'll have to crawl to safety on the floor."

"Your dad used to cook steaks so rare I used to tell him, 'Give this one a shot of penicillin, it'll bawl and run off.' "

"It's criminal," she said, imitating her dad's voice, "criminal — ruin a damn good piece of meat."

After they had eaten, they sat out on the steps. The slow summer sun was still high.

"Your dad's a strong man," Dill said.

"He needs a shave."

"I could take care of that."

"Could you?"

"First thing. First thing in the mornin'."

All winter, she'd been thinking ahead to how she would get away. Get out of the valley. How Earl would never hit her again. And now, he was just an ugly, sick old man. There wasn't any reason she should leave. But her aunt was coming to get her.

As if he were reading her mind, Dill said, "We'll take good care of him. He'll make it."

"You don't think I should stay?"

"No."

Dill struck a match on his boot heel and lit a cigarette. He coughed, a raw sound churning in his lungs. "Need to quit these things," he said. He looked out into the sagebrush and the new green of the aspen trees. Late spring had been so unseasonably wet that saplings seemed to appear overnight.

"Why does he hate me so much?" Cynthia asked. "Do you know, Dill?"

Dill took his time, finishing his smoke.

"I suppose it won't hurt now to say," he said. "You came along pretty late, you know. You were the apple of his eye. Earl carted you everywhere. Never saw him without you. Then — must have been the year you started school, never thought of it that way before — Earl changed. I don't know quite what it was. I guess he knew right then you were bound to go your own way."

Cynthia thought, This is it? This is all? It was like Earl wishing she were a boy. It explained, and yet it didn't. How could he leave her just for going off to kindergarten?

"Doesn't make sense," she said. She fought to hold back tears. "I must have done something."

Dill wrapped his arm around her, pulled her close. "Nothing, sweetheart. Not a thing."

"Tell me."

"Settle down. It's okay now."

She mashed her face into Dill's shirt and cried.

"Quit now," Dill said. "Quit now."

He pushed her away and looked into her face. She felt her mouth contort and another wave of tears start to come. Then there was something. She saw it in Dill's face, and suddenly she was alert. Angry.

"What? You tell me, Dill. You have to tell me now."

"There was an incident," Dill said.

"What did I do?"

"You were just a little girl. You didn't do a thing. We were playing cards up at the mill. Earl let you wander off. You know it's dangerous, a mill. A kid can drown in grain. When he went lookin', your dad found you with Harold Cray."

"What was I doing?"

"No one is sure, to this day. Harold was a big boy, nearly grown. But your dad gave him a beating, right there on the loading dock."

"Is that why Harold is slow?"

"No, there's nothin' wrong with Harold's mind. He was a bright boy, even then. But that day he never had a chance to speak. He went into the service, to Vietnam I believe, not long after.

"It's not that Earl wanted you to be a boy," Dill said. "It's just he didn't want a girl."

Cynthia drove to Harold's shop. The antique glass and dark oak door was locked, the counter and the rows of saddles on their stands filmed with a layer of dust. It looked as if the shop had been closed for weeks.

She drove out to Harold's house. It was a shack, really, built by Harold of scrap lumber over the years. Just one room and two glassed-in porches, front and back, constructed of mismatched windows. Weeds grew up the outside of the foundation, and two dung beetle-shaped old cars and a truck frame were rusting in the sagebrush yard.

She knocked on the door, then called Harold's name. When nobody answered, she walked around to the back. Beyond

Harold's house, there was nothing but chewed-down grass, the fences past repair. Black TV sets had been set up along the fence line, on stumps and ammunition boxes.

Harold sat in a folding lawn chair, beside a wooden table made for spooling wire. Without a hat, his bald head shone, burning pink in the sun. He looked up at her and nodded at a second chair.

Cynthia sat down and looked out over the pasture. From a bare mound of dirt, chizzlers, fat ground squirrels, sat up and chattered. They popped in and out of burrows like puppets in a show.

Harold pointed just beyond the mound. Three young foxes watched the chizzlers. One leaned back on his haunches to scratch has neck with a back paw, lost his balance, and tumbled over backward. Cynthia laughed.

"The peaceable kingdom," she said.

"Fat summer," Harold said. "Plenty of food to go around."

Harold squinted out at the row of TV sets. Before she could speak, he hoisted an ugly automatic rifle to his shoulder and fired, blowing out the glass in one screen after another.

The foxes and the ground squirrels vanished. Cynthia sat unable to move, staring at the gun, a flat, black machine gun. Her ears rang.

"What are you doing here?" Harold said. "What do you want?"

"Put the gun away," she said.

Harold looked at it, cradled in his lap.

"All right," he said. He stood and motioned her to follow. She went through the screen door into his back porch. There had to be two dozen guns there. Rifles and handguns. Harold laid the machine gun down in a row of other guns. The room smelled like gun cleaner and stale beer and cigarettes. Harold opened a refrigerator and took out one beer. He twisted off the top, but didn't drink.

"Okay," he said. "What do you want?"

"I want to know what happened when I was five. What happened at the mill."

"Nothin' happened."

"Why did Earl give you a beating?"

"Lost his temper."

"Why?"

"Why'd he beat on that boy Ken?"

Harold walked over to a wall he'd paneled with rough gray barn wood. On the wall, he'd pinned up photographs.

"Look here," he said.

Cynthia stepped up, and he pointed at a blurred photograph of a skinny boy in jeans and a white cowboy shirt, leaning on a car.

"That's Cal Haverford. He died, not ten miles from here. Shot himself in the head. His dad said it was a hunting accident. I grew up with Cal."

He pointed to the next picture. "Walter Johnson, 1948–1972," somebody, Harold, she guessed, had written underneath.

"OD'd," Harold said. "Heroin." He looked at her as if she might not know what that was.

There were more pictures on the wall. Narrow-chested men in T-shirts and fatigues, wearing dog tags and posed in front of jeeps. Some were shirtless, and she could see the outlines of their ribs.

"I've got my own memorial," Harold said.

"Earl's all right," he said. "I understand Earl. It's generally the other ones you got to watch out for. The little old lady driving to the store. She's the one who takes you out."

"Why'd he beat you up?"

"We were up on the loading dock. You could sing, even then. You used to sing this little kid's song, about a kitten and a pussy willow. . . . It was my fault. I started teasing you, singing along, and you got to laughing. Laughed so hard you peed your pants.

"Then you were ashamed and mad. You took your underpants off and threw them in the dirt. You followed me down to get 'em back. Just about that time, your dad showed up.

"Earl was scared. I guess he saw how something bad could happen to his kid, and not a damn thing he could do."

"Why don't you hate him?"

Harold looked at the pictures on the wall.

"I owe him," he said. "He taught me the one thing. Watch out for yourself. Nobody else is goin' to. It's just like that." He snapped his fingers. "Whether you're alive or dead. You got to decide for yourself. You want to live? or you want to die?"

Harold moved so close she could smell the beer in the bottle in his hand. "Whatever you do," he said, "don't start feeling sorry for yourself. That trap will snap shut with you in it, just like that."

"It doesn't make sense to me," she said. "It's not enough to make Earl hate me."

Harold squinted, as if he were coming to a decision. He started to speak, and stopped.

"You tell me," she said. "Please."

"Earl didn't go after me," he said. "He went after you. Hauled you up on the dock by an arm. I heard it pop out of the socket. You were screaming. You were so scared. Then I thought he was goin' to kill you. He shook you like a dog shakes a rat, and slapped you so hard blood flew out of your mouth.

"I remember standing there thinking, I can't interfere. A person doesn't interfere in family.

"But you had blood smeared on your cheek, like you'd been

picking cherries. I saw that. I couldn't stand to see that. I had to stop him."

Without warning, Harold's face softened. He gave her a quick hug, as if she were a man. A pat on the back. And he stepped away.

"It's not your worry," he said. "You go on . . ." He almost pushed her toward the door. "You go on," he said. "You're stronger than you think."

Driving home Cynthia felt like she was made out of tears. The bones in her face began to ache from crying. She cried because all this time Earl had held it against her, something she'd been too little to understand. Something she didn't remember. And because her dad would die. But not now, she thought, not right now.

34

On the Fourth of July, the hotel hired enough bands to keep the music pounding all day and most of the night. At some time during the day, the entire county showed up at the café or the bar. Roddy Moyers should have been out on the circuit. But he'd been working this rodeo since he was a kid. He couldn't ride in an amateur show anymore, but he'd stick around and help out around the chutes.

He sat in the back of the café jammed in by six other bodies in a circular booth. Friends and acquaintances had been buying him beers all afternoon. The band in the bar started up again, so loud the whole place shook with every bass note and drumbeat, and the waitresses had to yell over everyone else yelling over the band.

"What's that?" an old-timer bellowed from across the booth.

"Why don't you get a *hearing aid*?" Dolly McReynolds demanded.

"Ain't found one that's worth a darn!"

"That's why I don't get one!" Dolly hollered back, getting a big laugh from the table.

Roddy wondered if his own ears were being damaged. He squeezed out of the booth and started for the door, turning sideways to get by the people standing in the aisles.

He walked down the center of the street, kicking at crushed paper cups and beer bottles left from the parade. Across the railroad tracks, a makeshift town of cars and trucks and horse trailers had grown overnight in the dusty pasture around the new arena.

Horses, most already saddled, stood tethered to trailers, and he felt the steady flow of movement, like an eddy in a river. People passed on horseback, going nowhere, just kicking up the dust. Barrel racers rode the periphery on thin-necked horses. A girl wearing gold shorts and a halter top rode by, her face and long brown arms painted up in war paint. Even the horse had ghost-white circles around his eyes.

The arena was crowded, half the riders loping in one direction, half in the other. He witnessed a near collision and shook his head. If they aren't ready now, he thought, they aren't going to be.

He climbed up behind the chutes, where cowboys had stretched out on the boards, checking gear and working stiffness from their legs. Al hollered at him from the arena, where he was down checking gates. Kenny Swanson perched on the top rail with his knees pulled up. The number 12 was pinned to the back of his shirt.

"Aren't you a little young for this?" Roddy said.

"How old were you?"

Roddy laughed and climbed up next to the boy. "Old enough to know better," he said. "Your mother here?"

Kenny nodded at the stands. They were filling up with spectators.

"How's she takin' it?"

"What?"

"Earl's still in the hospital."

"She's okay. She's okay with it."

"How're you?"

"Be all right."

"Scared?"

"Not of the horse."

"What's your ride?"

"Horse called Hailstorm, out of Texas."

"Oh, boy."

"What?"

Roddy shook his head.

"You know that horse?"

"Texas, huh? Hey, Al, you hear that? Kid drew Hailstorm."

Al looked up from the arena, worry showing on his face. "Oh, boy," he said.

"Bullshit." Kenny looked from one man to the other until they laughed.

"Hailstorm," Al said. "Never heard of him."

Roddy had heard of him, though. He was a solid, healthy horse, a thick-muscled, brown gelding with a jagged scar across one eye. Looked like someone tried to break him with a two-by-four. But he gave an honest ride. Went out and did his job, no tricks.

Roddy lowered himself down in the sawdust beside Al. "Take it easy," he said to Kenny. "We'll buy you a beer if you live."

"Sure," Kenny said.

Kenny couldn't sit still anymore. He climbed down off the fence and walked back and forth to stretch his legs. He dangled his arms and shook. He wanted to go take another look at Hailstorm, but he knew it would only spook him. Spook him, not the horse. It was better not to think too much.

But he hated waiting. If it were up to him, he'd go to town until they called for bronc riders. He wondered if Cynthia was there. He'd been looking all afternoon. Watching for her hair in the hot sunlight, waiting for a signal like a mirror flash. He pretended he wasn't, but he was searching for her in the crowd. He walked back through the parked outfits.

He didn't find her until just before the anthem. She was sitting in the stands beside a woman wearing a dress and high-heeled sandals. When Kenny climbed up, he saw the woman's toes were brown with dust. Cynthia stood and introduced him to her aunt Helen. He stood with them with his hat over his heart while they sang and the queen and all the princesses rode flags around the arena.

Aunt Helen had gray hair, but she looked young. Even in the heat her dress was crisp, and she smelled of cologne. Kenny tried to tell from looking at her if she knew about his fight with Earl, but if she did, she didn't show a sign. When he had to go, she shook his hand and wished him good luck with his ride. Cynthia winked and gave him a high sign.

He wanted time to go say hi to his mom, but at the last minute he decided not to. It would just make her worry, and he was worried enough for both of them. Mr. Gallagher and the whole team were at the chutes. Every person he knew was there. He had to make his ride.

"Cowboy from Montana next, ladies and gentlemen, and Kenny Swanson in the hole. Eight long seconds here, that's all we're lookin' for."

Kenny waited, all set, and then the crowd noise swelled like something natural, a high wind in the trees, and Kenny was only aware of hands on him and voices. He sucked in a deep breath and held it. Hailstorm bucked before the chute opened, ready to go, and they just let him out. He arched up in a hump and twisted. Kenny raked his spurs into the shoulder, jerking his knees, one arm in the air. He clenched his teeth to keep his jaw from taking the shocks. There was just that one, pure moment, when he felt all of his muscles work. As if the horse and he were spinning, up above the ground. Then the bronc bucked him off.

But he couldn't twist his glove loose, and he flopped along the withers of the horse like a grain sack. He felt more than he heard the scare come up in the crowd. Finally his hand came free, and he landed on his shoulder blades, so hard he couldn't breathe. Then his lungs sucked in dust.

Lenna wanted to jump the rail, race across the arena. She saw the clown run out, lift Kenny from under the arms in one motion, drag him to the rail. She didn't see the rest. The crowd made way for her, and she ran to the gate where the ambulance had been parked all day, its rear doors open. By the time she arrived, Roddy Moyers was holding Kenny's forehead while he sat on a canvas cot and threw up in the dirt. His face had taken on a pearly blue color, and his hair was flattened by sweat.

The male nurse from the ambulance grinned down at her. "He didn't take no harm," he said. "Just shook up."

She stood beside Roddy and waited for Kenny to stop coughing. Kenny waved a hand at her. He couldn't talk.

"We don't think he broke anything," Roddy said. "But he needs to go for pictures anyhow."

Kenny coughed and tried to speak.

"Take it easy," Roddy said. "Soon as you can walk, we'll take a trip to town."

Kenny held his breath and his words came in a slow croak. "What did the judges say? Did I make the ride?"

"You sure as hell did," Roddy said. "Damn near rode that horse to death. We couldn't get you off."

"First *twelve*-second ride we've had in years," one of the men joked, and everybody laughed. Lenna felt the tears before they came, tried to smile at Kenny. Someone handed her a crumpled, warm bandanna from his back pocket. She tried to look away, but Roddy put an arm around her shoulders.

"He's all right," he said. "Just the scare. Happens all the time."

From the corner of her eye, she saw the girl Cynthia walk near and nod at Roddy.

"Nice ride," she said to Kenny.

He looked up and grinned. "Thanks," he said. The color was coming back into his face, and he stood up, wincing. His shirt was torn from the cuff to the elbow, the skin rubbed raw and dark with dirt.

"We better get you into town," Roddy said.

Cynthia looked at Kenny. "You want me to come along?"

"Yeah. Sure."

"Well, whoever's goin', let's go," Roddy said. His truck was pulled up close, and he reached with one arm under Kenny's shoulder to help him walk. Lenna saw there wasn't room for four. She took a step back.

"Mom?" Kenny called back to her.

"I'll follow you," she said. She waved. "Go on ahead."

When the truck had pulled out toward the road, she folded the borrowed bandanna and handed it back to the fellow who had lent it to her.

35

Kenny stood in the emergency room, waiting for his mom to finish filling out papers. His ribs had been taped so tight he could hardly breathe, and already he had itches underneath the bandages.

"Nothin' hurts so bad as a cracked rib," Roddy had told him. "But there's really not a lot to do. Gets well just as fast if they tape it or they don't. Hurts a little less with tape." He'd gone back to the rodeo but said he'd stop back later on.

Cynthia stood out on the ambulance dock, drinking water from a paper cup. Kenny filled a cup at the cooler and followed her out. "I've spent too much time in here," she'd said.

He always asked her, "How's Earl," but this time she gave him a different answer. "I think he's going to make it. I don't know why. I just do. But even if he does, it will be a long time before he can work again. He might not work again."

"Who's going to run the ranch?"

"Dill and the hired man. They'll take on more hay crew. Earl can still give orders. As soon as he could talk, he started yelling for the nurse. My aunt Helen just laughed. 'Not a thing wrong with his lungs,' she said."

Kenny drank his water and crumpled the cup in his fist. He tossed it down on the asphalt, where the orderlies had dropped a mess of stubbed-out cigarettes.

"You sure?" Kenny said. "You sure you have to go?"

She turned and looked at him, just looked without smiling or blinking. "You think I won't miss you?"

The sound of her voice was different, sad and serious at the same time. She wanted an answer. He put his hand on her shoulder, for balance, and so she couldn't hug his ribs. He kissed her on the mouth. He felt no hurry and no fear. When he stopped, he stood back. "I'm going to miss you more," he said.

Roddy's truck pulled in just as his mother came out the swinging doors.

"Roddy's giving me a lift home," Cynthia said.

Kenny was surprised. But his mother nodded.

"Good luck," Lenna said. She reached out and touched Cynthia lightly on the arm. "Good luck," she said again.

Cynthia started to leave, but Kenny stopped her.

"You ever need anything," he said. "Anything at all."

"I'll call you," she said, winking at him. "I'll call you."

She walked down the steps to Roddy's truck. Kenny waved as the truck pulled out, and Roddy honked.

Kenny told his mother he had another question for the nurse. Could she wait there one more minute? In the hospital, it wasn't hard to find Earl's room. Kenny listened outside the door, then, as quietly as he could in boots, walked close to Earl's bed. The old man's eyes were closed, and his breath made a soft, wheezing sound, like wind at the edge of a field.

Kenny couldn't really sit, so he leaned against the other bed, planning to watch this man who might die. For Cynthia, he had prayed that Earl would live. But this man could send him to jail.

The old man's eyes opened slowly. He looked from side to side, hardly moving his neck. "Cissy?" he said. "Is Cissy here?"

"Not now," Kenny answered.

Earl suddenly fixed his eyes on Kenny's face. An anger sparked through them that made Kenny fear he would have another heart attack. He started to back out of the room, to go find help.

"No," Earl said, and the look faded into a simple tiredness. "I'm not going to die yet. I just want my girl."

"I'll get somebody to tell her," Kenny said. "First I have to ask you what the sheriff said."

The old man winced. "Said to throw the book at you. Two-time offender."

Kenny stared directly into Earl's eyes. "No," he said. "I was trying to help her."

"We'll see about that."

Kenny left the room and met his mother back at the emergency entrance. She tried to give him a hand, but he waved her away. His ribs hurt so much it was all he could do to keep his balance going down the stairs.

In the truck, Roddy tried to talk Cynthia into stopping at the café, but she shook her head.

"I don't want to see all those people," she said. "Have to say good-bye again."

"You have to get right home?"

"No," she said. "I'm packed. Dill's driving us to Bonneville Falls in the morning."

"Might be your last time," he said. "Let's catch the fireworks."

They left the truck on Main Street and walked down among the parked horse trailers. Families were picnicking in fold-out chairs set up in half circles. A trailer filled with tack for sale was open, saddle blankets hanging on the guy wires of a tarp. They found a place to sit on a stack of hay bales piled behind the fair building. From there, they had a clear view of the sun going down over the mountains and of the new arena where the fireworks would shoot up over the grandstands.

"So," Roddy said, "you're going."

She didn't answer. She leaned away from him, her elbows resting on her knees, her long back curved. In the dusk, her hair gleamed silver, and Roddy felt an almost unbearable urge to touch her.

She had changed so much since he'd been gone. It took him some time to figure out what it was that was so different. She was calmer. It was something in her voice, he realized.

"Any way to change your mind?" he said.

She turned around, surprised. Just then, the first of the rockets hissed out in the dark and blossomed in a spray of light above them. The horses tethered to the trailers lurched and whinnied, and a dog barked, then whimpered and began to howl. A muffled *pop, pop, pop* went off, and molten-blue comets arced into the sky.

"Let's go," he said. He couldn't stand to sit there while the rockets scared the horses half to death.

"Where?" she said.

"Come play for me? Just one last time?"

He drove her to the ranch house and watched while she sat down at the grand piano. He loved it that she could play anything, songs he'd heard on the radio. Tunes he could only hum for her.

Afterward, she told him what had happened with Kenny and her dad, and about going to see Harold.

"It was nothing, really," she said. "But my dad punished me for all those years."

"You're leaving something out," he said.

She looked at him, confused.

"It started with your dad," he said, "but then it was you, too."

She reacted, pulling back, a look of anger on her face. "How is this your business?"

"That's what I mean," he said. "It's one thing to want people to love you," he said. "It's another thing to *let* them."

"Who exactly loves me?" she said, her voice caught between anger and tears.

He reached out and pulled her close. He lifted her and carried her into the darkened room where he'd been staying. He kissed her face, her neck, the soft hollow just above her collarbone. He wanted to tell her, "I love you," but instead, he helped her with her clothes and ran his hands down her long arms. For the first time, it seemed to him, she turned her body in toward his and moved like a grown woman, her mouth and fingers speaking to him as if he were — as if they were — an urgent, complicated piece of song.

He awoke in the silver before dawn, watching the light beyond the windows fade from dark to softer gray. He woke her and drove her across the valley. They crossed the river, and he let her out at the foot of her own road. He sat in the car and watched her walk up the ranch lane. Halfway up, she turned around. Her old dog loped over the rise and sank down at her feet.

36

Kenny felt as if he might be a hundred. Every place on his whole body hurt. His bruised muscles hurt just under the skin, and he couldn't find a way to sit or sleep that didn't cause a stabbing pain. His mom brought him two aspirins and a glass of water.

"Come on," she said. "We'll walk downtown and get an ice cream. Be good for you to walk around. Doctor said, 'Get up and move around.'"

The aspirin caught and dissolved in the back of his throat. He gulped from the glass of water to get rid of the bitter taste.

"After a while," he said, and his mother went back to the kitchen.

He lay on the couch propped up on pillows, looking out the window. The sky was a kind of blue he only saw in the heat of summer, an empty blue with too much white in it. The whole rest of the summer seemed to him like that blue sky, no clouds. A flat, empty place where nothing happened. He could smell it in the house. That summer smell of dust and dampened floors where his mom was cleaning.

He had a sense that Roddy would be leaving again, and Cynthia had gone to the city, a place Kenny thought of as very far away. A dark, cold place crowded with hundreds and hundreds of people.

More than anything, he felt left. Left with all the plans he didn't even know he'd had. It was as if he'd gone to sleep and had a dream where he forgot to go to practice. Where the buzzer went off, and he didn't even hear it. When he did sleep and dream, he dreamed about riding the horses in the Moyerses' far pasture. The dampness and the river smell of the grass. He thought of the white goat, the shimmering hide his dad had never sent him.

The sheriff and the county prosecutor had talked to his mother at work. Earl was on his feet but talking about pressing charges. His mother didn't know where the money would come from if they had to hire a lawyer. Kenny knew the county didn't have much evidence; it was his word and Cynthia's against Earl's.

When Lenna was called upstairs, the prosecutor sat behind his scarred oak desk and told her what charges could be filed. He took statements from Mrs. Dustin and the paramedics on the scene, considered that Kenny had been trespassing and that he'd been accused of trespassing before. Jeff stood by in his sheriff's khakis. They looked at her with no apologies. When she demanded to know why Earl would do such a thing to a boy, they wouldn't answer. As she was leaving, the prosecutor warned her to keep her kid away from Earl. If he'd kept quiet, she probably would have, too. But she turned around and glared at them.

"No," she said. "You keep Earl away from my boy. I mean it. You try to hurt that boy, and I'll hire a lawyer and put you all to shame."

The next few days, she stayed home watching over Kenny, waiting for a call from the courthouse. Her threat had been an empty one, a bluff, and she knew those men would go a long way to save face. But it finally came to her, at first as a feeling, and then as certain knowledge. Earl would not ask Cynthia to testify. Still, she couldn't keep herself from dreading that the phone would ring.

She'd spent all morning cooking Kenny's favorite dinner, ham and white beans and cornbread, hoping he'd feel well enough to eat. But at noon, she couldn't bring herself to disturb him. She stood by the couch and watched him sleeping.

Kenny awoke to the throaty sound of a rusted muffler outside and the clank of metal on a gate. He sat up slowly, craning his neck to see out the window. The throbbing engine died. His mom came in, a look of curiosity lifting her eyebrows. She shrugged an "I don't know."

They walked together out into the yard. Dill's old pickup and a brick-colored trailer were parked on the far side of the yard. Two men stayed in the cab, their hats pulled down low, and Kenny saw Roddy Moyers move to the rear of the trailer. He swung open the gate and disappeared inside.

Kenny followed his mother out to the curb. He was aware of how they looked, standing in front of the small gray house under the tall cottonwoods. The leaves on the trees hung dusty with summer. Roddy backed Goldie out of the trailer, led her in a circle and stopped. The colt skidded down the ramp, uneasy without his mother. He danced at her flank, afraid to approach Roddy, and afraid to be too far away.

Confused, Lenna looked at her son. Dill Nethercott walked around the truck and opened the door on the passenger side. It took a long time for Earl to climb out, as if his body might not bend at all. When he was standing, he walked up to Roddy and took the halter rope. With some effort, he led the mare to Kenny, the colt in his small halter following behind.

"My girl," he said, "asked me to give you the mare." He handed the rope to Kenny and, without seeming to move, snapped a lead rope on the colt. "And the horse colt, too."

Earl nodded at him and at his mother and made his way back

to the truck. He climbed in. Dill shut the door like a chauffeur and got back in behind the wheel. He looked to see if Roddy was coming, but Roddy signaled no.

The colt shone like oiled wood, deep red in the sunlight, his cream-colored deer fawn tail twitching. He lipped at Kenny's hand. Roddy stepped up to hold Goldie.

Kenny laid both hands on the colt and slid his palms along its quivering neck. He let the small horse nip at his shoulder, and mouth along the length of his shirtsleeve.

They stood together in front of the gray house, Roddy, the boy, and his mother. They watched the truck and trailer rattle down the street, turn toward town, and disappear.

Acknowledgments

I am very grateful to all those who generously gave me advice and encouragement during the writing of this book, especially Rod Kessler, Kristen Zethren, the Chambers families, Stephen Bellon, Mickie Morgan and Barbara Herman, Jeri Weiss, Bruce Macadam, Gaetha Pace, and the students I taught at Oakwood School. For help with all things rodeo, I am indebted to Dotty Bowen, George Quarta, and the inimitable Ken Chambers, who invited me along to rodeos of all kinds. I am very grateful to and have the deepest regard for my agent, Denise Shannon, and my editor at Little, Brown and Company, Pat Strachan. I also want to thank Pamela Marshall, the copyeditor from Heaven. Finally, I continue to be grateful to the Centrum Foundation and the Idaho Commission on the Arts.

About the Author

Christina Adam's short fiction has appeared in *Crazy Horse, Prairie Schooner, The Atlantic Monthly,* and many other periodicals, as well as in *Circle of Women: An Anthology of Contemporary Western Women Writers.* Her first book, *Any Small Thing Can Save You,* a collection of stories, was published in 2001. Before her death in the summer of 2003, Christina Adam divided her time between Venice, California, and a ranch in Idaho. *Love and Country* is her second book.